Turn Turn Turn

Nicholson Taylor

Turn Turn Turn

Table of Contents

Chapter 1 1

Chapter 2 3

Chapter 3 6

Chapter 4 8

Chapter 5 19

Chapter 6 22

Chapter 7 29

Chapter 8 42

Chapter 9 57

Chapter 10 71

Chapter 11 85

Chapter 12 96

Chapter 13 102

Chapter 14 108

Chapter 15 114

Chapter 16 140

Chapter 17 143

Chapter 18 159

Chapter 19 172

Chapter 20 185

Chapter 21 193

Chapter 22 207

Chapter 23 223

Chapter 24 236

Chapter 25 245

Chapter 1

Our story begins.

Colin Bucket is a successful businessman and lives in a 3-bedroom apartment in the Barbican in the city of London. He has been married for 6 years to a beautiful girl, Karen, and they have a 3-year-old son, Jonathan. In all aspects, life seems pretty good.

The only problem is that Karen wants to move out of the flat and buy a house in the country to give Jonathan the open spaces which she thinks he needs. Colin is of the opposite view. He works in the City and every day has an easy stroll to work. Buying a house would need all their savings and a mortgage, and instead of the easy stroll, he would have an hour or more each day both ways or more than two hours in a train or car, which would all cost money. It would probably be a car, as he is senior enough to be entitled to a car parking space at the office.

A little about our characters.

Colin is 34 years old. He qualified as a Chartered Accountant aged only 22, but he did not think the profession was for him, although he was offered a fast-track partnership. He moved into commerce. The first job was not so great as all the directors had the same name as the company, and it all seemed a bit slow, so he looked elsewhere and got his second job, where he has now been for nearly ten years. He works for a company itself listed on the Stock Exchange, which invests in new companies and develops them to bring them to the stock market. The investments are worldwide, and over the years he has travelled a lot to Europe, USA, South America and Australia. He is responsible for preparing companies for IPO's or Initial Public Offerings and then dealing with the IPO itself, working with the advisors on the prospectus, and then hopefully successfully bringing it to market. His status is Associate Director, and his salary is just over £100,000 per annum, but he also earns bonuses, and last year he made £60,000. His ambition is to be a director and earns the big bucks. His soundings indicate this could be in the next year, depending on performance, which he feels sure he can achieve.

He met Karen, who is one year his junior, just before he was eighteen in his last year of school. She was the first girl he slept with, and truth be told, the only girl still. He has been tempted a couple of times, but to date, he has resisted the temptation.

Karen trained as a solicitor, but she never found it very exciting. Colin took a long time to propose marriage, but when he did so, she had him down the aisle in 8 weeks. When they married, she felt that he was always going to make more money so she chucked it in and started working in a restaurant with a friend of hers not making a lot even with tips and the unsocial hours made home life a little difficult but Colin used it as his excuse to spend more time in the office. When she became pregnant, she decided to take permanent maternity leave and is now at home all day with Jonathan. She seems to complain a lot when he works late or goes on overseas trips, which these days seems to happen frequently.

To be honest, they have never had that great a sex life. Before marriage, they were both living at home, and sex seemed to be only on holidays or the occasional weekend. They moved into the Barbican when they got married, and it was fine until she got pregnant, when it all seemed to stop. After the newborn, it took a while to start again, but now it is only about once a week. Colin feels it should be more, but she doesn't seem so interested.

Chapter 2

Now that we have had the background, let's get into the story.

In Colin's office, he has a small team of only four: himself, a rather pretty assistant, Penny, another male assistant, and a secretary who is also quite pretty.

Penny has long blond hair, a fabulous figure and always seems to wear short skirts. She is also a Chartered Accountant and very ambitious, and is always telling him that she wants his job. Going back to what we were saying about sex earlier on, it has to be said that he quite fancies her. There are two problems here. Firstly, he wants to remain faithful, and secondly, the opportunity has never arisen. He often wonders what he would do given the opportunity.

We may be getting near the opportunity. They are currently working on an IPO for a craft brewery. For two weeks, the four of them have spent many hours working on the project and been in the office until nearly midnight most days and even worked on the Saturday until teatime. Needless to say, Karen has not been happy with a lot of moans about his time in the office. At long last, they are ready to go to market, and the offering is a great success. On Monday, there is a Board Meeting and Colin is summoned. The directors all clap their hands and tell Colin he has done a great job, and the firm has made a lot of money, and the least he can expect is a jolly good bonus. Colin is a little put out as he was really hoping he was going to be invited onto the Board.

Colin feels that he needs to reward his team. He can't really ask for them to get a bonus, so it will have to be something more personal. Colin thinks that a celebratory dinner would be a good idea. But where to go? He remembers some friends in Chelsea who had a birthday dinner at a local restaurant, Foxtrot Oscar, which had been a great success with a really good atmosphere, interesting cocktails and nice food, which would be perfect to celebrate. He decides on next Thursday night and invites the team. They are all up for it, and he books a table for 7pm. He tells Karen on Wednesday night that he has to go to a boring business dinner the next night and will probably be late. Moans as usual, but too bad.

On Thursday, the team all seemed to be looking forward to the night out. The girls are both impressively dressed, and Penny has the shortest skirt ever. At around 6 o'clock, the girls go off to do their make-up and both look stunning. At 6.30, they grab a taxi outside the office and head off to Chelsea. Something tells him this is going to be a good night.

They arrive at Foxtrot's and are warmly greeted. They decide to have a drink in the bar first, which seems quite full of loads of people who all seem in a good mood. They all look at the cocktail list, and everybody wants the margarita with salt. It is very good. He notices that the male assistant and the secretary seem to have a lot to say to each other, so he gets into conversation with Penny.

He cannot stop looking at her legs, and he is mentally undressing her and feels an erection coming on. She knows he is married and asks about his son. He has never really had a personal conversation with her, and asks if she is married, which gets a big laugh. Engaged then - no. At the present time, she doesn't even have a boyfriend as work seems to take up all her time. Colin cannot really believe there is no man in her life. He tells her about Karen moaning about the late nights, trips away and business dinners like tonight. Penny nods and says she can see her point of view. Colin feels he knows her a little better, but that erection will just not go away.

Time to go and sit at the table. He suggests they start with the oysters, which come from Falmouth in Cornwall. He wants to see if it really is an aphrodisiac. The other two decide to share a

Chateaubriand; they are sure getting close. Penny doesn't want to share and goes for the Ossobuco, and he decides to have the same. He decides they need red wine and orders two bottles of Frappato from Sicily.

The oysters are a delight. The Chateaubriands enjoy their food together and seem very chummy. Penny loves her Ossobuco, and he thinks it is not too bad. The wine goes down very well. Nobody wants dessert. He is wondering where they are going to go from here, as it is just after 9 o'clock. The assistant and secretary are giggling together and say it has been great, but they are going to make it a night and leave. He is not sure if the secretary is married, but he thought she was, and he wonders what they mean by making it a night. They leave, and he gives the secretary an air kiss and the assistant a man hug. Penny is looking a little anxious and wonders out loud what they mean by a night. Colin asks for the cheque.

Penny says it's still really early, perhaps we should do something. I live a short cab ride from here, and I have a special bottle of Calvados which I would like to share with you after such a great dinner.

They leave the restaurant and grab a cab to her place, which takes about 5 minutes.

Chapter 3

They arrive in Rosary Gardens, and her place is a basement flat in a Victorian conversion. They are soon inside and it is tastefully modern. She sits him on the settee and goes to get glasses and the bottle. She goes to her CD player and puts on Norah Jones, which suits the mood, for his erection returns.

She comes back in and pours them both a good measure and sits next to him, close, and they clink glasses. Then she says to him, 'I think I would like you to kiss me, but not one of your air kisses.'

This is some invitation, and he gives her a real tongue kiss. She lays back and sighs.

We are not going to go into details about what happens next, but they are very quickly naked and in her bed, and she tells him she is on the pill, so no need for protection. She seems very happy and seems to have an orgasm at the same time as him. She tells him it was great, and hopefully, this will not be a one-night stand. In his joy, he tells her certainly not, and he is already planning the next time. He takes his leave sadly and gets a cab home, arriving just before midnight. Karen is asleep in bed. Penny is not going to bed and dreaming of a great evening, and wondering when it is going to happen again. Oh no, she is planning the downfall of her boss. The first thing she does is get a rope and make marks on her wrists. Then she makes herself cry by putting salt in her eyes. Satisfied, she then leaves her flat and catches a cab to the police station. There is a friendly looking sergeant and she tells him that she needs to report a rape. The sergeant is very concerned and says he will need to call a doctor and take a statement from her. He calls the doctor and takes her into a separate room. He sees she has been crying and asks if she needs anything. She declines. The sergeant asks her what has happened.

'Tonight I had dinner with my boss and two colleagues from work in a restaurant in Chelsea. My two colleagues left early, and I was left with my boss. He knew I lived quite close, and he invited himself to my place. We had a good dinner with him, and I always thought he was all right and a happily married man, so I thought, why not, and we got a cab to my place. As soon as we arrived after I had closed the door he grabbed my arm and dragged me to my bedroom where he tied my wrists to the bed, took off my clothes and then raped me. You can see my wrists here where he tied me. I am very worried, I am not on the pill and I hope to god that I am not pregnant.'

The sergeant tells her this is very disturbing and asks if she knows where he lives, to which she has to say no. But she tells him his name and the address of the office where he will be tomorrow. The sergeant says, I will see if the doctor has arrived. He returns shortly with a lady doctor who tells tells her is appropriate in cases of rape. The sergeant leaves, and she is left with the doctor. She has to tell the same story to the doctor. The doctor examines her wrists and makes a note in her notebook. She then undresses Penny and does the doctoring things associated with alleged rapes.

The doctor tells Penny from what she has been able to determine she has semen in her vagina, unexplained injuries to her wrists and she will most certainly be reporting to the sergeant that this prima facie looks like an aggravated rape. She leaves the room, and the sergeant returns. He thanks her for her time and says that tomorrow morning they will be going to Colin's place of work to arrest him for his crime. In the meantime, he will arrange for a car to take her home. He advises her not to go to work on Friday.

She is taken home in a police car. She lets herself in and gives herself a big pat on the back. It certainly looks like her plan is going to work. The doctor and the police are on her side, and his job has to be hers.

Chapter 4

Colin is feeling a little hungover. Karen asks about his night and comments that he was late home. Another moan. He just has a coffee for breakfast and sets off for his short walk to work. He is feeling pretty good about himself. He has been unfaithful, but what a way to do it. A truly great girl and a body to die for. He gets to the office just before 9 o'clock. The receptionist tells him two police officers are waiting to speak to him in the boardroom. He thinks this is very strange and cannot for the life of him think what this can all be about.

He enters the boardroom, and two men in plain clothes introduce themselves as an Inspector and a sergeant. They come straight to the point and tell him that he is under arrest for the rape last night of Miss Penny Weathers. He is astonished and a bit dumbfounded, and all he can say is, 'I am very sorry, but this seems like a huge mistake. I do admit that I had consensual sex with Penny last night, but in no way was it rape, and in fact, if anything she took the lead. I think the best thing we can do is bring Penny in here so we can clear the whole thing up.' The police tell him that Miss Weathers has been advised not to come to the office today, and he is under arrest and is coming with them now to Chelsea Police Station. He tries to complain but is told it is better to leave quietly without handcuffs, to which he has to agree. As they are leaving, the receptionist gives him a very strange look. He tells her just a routine enquiry, and I will be back shortly. The policemen raise their eyebrows but do not comment.

He is ushered into the back of a police car, and after about thirty minutes, they arrive at the station.

He is taken into a room where he is formally charged with the rape the previous night of Miss Penny Weathers. They then take his fingerprints and put something in his mouth to get his DNA. He assumes that he will now be free to leave, but they tell him this is not the case, and he will be put in a holding cell for the time being. He wants to protest, but what can he say?

He is put in a holding cell with no offer of a drink or anything to eat. With no breakfast, he is feeling a little hungry. He wonders what is going on here. It takes a while, as it is all so unexpected. At long last, he thinks he has worked it out. He has always known that Penny was ambitious, and she probably wants his job. What a clever girl, have sex with the boss and then cry rape, all angles covered and he is really in the shit.

It is a very long morning, and he is left completely alone. At midday, he is given a cheese sandwich and a bottle of water. The person delivering is not able to tell him anything.

At around 3, he is taken back to the two policemen. They tell him that DNA has confirmed his sperm was in the vagina of Miss Weathers and that he will be appearing in the Magistrates Court on Monday and is given details of the hearing. In the meantime, he will be released on police bail. He blurts out, 'This is all a terrible misunderstanding. The DNA only confirms what I have already told you: we had consensual sex. I do not know why we cannot get Miss Weathers in here and clear up the misunderstanding. 'The police only respond by saying that he is required to be in court as set out.

He takes the tube home. Karen is surprised to see him so early. He mumbles about business not being so busy and, for a change, spends some time playing with Jonathan. They have dinner at home and watch a bit of TV. There is no way he is going to tell Karen about the charges. They go to bed, but he cannot sleep. He has worked out what her game plan is. At the end of the day it will probably go to trial and a jury will have to decide whether it was consensual or rape. She will no doubt have a great sob story, but he will beat her. He has a lot more money than her and he will make sure he gets the best rape defence lawyer there is. A problem is how to keep this from Karen, not sure on that one. Then there is work. In this situation, they cannot be expected to work together. She will have to resign, but she wants my job. I am not going to resign as I am innocent and so close to being a director. Is this going to impact my ambition? With all these things going on in his head, he cannot sleep.

He gets up before Karen and makes coffee. She tells him he is looking tired. What can he say to her?

He manages a little sleep on Saturday night. Sunday is terrible, and he and Karen hardly have a word to say to each other. He doesn't sleep too well on Sunday either and gets up on Monday morning looking like a wreck. Decides to have toast and coffee for breakfast to give him some energy. Takes the tube to Sloane Square and walks to the Magistrates and gets there just in time. He has no lawyer, but he is innocent, so not need one. He finds the daily list, and he is number 7, so he will have to wait for a bit. Eventually, his case is called, and he enters the courtroom. There is no sign of Penny. The magistrate looks very stern. He asks Colin if he is represented, to which he replies in the negative. The magistrate asks a man whom he assumes is the prosecutor to open.

He says, 'We have in front of us a very serious case of rape. It is alleged that the defendant tied Miss Penny Weathers to her bed and then raped her. A doctor has examined the victim and confirms ligatures on her wrist and DNA has confirmed semen found in her vagina is that of the defendant. This will need to go to trial in the Crown Court, and we ask the magistrate thus. In the meantime, we also ask the magistrate for an order that the defendant should not approach or in any way contact the victim. They both work in the same place, and this means that prior to trial, the defendant should be excluded from their place of work. We are agreeable to bail but request the defendant forfeit his passport and be required to report weekly to the police.'

The magistrate says that it is all in order. The defendant will report tomorrow at his local police station and surrender rather than forfeit his passport and make arrangements for a weekly report. Colin is shown out of the Court.

He cannot believe what he has just heard. She really is a calculating bitch. There is no way he tied her up, but she has managed to engineer ligatures. This case is not going to be so easy. He has no proof that he did not tie her up. Even if he denies this to be the case, the marks on her wrists tell a different story. Meanwhile, let's talk about Penny. She did not go to the office on Friday and considered her position. She has no idea if the police went to the office. She decides to make a call and gets through to the secretary and reports she is unwell, but nothing serious, and she expects to be okay by Monday. Anything happening. Yes, there is.

Two police officers came early this morning and escorted Colin from the building, and he has yet to return. Nobody has any idea what it is all about. Penny expresses her surprise and ends the call by saying, "Get well soon." The secretary wonders if it is just a hangover. Penny continues her reflections. It seems he has been arrested - good. It will be difficult for him to come back to the office, which will make it easy for her to replace him. It all seems to be going to plan. There is one slight problem which she ponders. In order to prove her case, they had unprotected sex as she wanted to be able to provide a specimen of his semen; a rubber would have been no proof. But she is not on the pill. Is there a risk of pregnancy? She has heard of the morning-after pill, but she has no idea how or where to get it. She decides to wait a couple of days and then do a test. If she is pregnant, she will have to have an abortion for two reasons. She in no way wants his child, and pregnancy would interfere with her career ambitions and after all, this is what this is all about. So far, it seems to be going very well. She does not feel sorry for him in the least. A married man sleeping around deserves to suffer.

Colin now has to decide what to do. Should he go back to the office, perhaps tomorrow? Should he tell Karen? Maybe not. He gets home early again, as not much is happening at work, and spends some time with Jonathan. At around 7pm, his mobile rings, a number he does not recognise. He picks up, and a serious voice asks if he is free to speak privately. He says yes and goes into the bedroom. The serious voice says, 'Good evening. My name is Burns, and I am instructed by your company to deal with the matter at hand.

You have been accused by a member of your staff Miss Weathers, of aggravated rape.

My assistant was in court this morning, and I have full details of the charges. The magistrate also specified that before the trial, you should be excluded from your place of work to avoid any interaction with the victim. I appreciate that this case is in the early stages and will eventually come to trial, and that you are, of course, innocent until proven guilty, but with great reluctance on behalf of your company, I am instructed to inform you that from this moment, you are formally suspended from your position with the company. Furthermore, under no circumstances are you to attend the office or make any written or verbal correspondence with the company. In your absence, your salary will be stopped, credit cards and the office telephone – the one we are now speaking on - will also be stopped. I will be writing to you formally tonight, setting out the arrangements and will have it hand delivered tomorrow. If you have any personal effects that you wish returned, I would be grateful if you would contact me and only me directly for their return of such. Similarly, your only contact with the company will be through me, and I would hope you are going to be sensible and not try anything else. I hope I have made myself clear. Do you have any questions? Colin doesn't really know what to say, and his only response is, 'Thank you.'

He goes back into the living room, and Karen asks what that was all about. He can only say, 'Just business.'

He again doesn't sleep too well and thinks a lot about what is happening. Penny wants his job and has set him up. The company have got the legal boys involved, assuming he is guilty, and effectively kicked him out. He cannot go to the office. He guesses that tomorrow he will have to go to the police station to report and hand in his passport. He will then have to find something to occupy him for the rest of the day. At this time, there is no way that he is going to tell Karen what is going on. So what is he going to do every day? It is a real bore that his salary has gone and his credit card, and phone. They are reasonably well off and have over £100,000 in the bank and a similar amount in ISAs and investments, so in the short term, not much of a problem. The real question will be the Court. The evidence against him might be very strong, but it is all a lie, particularly the ligature. He is going to need a very good lawyer. He sneaks out of bed and does not disturb Karen, and goes to his iPad. He types in rape lawyer. There are quite a lot, but he selects Olliers who have an office in Berkeley Square. Their website has a number of interesting case studies. He takes down the phone number. He will call them tomorrow. He returns to bed but cannot sleep. Karen seems very peaceful. She wouldn't be if she knew what was going on. In the morning, he finds his passport in the normal place, dresses as if for work and leaves. The police station is fairly routine, and he agrees to report weekly on a Tuesday. He leaves the police station and goes into Starbucks and orders his favourite cappuccino. He uses his own credit card to pay. He sits at a table and turns on his phone. He has no line; it has already been disconnected. There is no payphone in Starbucks. He decides to just go to Olliers and takes the tube to Marble Arch and walks down to Berkeley Square. The offices are quite large and very modern. He goes to the reception. A very pretty girl. He explains he has been wrongly accused of rape and he needs a lawyer. The girl takes his name and asks him to go to the waiting area, and she will get somebody to see him. She hopes it will not be too long. He doesn't care as he has all day. After about 30 minutes, his name is called and he is shown into a conference room by a young man in shirtsleeves. He introduces himself as Chuck. Colin declines tea, coffee or water.

Chuck tells him that he is thirty years old and that for the last seven years since he qualified he has specialised in rape cases. He is an associate. He asks Colin to tell him his story.

'Well Chuck, I have been wrongly accused of rape.' Chuck butted in, 'I am sorry, that's what they all say. Please explain the circumstances.' 'Sorry, Chuck, to start off in the wrong way. My story is that last Thursday evening, I had dinner with four of my team at work to celebrate a successful IPO. There were four of us. We drank cocktails, good wine, and ate excellent food. Two left quite early, and I was left with Penny, who is quite dishy and wears very short skirts, and whom I have always rather fancied. Penny suggested that we go back to her place as she had good calvados. She was very leading, and we had unprotected sex as she said she was on the pill. She seemed very happy with the sex, and we sort of promised to do it again. I went home to my wife just before midnight. The next morning, I had a spring in my step, which didn't last long, as soon as I got to my office I was arrested by two police officers and taken to a police station where I was fingerprinted and had my DNA taken and then charged with rape. I had to go to Court on Monday where it was alleged that I had tied up Penny and then raped her. The magistrate gave me bail, but I have had to surrender my passport, and he also made an order of no contact. I have been suspended from work, and now I am here with you. I can tell you that with her leading, I did have consensual sex with Penny, but there was definitely no bondage. You have to realise that Penny is my number two and very ambitious, wanting my job and the bitch has set me up without a leg to stand on.'

Chuck strokes his chin. 'Firstly, I think we should not be calling Penny a bitch. But no matter, it seems you have a real problem. A doctor would have seen her ligature marks and recorded them accordingly. If what you are telling me is correct, then the ligature marks would have been self-inflicted.' 'Suppose we are in Court. She says you tied her up and then raped her. You say you did not, and she must have done it herself. The Court will have evidence of your semen in her vagina. It is my belief that 99 juries out of 100 will believe

Penny and find you guilty. It looks like a watertight case - a clever girl who has really caught you out and will most certainly get your job. 'Then there is the prison term, which can be between 4 and 19 years. I am afraid to say that in this case, tying up and then raping the victim could result in something like 15 years.'

Colin is shocked by this. A discussion about Penny ensues. Does he have any proof that she is a liar? No. Is there any way that we could get that proof? Probably not. Chuck says he is prepared to take on the case. His initial fee will be £5,000, with extra costs when it comes to the trial on a time basis. In addition, at Colin's expense, he would like to employ a private investigator to look very closely at Penny and hopefully find something useful to the defendant. He has a man in mind who has a good track record in this respect. The cost will be £500 per day, and he would recommend two weeks, which would cost £7,000 working 7 days a week. Colin reluctantly agrees to all this. He uses Chuck's iPad and transfers £12,000 to Olliers. They agree to meet at the same time tomorrow.

A bit early to go home, so Colin goes to see a movie. He arrives home a little late and can only mutter, 'Busy again.' That was the wrong thing to say as it means he will have to be always busy again, even though he now has no job. Karen hands him the post, but luckily, she doesn't mention that one was hand-delivered. The letter from Burns is just a repeat of what he said on the phone. Sleep is again difficult. £12,000 is a lot. He hopes Karen is not checking the bank - he will just say investments. The main problem is when to tell Karen - not yet. The other real problem is that he could be looking at 15 years in prison. One thing he is certain is that there is no way he is going to prison for 15 years just for a consensual shag with a pretty girl. His mind then wanders. Perhaps we need to get rid of her. How do you go about that - he has to admit to himself that he has no idea, but worth exploring? Then he has an idea. He should write to his Managing Director and set out Miss Weathers' play. This will have the effect of putting doubts in their mind. He knows that Burns has told him not to correspond, but he feels he has the perfect right in the circumstances.

He has trouble sleeping again and sneaks out of bed and gets out his iPad to write the letter, which goes as follows:

Dear Jim (the name of the Managing Director with whom he has always been on first-name terms)

I hope you will forgive me for writing to you despite the instructions I have received from Burns, but there are matters involved in this case which I feel it is important to bring to your attention. Miss Weathers, whom I used to have a lot of respect for, is playing her own game here. She has always been ambitious and after my job. The events of last Thursday evening gave her the ideal opportunity. I took my team out for a celebratory dinner to thank them for all the work on the recent craft beer IPO, which I am sure you will agree was the correct thing to do. Two of my team left early, and she took the lead, inviting me to her flat to drink a special calvados. She was always taking the lead and took me to her bed, where we had consensual sex. The sex was unprotected, as she said she was on the pill. I am a married man, and I know this was wrong. As I was leaving, it was all very pleasant, and we talked about the next time and the times after that.

After I left, she must have made the ligature marks and then gone to the police and told them that she had been tied up and then raped, which led to my subsequent arrest and appearance in the Magistrates Court when I know you had observers. I can tell you categorically that all I did was have consensual sex with one of my team members. I understand and agree that this was probably not the right thing to do, but I never tied her up or forced her to have sex. It is clear to me her game here. With her leading, she made me have sex with her. On my leaving, she made ligature marks and because it was unprotected sex, she had my semen in her vagina which she would have produced to the doctor. The police took my DNA, and of course, it can be proved that we had sex. She has always been ambitious and probably wanted my job. I think you have a lot of questions to ask here. Can it be right to allow an employee to take advantage of her boss to further her own ambitions?

Is this employee as good as her boss, and will the company be less effective without him? Is this employee trustworthy? Given what I am telling you, would you trust her integrity?

I truly hope that you find ways to answer these questions.

In all the circumstances, I believe it is wrong for me to be excluded from the company, and I would be grateful for your consideration.

Yours Sincerely

Colin

He printed two copies. One for the post and one for Chuck.

Chapter 5

He is up next morning, pretending to go to work. He posts the letter to Jim first class. What is he going to do with the morning before going back to Chuck? He ends up in the library reading the Telegraph and the Times and does both crosswords, but not very well, as he has other things on his mind. It is still early. He takes the tube to Marble Arch again. He wonders about a pub lunch but decides to remain sober for his afternoon meeting. Instead, he goes to Selfridges and have a pretty boring lunch surrounded by middle-aged ladies on a shopping spree. How boring can you get? He finds he is missing the buzz of the office and wonders what Penny is up to. Probably being the perfect bitch and enjoying her glory.

He manages to waste another hour and then goes back to Chuck.

Back in the same room. Chuck looks very grave and says,

'Colin, I am not going to beat about the bush. I can sum up the situation by saying you are in the real shit here. From my reading, Miss Weathers is an *extremely* clever, calculating lady, and she appears to have covered all the angles, leaving you with no defence. As we talked about yesterday, I have instructed the private investigator who reports that she left home at 7.30 and he followed her on the tube to work, where she arrived shortly after 8.00. He will return before 17.00 and follow her when she leaves the office. My team are considering all aspects of your case, looking at case histories, but I have to say that unless our investigator is able to come up with something, the odds do not look good.'

Colin tells him that it was short and sweet, but suddenly has an outside-the-box idea.

'Chuck, I have told you that I did not tie her up and that her ligatures would have been self-inflicted. I am not sure that she will have been so clever as to have got rid of the rope or whatever she used. Do you think it would be possible for the investigator to gain entry to her flat and find the rope or whatever, take it away and have it analysed to show that my DNA is absent, which would prove my version of the events?'

Chuck replies that it is a great idea, but he is not sure the investigator would be up for illegal entry, but he can always try. He does not think under the circumstances that they would be able to get a search warrant.

Colin then gives Chuck a copy of his letter to Jim. Chuck reads it carefully, 'I think your letter was a good idea. What you are doing is casting doubt. It could have been a little more legal. As a follow-up, I believe we should also write, thereby casting more doubt. I will draft it myself and email it for your approval. I will need the full name of the Managing Director and office address, and your email. What you say about the pill is interesting. Suppose she is not on the pill and only had unprotected sex in order to get a DNA specimen to prove sex had taken place with you. I will ask the investigator to look into it.'

They agree to meet again on Friday at the same time. Colin goes to see another movie. Karen seems very nice tonight and wants to make love. He has to decline - pressure of work. We know that he has still not told her, and for the time being, he decides to keep it that way.

Back to Penny. She has now been in Colin's seat for 3 days. She had rather hoped that a director or personnel would have called her into a meeting to confirm her appointment with a good salary and benefit increase, but it hasn't happened. She wonders if she should push, but decides it is better to wait and see. Her plan, though, seems to be working with Colin out of the office and probably in jail and never to return. She tries not to feel guilty for what she has done to him, but in the end, he deserved it for being unfaithful to his wife. She is still a little concerned about the pregnancy question and decides to get the contraption and test it later.

On the way home, she pops into a local late-night chemist and buys a Clearblue pregnancy test. The first thing she does on arriving home is do the test. Oh my god, it is positive. It must be Colin because he has been her only sexual partner for ages, and anyway, in the past, she was always careful.

A lot to think about here. Does she want a baby? Definitely not. It would interfere with her career. Should she have the baby and have it adopted - definitely not for the same reasons. There is no way she is going to tell Colin, so the only thing to do will be an abortion.

She goes on the internet and finds 132 Healthwise at Chelsea and Westminster Hospital on the Fulham Road, just round the corner. It is all very simple, and online she books an appointment for Saturday morning.

She sails through Friday, but still no Director or personnel and gets home quite early. She thinks she needs some courage for tomorrow and has a salad and a bottle of wine to prepare.

She comes out of her flat feeling a little hungover and does not notice the investigator who follows her to the hospital. She has her abortion, and he follows her home. He immediately reports to Chuck that Miss Weathers has had an abortion.

Chapter 6

Since their last meeting, Chuck has emailed the draft letter to Jim, which Colin has approved. Colin has had no response to his letter.

There is not much to discuss in their Friday meeting.

Colin spends Saturday morning trying to be a good father and takes Jonathan to his Saturday Club and tries to talk to the other parents, but with what he is going through, finds it a little difficult.

Just after lunch, he gets an email from Chuck:

'Just had a notification from the investigator that Penny had an abortion this morning. Need to meet. Come in first thing Monday morning.'

Very interesting, he spent the rest of Saturday and Sunday with his own thoughts.

On Monday, he is back with Chuck.

Chuck opens the conversation, 'This is good news and bad news. You have maintained that she told you she was on the pill so that you could have unprotected sex. The fact that she has had an abortion shows that she lied to you. The bad news is that she says you tied her up and then raped her and in these circumstances the question of the pill would not have arisen. To be honest, we are still at square one, and all we have is your word against hers, and to be honest with you, I do not think it will take our defence any further. She had to have an abortion because you raped her.'

Colin does not really like what he is hearing and can only respond,

'I see the good and bad news. She most certainly did tell me that she was on the pill and I cannot know if I was a rapist why I would have made this up. Is there no angle we can use here to improve my defence?'

All Chuck can say is that 'Unless you wiretapped her making that statement, I cannot see anything. We will continue to work on your case and try to find something.'

Colin leaves feeling very low.

The bitch really seems to have got me.

He goes and sits on a bench by the Serpentine in Hyde Park and thinks about the future.

He really has been set up. His defence is nothing. He is not going to prison for 15 years because he is innocent. He will just have to leave this all behind him.

But where will he go? He cannot flee overseas as he has had to surrender his passport. It will have to be somewhere in this country, nowhere too obvious, where he would be noticeable. A tourist place would be good, maybe Cornwall. If he is fleeing justice or injustice, he will have to be a nobody and have no identity. But he will need money. Can you work with no identity? Casual cash work, maybe such as gardening. He has never been in a garden in his life and would not know where to start. In the meantime, he will need a float to get him going, and he determines to go to the ATM every day and withdraw the maximum amount and build a nest egg. Hoping Karen is not checking the bank.

When he gets home later, he logs into his bank and finds he can withdraw £500 per day. He transfers £5,000 to the current account.

It is now Tuesday, and as usual, he pretends he is going to work. First stop is the nearest ATM, and he withdraws £500. He then goes to Starbucks for a coffee and then to the library to read the papers and do the crosswords. He finds a cheap cafe for a sandwich lunch and reflects on what he intends to do. It must be the right decision, as it cannot be right to go to prison as an innocent man. In a couple of weeks, he will have £5,000, but he thinks maybe this is not enough to start his new life. He should perhaps delay his departure for another two weeks and get £10,000, which he feels more comfortable with. But he will need to get away before he is due to appear in Court. He has no idea of the process but thinks he will probably get a letter inviting him to Court. He has no idea when this will be, but from experience, it is likely to be some time away. And now he thinks about the money. The best thing would be to keep it on his person or maybe in his briefcase, which he still carries with him every day for the pretend office or hide it in the house somewhere, which he prefers. He will decide when he has a little more.

What can he do with his afternoon? Another movie, which is probably what he does.

The movie ends at 5pm, and he can't get home too early. He thinks about going to a pub, but Karen would notice, so not a good idea. He could go walking, but then he might be easy prey for muggers. This is a real problem, so he just goes to another cinema and sees another movie.

He gets home around normal time, and Karen still seems very good-humoured and has made him a nice dinner. He tells her weekdays, so maybe we will leave the wine until the weekend. After dinner, he checks his emails, and there is one from Chuck suggesting a Friday afternoon meeting to which he replies in the affirmative.

Another sleepless night. He thinks to himself that he has really been set up by that bitch but at least he has a plan. In four weeks, he is just going to run away from it all. But what is he going to do in those four weeks whilst pretending to go to work? At work, he is always busy and has too much to do, but now he has nothing. He really does not want to spend his days in Starbucks, the library doing crosswords and seeing two movies per day, with the only respite an occasional meeting with Chuck to hear some more bad news. One option would be to tell Karen everything and apologise for being unfaithful, and explain to her how he has been set up. Give her the lawyer's bad news that he will be found guilty even though completely innocent, and is likely to spend up to 15 years in prison. Tell her that for the next couple of weeks, he will be at home, and then they are going to run away, taking Jonathan. There are some good things here. Despite being unfaithful to Penny, he thinks he still loves her, and he quite likes Jonathan, although he has not had so much time with him. They can still be a family. Then he thinks of the bad things. He has never wanted to confess what went on with Penny, and he thinks he still does not. How will she react? Ask for a divorce, maybe. Then there is the money. He has planned to get £10,000. He will be able to exist on that for a while and supplement it with his cash job. If he has to support three, it will be a lot more expensive.

He then starts thinking about what will happen if he runs away. Karen will be left a single mother, but in essence, that is what she is anyway. Financially, there will be a big pot of cash and investments, and when Jonathan goes to school, she can go back to being a solicitor. She will probably inform the police that he has gone missing. He feels sure that they will assume he has absconded and do little to try to find him or start a murder inquiry. He is not sure what efforts they will make to trace him. He has no mobile phone, so that will not give him away. Debit and credit cards can be traced, so he will just leave those behind. There will be nothing for them to go on.

But what to do in the meantime? He has a sudden bright idea. A holiday. It has been ages since they were away. They had a weekend in Rome about a year ago. It will have to be the UK as he has no passport. We are in early June, the start of the holiday season. He could say not much is going on at work, naturally true as he is excluded, and he thinks they all need a break, and he has booked a fortnight in Cornwall for the three of them. He will have to get police permission, but it should not be a problem. Thinking carefully, he decides to tell them he is going to Suffolk, as when he does run away, that is the first place they will look. But then Karen will probably tell them about the holiday in Cornwall, which might place the emphasis back there. He decides Suffolk will be the best bet to cover all the angles. It would have been good to go to Cornwall and check out the possibilities where he has not been since his teenage years, but it is a dangerous route.

Off to the office again, but today he takes his iPad. His normal Starbucks start to the day and then to the library, but no papers today. He starts searching holiday rentals in Suffolk. Suffolk is a big place, but he settles in Southwold. He finds a penthouse with a terrace and sea views for £950 per week and is available for the next two weeks. He books it and pays the whole sum by credit card.

A short time later, he gets a confirmatory email with all the details. Access is by the porter. Sounds very smart.

The next thing to do is think about eating. He needs to make this holiday special, and some good dinners out will help to achieve that. Back on the internet to find Southwold restaurants.

TripAdvisor has a lot of options. He books the Swan Hotel for Saturday, the Crown for Sunday, and Coasters for Monday. After that, they can check out the scene and maybe even eat at home some nights. He feels the job is done.

Another sandwich lunch and another movie, but he gets home very early at 5.30. Karen is a little shocked to see him. He says:

'Good news. I have managed to negotiate two weeks' leave, and I have booked us a fantastic sea view penthouse in Southwold, and we leave Saturday morning. You will need to pack your bikini and a bucket and spade for Jonathan.'

Karen looks very pleased and says:

'I have never heard of Southwold. Is it in Italy or Greece? Which airport are we flying from, and what time is the flight?'

This amuses Colin, and he tells her that Southwold is in Suffolk and they will be taking the train.

She seems a little downcast and replies:

'What is the point of going to Suffolk? It will be cold and dreary, full of fish and chip shops. We haven't been away for nearly a year since we went to Rome. I really think that you should be taking us to Italy or Greece.'

Colin is a little put out by this as he had rather hoped she would be excited by a sea-view penthouse, and he can hardly tell her his passport is with the police because he is out on bail. What excuse can he make?

'It is June. This holiday is very short notice, and I did try to find something in Italy or Greece, but all the flights were full, and I could not find anything. I am sure that the weather will not be dull and dreary, and I have already booked expensive upmarket restaurants for the first three nights.' He is hoping that this is going to satisfy her, but it seems not.

'You are a very busy man, and I am sure you have little time to investigate holidays. I am going to get on the internet right now and find us the perfect holiday in Italy or Greece, and I bet I will come up with something splendid.'

Colin feels exasperated by all this.

'I am sorry, but there is a problem. The penthouse is quite expensive (no need to tell her how much) and I have paid the full amount for the two weeks, which we will lose if we are a no-show.'

And now, being a woman, she wants to know how much. He tells her £1,900.

All she can say is, 'It better be good then.'

This wasn't quite what he had been hoping, but at least it now seems settled.

By the end of the week, he has £2,000 in cash. He decides to hide it in a suit pocket. He will have to carry on with the ATM in Southwold.

He does have his meeting with Chuck. Chuck is still very negative. The investigator has found nothing else. Her life seems to be work and back, usually late, and she never goes out unless after midnight when he clocks off.

He has booked their train tickets first class from Liverpool Street to Halesworth, the nearest station. They will get a taxi to Southwold. The train journey is nearly three hours. They leave Liverpool Street at 10.05, so it looks like a late lunch.

Chapter 7

And now we are off on holiday.

It is a very cloudy, cool day. Colin has not checked the weather forecasts.

Liverpool Street is not far in a cab.

The train is late and does not leave until 10.30, which means an arrival time of 1.30. No restaurant car on the train, just a buffet.

They only use the buffet for two coffees and orange juice for Jonathan.

Eventually, we are all in Halesowen and everybody is hungry. They grab a sandwich at the station. Not another sandwich and no match for London.

There is drizzle and it feels cold.

They find a taxi that quotes £40 for the fare to Southwold - a real rip-off. It is only 15 minutes and they arrive at their location.

The porter is very friendly and takes them up in the lift to the top floor - 6. He opens the door. There is a great view of the sea and drizzle. He shows them the two en-suite bedrooms and leaves them to themselves. All Karen can say is that there is no bath for Jonathan. Not a great start. They decide to give Jonathan his afternoon nap as they will be having dinner later. Colin and Karen open the doors to the terrace and venture outside. It is large with great sea views, a table and four chairs and four sun loungers. All Colin can say is that the sun will be out soon, and we will really be able to enjoy it. Karen just grunts and says she will unpack. Colin just sits looking at the sea. He forgot to bring a book. In reality, this seems just as bad as his non-work days. Karen returns but says nothing. He tells her he forgot to bring a book and is going out to find a bookstore, and leaves.

He braves the weather and starts to wander through the town. He finds a small bookstore. He has a chat with the friendly salesman and eventually selects 'The Honourable Schoolboy' by John Le Carre, which looks quite long. He finds a bank and takes £500 from the ATM and returns to the penthouse. Karen is reading and does not acknowledge his return. They just sit there reading and not conversing. Eventually, she goes to get Jonathan up. Colin spends some time with his son.

He has booked an early dinner at 7pm because of Jonathan. They both have a shower and change. Jonathan just gets a face wash.

They ask the porter for directions to the Swan. He tells them that he will be off at 8pm and shows them the key to gain re-entry.

The Swan is a nice-looking old building. They enter the restaurant and go straight to the table, and are given menus. Would they like an aperitif? Karen says, 'Two orange juices, please.' Colin orders a pint of the local Adnams' ale, which is recommended. This is not looking so good as Karen is not really speaking and is sticking to orange juice. Jonathan is very quiet, too.

They look through the menus. There is nothing for kids. They call the waiter over and ask about food for kids. There is none. Not a good start. Karen says she will share hers. Colin orders Gazpacho and the Fish Platter, which has cured salmon, crab, herring and cod's roe. Karen orders only a main course of duck. He is given a wine list. Karen does not want wine. He cannot drink a whole bottle, so he asks about wine by the glass and orders a Pinot Noir. Their drinks arrive. It does not seem appropriate to clink glasses and say cheers.

Colin tries to open a conversation. 'It all seems great here in this lovely restaurant, and I really like the penthouse. It is so modern and has everything you might need, and the terrace is fantastic and pretty soon we will be out there sunbathing.' Karen looks like she is not going to reply, but eventually says, 'I am glad you like it. I hate everything about this place, particularly the weather. I told you I wanted to go to Italy or Greece, where the sun would never set. But you made up your mind, and here we are.' Colin has nearly finished his beer, and his wine arrives. Jonathan starts moaning and says he hates it here, and why can't they be at home? Colin tries to placate him by telling him that he is going to love it here. Tomorrow they will go to the beach and he can play with his bucket and spade and paddle in the sea. His response is that it will not happen as it is sure to just keep on raining.

Colin's Gazpacho arrives, and it is very good. He finishes but cannot think of anything to say, and Karen is not talking. The only good thing about this situation is that Karen seems unlikely to be sexy tonight, so he will not have to think up an excuse.

Their main courses arrive, and Karen orders two more orange juices and Colin another Pinot Noir. His Fish Platter is very good. Karen makes no comment about her food, and Jonathan does not like the duck or the vegetables and eats hardly anything. Their plates are taken away, and they are offered the Dessert menus. Karen declines, Colin does not really like puddings, but they do order a vanilla ice cream for the boy, which he seems to enjoy. It is only 8.30 but they get the bill, pay and return to the penthouse. After his beer and wine, Colin feels quite well, but Karen, who is still silent.

They get back in okay, and Karen says she will put Jonathan to bed. Colin turns on the television, but there are only five channels. No Sky or anything interesting, and no DVD player. Colin watches a bit of Casualty, which is so boring. Karen seems to be taking forever, but comes back and announces, 'Jonathan is very unhappy in this strange new place. I think I should spend the night with him to give him comfort. I will go into our room and get my nightdress and bid you goodnight.' All Colin can do is say goodnight back.

So, here he is in his expensive, smart penthouse all alone. Karen is truly pissed off and is not going to hide her displeasure. The worst part is that they are going to be here for two weeks. He could say he has an urgent message from work and has to immediately return. Leave them here and have the Barbican to himself. But that won't work as she would no doubt come back with him.

He is just going to have to stick it out.

He turns off the television and gets his book out. He would like another drink, but he searches in the kitchen and the cupboards are bare. Oh no, there is nothing for breakfast and no coffee either.

In very low spirits, he goes to bed at around 11.30.

He seems to be first up in the morning, as there is nobody around. He will surprise them with breakfast out. He looks out at the sea. It is still very cloudy, but it does not seem to be raining.

At long last, Karen appears in her nightdress. The boy is still asleep, but she didn't sleep too well. Join the club, but for different reasons. Where's breakfast? He explains that they forgot to stock up and will have to go out and then find a place for food and drink to stock up. Her reply is 'Brilliant' and she goes into their bedroom. Again, she seems to be taking ages but eventually comes out and looks at the weather, another 'Brilliant.' She goes to wake up Jonathan and is gone for ages again. When she comes out, she tells him that she had to wash him with a flannel due to the lack of a bath. He looks as downcast as her, and all he can say is that he is hungry. Not surprising, as all he has had since a poor lunch sandwich is ice cream.

They leave the penthouse and wander into town. It is Sunday, and everything seems to be closed, and they do not see any supermarkets for provisions. They spot the Crown Hotel, where they will be going for dinner later and go in for breakfast. It is very grand. Breakfast is £20 per head and there are no reductions for children. They have a reasonable breakfast and so it should be at that price.

They ask the waiter about supermarkets. He tells them there is a Co-op in the Market Place and gives them directions, and says it should be open by now. 10-4 on Sundays.

It is quite easy to find. They buy orange juice (crucial), milk, tea, coffee, tea, sugar, bread, cereal, butter and jam, which should do them for breakfast. Colin says he wants to get some beer and wine. Karen objects and says no real need and too much to carry. They just buy breakfast things.

Back to the penthouse. The weather is still cloudy. Colin says this cannot be a home without beer and wine. I am going back, which is what he does.

He gets back just before midday with 12 Peroni and three bottles of Pinot Noir. Karen asks if he has bought lunch. There is some discussion about what we all want for lunch. Jonathan wants crisps and a Kitkat, Karen wants a smoked salmon sandwich, and Colin has no idea. He is sent back to the Co-op. He forgot to ask what sort of crisps, so he bought salted. There is no smoked salmon, so he gets tuna for both of them. Back to the penthouse. They are not going to be having lunch on the terrace, so they sit around the dining table. Colin produces the goodies. Karen, 'I asked for smoked salmon and all I get is bloody tinned tuna, which you must know I hate. What sort of place is this with no smoked salmon?' 'Jonathan, I hate salted crisps. At home, I always get salt and vinegar. Don't you know that? I suppose not because you are never there.' Colin can not believe it can all go so wrong over a simple thing like lunch. He is going to have to make this a lot better.

Karen announces that it is time for Jonathan's afternoon nap and takes him off.

She comes back with her book, and they read in silence for a couple of hours. It is still cloudy but not raining. Karen says she will get Jonathan up. He suggests they should go for a walk and explore the promenade. Surprisingly, she agrees.

At about 4.00, they leave the penthouse and make for the promenade. There are not a lot of people about. They walk along a bit and then go on the pier. It is not very exciting with just a couple of restaurants and not much else. They get back just after 5.00.

Karen says she is going to take a shower and then change. Where are they going tonight? He says back to the Crown, and she says she'd better dress up. He guesses he will need a jacket and tie, which is a bore. Colin has a Peroni and spends a bit of time playing with Jonathan, but is not really into it, given all the difficulties.

Karen reappears, and he goes off to shower and change.

To the Crown. He was right to wear a jacket and tie because all the gentlemen are so attired. Last night seemed much more relaxed. Again, they go straight to their table and are given menus. Sunday Roast. Soup of the day to start, your choice of beef, lamb, pork or chicken with all the trimmings, Dessert Trolley. £45 per head excluding service. Will they be having wine? Karen says, 'No, just two orange juices,' and Colin orders a pint of beer and a glass of Pinot Noir. Karen declares that due to the expense, she will share again and will have chicken. Colin enquires if the beef is rare and is told no, so, he orders pork.

Again, it is a mostly silent dinner. The food is pretty good. Colin only has the one glass, and they both declined dessert, and no, there is no ice cream.

Back to the penthouse before 8.30. Karen goes off to bed with Jonathan again, and he is left alone. He drinks a whole bottle of Pinot Noir all to himself.

He wakes up to another cloudy day with a bit of a hangover and makes himself a Nescafé. No sign of the others.

Karen appears and all she can say is 'another cloudy day.' She makes tea and gives herself cereal to eat. Still silence. Jonathan appears and has OJ and cereal with his mum.

Colin wonders what on earth they are going to do today. And has another thought. Maybe they should get a babysitter and have a Date Night. That might improve Karen's mood. He will ask the porter and also see if he has any ideas about what to do on a cloudy day. He pops down to see the porter. No problem, his daughter is a babysitter, and on a day like this, they should take the ferry to Walberswick and have a nice lunch in the pub. He gives directions.

Colin goes back and says, 'All sorted, we are going on a boat ride.' Jonathan claps his hands, so making progress then. He decides to keep the babysitter a secret, but they will need to get something for the boys' tea.

They head off for the ferry. It is a short ride at only £2 with under 5s free, but quite nice, and he can feel the spirits lifting a little. The place is pretty small with not a lot to do, so they are early in the pub. The bar menu has smoked salmon and cream cheese sandwiches, and local crab, which is what they order. Jonathan chooses Chicken Nuggets and Chips, which he is given to understand are his favourite.

Back to the ferry. Whilst they are waiting, he tells her about the babysitter. She says, 'I cannot believe you. We are in this foreign place, and you want to leave our boy with a complete unknown. Anything could happen.' Colin is a little taken aback. 'It is very late for such a little boy to be out. The babysitter will be the daughter of the porter. You have met him and he seems a very decent chap, and I am sure his daughter will be likewise, and there is nothing to worry about.' To which she replies, 'Over my dead body. It is not going to happen. If you are so concerned about the little one being out so late, then we will just have to eat at home. We will get dinner on the way back.'

There seems to be little point in arguing.

On the way back, they return to the town. The Co-op seems to be the only place to buy food. They get a frozen Lasagna, Chicken Nuggets and chips and head home. They speak to the porter and cancel the babysitter to his disappointment, but tell them to let them know if she will be needed another time.

Jonathan is put down for his siesta.

They sit silently reading. Jonathan is back in play, and he spends a little time with him, but there is no feeling. This all seems to be going so wrong. They were supposed to be in a smart seafood place tonight, and now all he is going to have is frozen lasagna.

At about 6.00, Karen says time to get dinner ready and goes into the kitchen. He gets himself a Peroni. She enquires what he is doing with himself and commands him to lay the table. He asks if she will be having wine with dinner, to which he gets a negative response.

There really is nothing happening here, and he can almost feel her loathing. She would loathe him a lot more if she knew the real story. Perhaps tonight he should tell her the whole story. How he has been set up, what trouble he is in, why they are here and not in the sunshine, etc. She might be compassionate and get on his side. Fat chance, he will have to keep his secret to himself.

The dinner is not a great success. The lasagna is overcooked and burnt at the edges, and Jonathan says his chips are not cooked properly. Karen puts the boy down for the night.

She returns to the living room and stares at him. He is sitting with half a bottle of wine beside him. She mutters, 'You have had a beer and now I suppose that you are going to drink that whole bottle, caring nothing about me or your baby.' He is not sure what the response should be here. Declare his undying love or talk about practical things like where to get some decent food. He decides the latter. 'I am only drinking because I did not really enjoy the dinner. The Co-op does not seem to me to be the greatest place to source dinner, and a place like this must have great butchers and fishmongers and indeed vegetable shops where we can do much better. You have always been a great cook (flattery can never hurt), and I am sure you could make us dinners better than any restaurant round here. I will go to see the porter in the morning and find out where we need to go.' She seems quite pleased with this, and he suspects she liked the cooking flattery.

Her reply, 'Good idea. I will leave it to you. Shall we see what is on the television?' Making progress, then. The television is dreadful, and they spend an hour flipping channels, and she retires to bed with the boy.

Colin has not touched his wine since her comment, but after she has left, he finishes the bottle.

The next morning, the weather is the same. He cannot check the weather forecast as there does not appear to be an internet connection. He had better buy a newspaper to see what is going to happen. He has his Nescafé, and later Karen and the boy have the same breakfast as the day before. What on earth can they do today in this inclement weather? He goes to see the porter and finds the food information he needs.

Goes back to them and reports that he has a butcher, fishmonger and greengrocer. He is going shopping, what would they both like for dinner? Karen looks thoughtful. She would like an Artichoke followed by a fish such as Skate. Jonathan wants Chicken Nuggets and ice cream. He tells Jonathan it must be otherwise. Karen just says, 'Let him have what he wants.'

He goes off and manages to source Artichokes and Skate, and in the Co-op gets potatoes, Chicken Nuggets, chips, peas and ice cream and the Daily Telegraph.

He gets back and, for want of something better to do, suggests a repeat of yesterday's ferry ride. Everybody agrees. But first, he looks at the weather on the back page of the Telegraph. Today is Tuesday, and the first sign of any sun is Friday. Not good.

The ferry trip and pub lunch are a repeat of Monday. Surely, they can't do this every day until Friday. On the way back, Colin goes into the Co-op and buys 4 more bottles of wine in case Karen wants to be sociable.

They put Jonathan down for his siesta and revert to their silent reading. Karen goes to make a cup of tea, but none is offered to him.

She goes to wake up the boy, and they watch Pointless. She says she watches it most days, and it is really good. He watches and only gets a few answers. She keeps shouting out things but does not get a Pointless answer. Is this what she really does when he is at work, earning all the money?

It is over, and she says she will get dinner ready and then change, as this will be a special dinner.

He asks her if she would like a glass of wine or beer while she is working, and she asks for a beer.

Maybe things are looking up at last.

A little later, she says, 'All ready,' and goes off to change and comes back in a black dress and full make-up. It is getting better.

He lays the table with two wine glasses. She comes out and says yes, she will have a glass of wine, but she would prefer white. He has to rush back to the Co-op and manages to find chilled Chardonnay and buys three bottles. He gets back and pours her a glass, and gets a thank you and a smile.

They have a reasonable dinner with some conversation, but all about nothing. Jonathan is put to bed. They sit down in front of the TV and are channel-hopping again. She finishes her bottle of wine, and he still has about a third left. He wonders if something good is going to happen. This is not to be, as she declares that she is tired and will go and join Jonathan. Some hope. He sits alone and slowly finishes his wine.

He goes to bed. At least she did talk a little today and drank beer and wine. It can only get better.

In the morning, he is first up, and it is still cloudy. Only two days to go before we might get some sun. He makes his Nescafé as usual and waits for her to make an appearance.

It is after 10pm when she surfaces with Jonathan, and he wonders if she is a little hungover. He asks her what she would like for dinner. Steak is the answer, and what should we do today? She has no idea. He says he will go and get the shopping and get something interesting for starters, and we need more milk, OJ and bread.

He goes off. The fishmongers have cooked langoustine, and he buys two fillet steaks and a hamburger in the butchers and gets supplies in the Co-op and another Telegraph. He gets back and checks the weather. The forecast has not changed. He tells Karen that he will take Jonathan to the beach to build sandcastles.

She gives him a stare, but says, 'Why not?' which is what he does.

Jonathan does not seem to like the beach that much and shows little interest in castle building. Colin has to do all the work, and after what seems like ages, he has built a massive sandcastle with a moat. He asks Jonathan if he would like to fill up his bucket with seawater and fill the moat. He is not interested, so Colin does it. The sandcastle looks great, and it is a shame he hasn't got any flags to decorate. He then notices that the tide is coming in rather fast. They have built the sandcastle in the wet sand below the tide line. Within about 15 minutes, the sea is lapping around his structure, and 5 minutes later, it is washed away.

He reflects that it just sums up life. They return to the penthouse. Karen puts down her book and asks how it was. Jonathan sort of mumbles something unintelligible. He has gone to a lot of trouble to amuse and seems to have failed. He doesn't know that he will soon be gone from life. Will he miss his dad? He is not sure he will miss his son, who seems so dull.

They go and have fish and chips for lunch. It is not too bad, but Jonathan hates the fish and only eats chips and tomato ketchup.

They take him back for his nap, and they revert to reading.

Karen declines a beer before dinner and has no wine. The food is rather good, and the langoustines are superb.

She retires early to bed again with Jonathan.

I am sure you will agree with me that this is all getting a bit dull. We will sum up the rest of the holiday in a short paragraph.

The weather gets better, and they go to the beach. Jonathan and Karen do not want to go in the water, so Colin goes for a swim alone. It is icy, and he doesn't stay in that long. All dinners are at home, and they have no more lunches out. Most afternoons, they sit in the sunshine on the terrace. Karen spends every night with Jonathan, so he gets no sex. He wonders if she knows he had been playing away. All things considered, he is not going to miss them. On Saturday, they take the train back to London. Nobody thanks him for a great time.

On Saturday night, Karen returns to bed, but there is no lovemaking.

On Sunday, he seems to spend it mostly alone.

He reflects on his situation. He has been really set up by Penny, and even with the best legal team, there seems to be no way out, and he risks a long time in prison, which he is not prepared to do as an innocent man. The fortnight away did nothing to change his resolve. Karen was so boring because she wanted to be in Italy or Greece, and he found that spending time with Jonathan did not do it for him. He finds that he will be glad to get away. He decides that he will do it tomorrow. By multiple visits to the ATM, he calculates that he has now over £8,000, which will be a good starting point before he is able to earn. But there is one problem. He would like to take a small bag or even a suitcase with some of his favourite things: jeans, shirts and sweaters and maybe a couple of CDs. He can't do that with Karen observing. He will just have to leave late in the morning after Karen has taken Jonathan to the nursery. He also wonders why there is no letter giving him a court date, but it doesn't matter as he will not be going.

The next morning, he forgets to set the alarm and they do not wake up until 8.30. Karen is very flustered and says it is so late, Jonathan had better have a day off today. With some gentle persuading, she agrees to take him even if he will be a little late. Colin retires to the shower, and when he comes out, they are just going. He gives them a cheery, 'have a nice day,' and they are gone.

He quickly finds a smaller suitcase and fills it with some of his favourite things. He hides his credit and debit cards and driving licence in one of his suits, and pretty soon, he's out of there.

Chapter 8

Colin makes his way to the tube.

This is his first TURN.

He gets to Paddington just before 10.00. There is a train to Truro leaving at 10.35, which will get there just after three. He buys a single ticket, which sets him back just over £70. He buys a bottle of water and a ham sandwich, and a paper from WH Smith and goes to find his train. The train leaves on time and does not seem that full. Monday morning, no holidaymakers. He reads the paper and realises he has no pen to do the crossword, and he forgot to bring a book. He scans the crossword and finds he can do most of it. Then all he can do is stare out of the window; it is going to be pretty boring doing this for the next three hours. Given his circumstances, he does not really want to get into a conversation. They will want to know "business or pleasure?" Neither am I running away. That is what he is doing; he is running away. He never thought in his life that he would ever get in a situation like this, but he has. Having taken good legal advice and weighed up all his options, it seemed the only alternative.

There is a buffet car, but he decides to just eat his sandwich and drink water. The sandwich tastes like it was made in a sewer. At long, long last, they are pulling into Truro.

He realises that he has nowhere to stay. He needs a bed and breakfast for a couple of nights while he sorts out something more permanent.

At the station, he asks a man in uniform about places to stay. He says that everywhere is probably full, but he could try the Townhouse and he gives him directions. It is quite a long walk, but eventually he finds it. He is able to book a room for two nights at £60 per night. The owners are helpful and tell him about local eating places. He goes to his room but does not unpack. He wanders back into town and looks around. He finds a couple of the places they mentioned, but eventually goes to Burger King, which is fairly busy. He thinks he needs some alcohol and wanders into a pub almost next door and orders a pint of Doombar, a local special. Nobody takes any notice of him, which is good. He is not standing out as a runaway.

He wonders about Karen. It is now 8.30 and she will be wondering why he is not home yet and he hasn't called or anything. Time drags on until 11.00 - still no sign. She just goes to bed.

When she wakes up in the morning, he has not slept in the bed. Is something wrong? Has he had an accident? She tries his mobile and gets the number unobtainable. It is too early to call the office, and she has no idea what to do. She takes Jonathan to the nursery and returns home. Calls the office. She is told that Colin has not been in for some time. That means he did not go to work yesterday. She would have thought he would be raring to go after two weeks' holiday. Where on earth can he have gone? It was a little strange that he left after them yesterday. That never happens. Did he have another agenda which he failed to mention?

She spends the day worrying about where he can be. Should she phone hospitals to see if he has had an accident - she decides against it. She picks Jonathan up from the nursery and returns home. Still no sign. And the same at bedtime and in the morning - he has not been back. After she has taken Jonathan to nursery in the morning, she decides to go to the police to report him missing. She is referred to as a young lady PC. She explains that her husband left for work on Monday morning and has not returned. She has tried his mobile (it's unobtainable) and she phoned his office but he was not in. The PC asks for name, address and date of birth and tells her she has to go and check a few things.

Karen is shown back to the reception area.

After a long time, a man dressed in civilian clothes asks her to accompany him to another room. He introduces himself as Inspector Edenridge and says, 'I think we may have a problem here. Mr Colin Bucket is currently on bail awaiting trial for a serious offence. He is supposed to report to the police. We understand he was away on holiday and his reporting was deferred to Monday last, and he failed to report. This has been noted on his file. We have checked with hospitals, etc., and there are no reports of any admission due to an accident or otherwise. It is our belief that he has absconded, and a report has been made to that effect. Likely, he is still in the UK, as we have his passport.'

Karen cannot believe it. They didn't go to Italy or Greece because the police had his passport. He never told me that he was on bail awaiting trial. She asks the Inspector, 'I am sorry, this is all a bit of a shock to me. My husband and I are very close, and I feel sure that he would have told me of any difficulty. Can you be sure it is him? And at the same time, can you tell me why he may or may not have been on bail?'

The Inspector tries to be sympathetic and tells her, 'I can tell you we are sure. What I cannot tell you is the offence for which he is on bail, as it is contrary to what we are able to disclose.'

Karen is still in a state of shock. He is on bail for an offence, but I am not allowed to know what he is supposed to have done. The lady leaves the Police Station a very worried lady. What am I going to tell Jonathan? He probably won't notice until Saturday. Who can I talk to about this? She hasn't really got any friends, her mother has never been any help, and she has no siblings. Nobody to talk to then, but she must have somebody. Maybe she could try the office.

When she gets home, she tries the office and asks to speak to personnel. All she manages is a secretary who is of no real help. She has no idea what to do.

Colin gets up on Tuesday morning and has a good breakfast. Today, he will find a permanent place to live. It is a lovely sunny day, and he wanders downtown and buys a local paper, the West Briton, and goes to Starbucks. Not so different then. He finds the accommodation section. There are houses to rent which seem quite expensive and too large for his needs. There are about twelve bedsits, which will do fine, but with no prices. Only three are in Truro, the others being in such places as Falmouth, Helston, etc. He gets some change and finds the phone box. He must get a pay-as-you-go mobile, which would be a lot easier. The first two have already gone, but the third is still available at £600 per month with a one-month deposit. He arranges to view at noon and gets directions. It is only just up the hill in Carclew Street, which sounds nice.

He arrives. There are 4 bells, so he guesses 4 bedsits. He tries the front door, which is open and enters and shouts hello. An attractive girl comes out of number 2 and says, 'Hi, you must be John. I am Jasmine. This is the available apartment.' The apartment seems a bit over the top, which it is. The room is pretty small. A double bed, one settee in purple velvet, a small table, a small television, a minute kitchen area with no cooker, only a microwave and a mini fridge and bizarrely a larger bathroom with a good-looking shower. Colin says, 'This looks fine. I'll take it.' She produces a one-page agreement, which he speedily reads and signs one copy. She gives him the other, and he hands over £1200. She gives him two keys. One for the front door and one for the room. He tells her he will be moving in tomorrow.

He gets himself a sandwich and water at Marks and goes to a nearby park.

He is feeling rather pleased. He is a runaway, but he has managed to find somewhere to live without having to produce any ID. Nobody knows who he is, and he signed the bedsit lease with a false name - John Sparrow. From now on, if anyone asks, that will be his name. Tuesday afternoon, Karen will notice that he has not come home. Has she rung all the hospitals to find if he has had an accident? Probably and has she gone to the police? Maybe tomorrow. They will tell her he is on bail and has no doubt absconded. Will they tell her why he is on bail? If they do, which seems likely, he wonders what she will think. Why is he thinking about her? She and Jonathan are past tense, and hopefully never to be seen again; he is going to forget all about them.

More important is getting a job to earn some money and pay the rent and eat, and have the occasional pint. He still has the West Briton and goes to work.

In his position, he has to be careful. No names, no NHS number, it will have to be cash. Before he got here, he had thought of gardening, but maybe there could be something in catering, pubs or restaurants. He has to admit he doesn't know.

There do not seem to be any job offers which meet his requirements. He wonders what to do.

Back to the Townhouse. He might as well stay one more night, as he has paid and will get breakfast. A boring afternoon ahead, so he goes back downhill and into Waterstones to buy a book. He spends the rest of the afternoon reading. In the evening back to Burger King to save money, but he goes to the pub again for another pint of Doombar. He keeps a low profile and avoids all the other punters. He realises that at some point, John Sparrow is going to have to talk to somebody about what can be his story.

He has come from London - true. He had a long-term relationship which broke down, and he decided he needed a change - half true. He used to have a boring job in admin - not very true as he was a highly paid executive. He is staying in a bedsit for the time being but hopes in the long term for something better - true. He does not have a job but is looking for a new challenge - only partly true, as his options are probably limited.

He sleeps alone quite well and has a nice breakfast. He gathers his gear and says goodbye, and makes his way to Carclew Street and lets himself into his bedsit. All things considered, it is not too bad. It is not the Barbican, but he is, after all, alone. He wonders if there is a garden. He finds there is a small garden with no grass and one unoccupied bench. A good low maintenance place.

Back into the bedsit, and he checks it out more carefully.

In the kitchen, there are four plates and two dishes, two mugs, four assorted glasses and some knives, forks and spoons. Nothing to make coffee in and no teapot, which he doesn't mind as not his favourite. No tea towels. The bathroom is completely empty. He will need towels, soap and shampoo. A glance in the fridge, which is quite small. And then to the bed. It has pillows and a dirty-looking duvet and a very old-looking blanket. He will need sheets and pillowcases..

It is time to stock up. He is carrying nearly £7000 in his pocket, not a good idea to go out with so much. He does not feel his bedsit is very safe, so he puts £300 in his pocket and the rest in his socks and slips on his shoes. It is not very comfortable, but no matter. He goes back to Marks, which should have everything he needs. He starts off in the Food Hall. Breakfast - OJ, milk, cornflakes and coffee. Lunch - he buys a sandwich for today but also buys some bread, butter and peanut butter for later in the week. Dinner - he will need to microwave so he gets Spaghetti Carbonara for tonight and Spaghetti Bolognese for the next night. He must find something else. He gets 6 bananas to help with his '5 a day'. Time for a drink, he just buys a 4-pack of Peroni and then looks at the wine. Lots of special prices and the pick seems to be a South African red at £7:99. He buys 3 to the checkout. It is nearly £100, which he finds difficult to understand, and hands over 5 £20 notes and gets little change. He has two rather full bags and decides to go home before he gets the rest.

Back home, he sorts out his shopping and heads back.

Will the £200 in his pocket be enough to buy everything? He seems to spend ages choosing. It all comes to nearly £180.

Back home again and nearly lunchtime. He will take his book, sandwich, banana and a drink into the garden. What to drink, he decides on a glass of water from the tap, which is not so bad. They probably have better water here than in London, and less pollution.

Over lunch, he reflects on his money situation. He started with £8,000, but he has paid rent, Marks, train fare and some sundries, which all amount to nearly £1,700, so he will have around £6,300 left. He will not have to spend anything for the next couple of days. He determines that he will try to live on £20 per day. Calculating that will be £600 for the next month and then £600 rent, it means that without work, he will be able to survive for only 5 months. It doesn't sound like much fun, penny pinching. Work must be a priority.

Midway through the afternoon, Jasmine appears wearing a bikini top and a sexy pair of denim shorts and sits on the bench beside him. She starts to apply sun cream in a rather suggestive manner. He wonders what is going on here. He says he thought she was just the agent handling the letting. She replies,

'I live in number 1, and my father owns the block. He also owns four other blocks here and in Falmouth. I handle all the lettings on his behalf and live rent-free and get a nice cash bonus every month to keep me going. As you can imagine, my work is quite flexible, which is why I am here now. The month is the worst for collecting all the rents, which have to be done at night or over the weekend. And what about you, what are you up to?'

Colin gives her the John Sparrow story, which we have already rehearsed and goes on to say, 'I only arrived here on Monday. I have my life savings, but it is not that much, and I urgently need to look for work.'

She asks him what sort of work he is looking for. He tells her certainly not an office job as he has had enough of that, and he would prefer something cash in hand because he hates the taxman. He seems to have spent his whole life paying tax. Colin congratulates himself on his clever thinking. A real reason for cash.

She looks thoughtful and says that she thinks cash jobs are difficult to find. On the other hand, at a couple of their properties, they do have a gardener who always insists on cash. She doesn't think he has anybody working for him, but he always seems to be busy and works weekends and all that. She could have a word with him and ask if he is looking for help.

At least that is something.

They spend the afternoon chatting about this and that. Colin finds that he is fancying her, but tells himself to be careful - you know what happened last time.

He is surprised when she says, 'I suppose you are now going back to your bedsit, microwave some dinner and watch crap tv on that crappy little box. Why don't you have your dinner and then take me for a drink in the pub? There is a great place up the road, the Thomas Daniel, which is well worth a visit (he has noticed it on his travels and it looks okay). We could give Rod, the gardener, a call and see if he wants to join us. If you're up for it, give me a knock around 8.'

He says he will most certainly give her a knock (nothing suggestive?).

They take their leave around 5, and Colin has his Carbonara and a Peroni. He has been in shorts and a T-shirt all day and changes into his chinos and a polo shirt. It is only 7, so he wastes time watching TV.

At 8, he knocks on her door. She opens immediately and is dressed in a short mini skirt, sleeveless top and what looks like no bra and nice make-up. He could enjoy this evening.

It is a short walk up the hill. They decide to sit outside. She would like an espresso martini (which costs £11 and he seems to be paying), and he sticks to beer.

The first thing she does is ask him about his failed relationship. In Colin's rehearsals, he had not thought he would have to explain this is trying, but he responds,

'It is very complicated (good start). Earlier this year, I turned 30, and I had a long-term girlfriend for a number of years. At some time, I was going to have to grow up and get married and have kids and be a proper middle-aged man with a good job and loving family. I needed a strategy, so I decided to take the plunge. I invited Katy, that was her name, for a weekend in Venice, all expenses paid, and she said yes - how could she refuse? We had a nice time there, travelling the canals by vaporetto and eating some great food. On the last evening, I took her to St Mark's Square and asked her to marry me. She burst out crying and said that it could never be, as she was in love with another. Before she met me, she had been engaged to the man of her dreams, but he dumped her and ended up marrying her best friend. She lost her lover and her best friend. She decided that if she could not have the man of her dreams, then it would be nobody. I was nowhere near the man of her dreams. She said that she was sorry to disappoint me, and things being as they were, we should stop seeing each other, and by the way, thanks for a great weekend. We got back, and as you can imagine, I was devastated and decided to change my life.' (For an off-the-cuff, Colin thought this all sounded pretty convincing.)

Jasmine looks as if she is about to cry, having heard his story, but she replies,

'What a terrible story, I feel so very sorry for you, and I really wanted to cry, but I never do. My story is much simpler. I am only 23 and an only child. I love my father, and he thinks he loves me. I have never loved any man. Nobody has ever asked me to marry them. I have had loads of boyfriends, but nobody has been the man of my dreams. Time for another drink, my round, I think.'

She goes off for the second round.

When she comes back, she suggests calling Rod and gets out her cell. He is going to join them for a drink. He learns that Rod is single and lives in a basement flat in Daniel Road, which is very close.

Very shortly, Rod turns up. He is well built with a shaven head and looks like he is in his gardening clothes. No dressing up for Jasmine then. She gets him a beer. There is a lot of harmless chatter, and then Jasmine gets to the point of the meeting.

'Rod, I wanted you to meet my new tenant, Colin. He has recently moved down here from London, leaving a good job in the City, looking for something new in his life. He hates the taxman and is looking for a cash job, which can be difficult. For some reason, when we were discussing this afternoon, I thought of you. You always seem to be busy, and I was wondering if you need somebody to help you.'

To which Rod replies,

'Funny you should say that. You are right, I am too busy, and I am always turning away work as I have built a strong reputation. I have been wondering about getting somebody else. Colin looks like a good sort, and maybe there might be an opening. I will need to think about it. Why don't you both come over to my place, number 17, about 9 tomorrow night, and we can talk it through.'

They all agree, and Rod leaves.

Jasmine and Colin leave soon after.

They get back to Carclew Street, and he thanks her for the introduction, and she says, 'No problem, I will come with you tomorrow. Give me a knock just before 9.' She gives him a peck on the cheek

Colin gets back in his bed, sits and feels a slight relief - maybe there is going to be a cash job here, good old Jasmine.

He goes to bed feeling a lot better. He wonders about the peck on the cheek. Did it mean anything? He has no idea, and he is glad she didn't want to take it any further because he is not sure he is up to it after what happened with Penny.

He spends the next day hanging around, but no sign of Jasmine; he guesses she must be busy.

At just before 9, he knocks on her door. Tonight she is in jeans and a T-shirt with not that much make-up. They take the short walk to number 17.

Rod seems welcoming and offers them a beer, which they both accept. He says, 'I have been thinking about our conversation last night. The sort of gardening I do does not need a lot of expertise, just hard work. I think I can get more work with a willing helper, and it would be good to expand. I expect you used to earn a lot of money, and I can only offer you a small amount of £10 per hour cash to be paid weekly with no tax deducted, which, from what you are saying, would be pleasing. I will not ask you for references, CV or any other of that crap. Can you start tomorrow? Be here at 9am, and we can get in my van, which is parked just over the way.'

Colin had not been expecting a job offer so soon. It will be good to be earning even though £10 per hour does not sound like much, but it could be £400 per week, which would be enough for him to live on and pay the rent. He says, 'That sounds great. I will be here in the morning.'

They finish their beers and head home. Again, he thanks her and gets a peck on the cheek.

He goes to bed wondering what he is going to wear. He decides on jeans, a T-shirt and trainers.

He is up early and has a good breakfast with cereal and toast as well as OJ and coffee. No use being hungry at work. He gets to Rod's on time. Rod is dressed like him, except he has on heavy boots. He says to Colin that he may want to think about the same.

Today is Friday, and Rod says they are going over to the Roseland on the King Harry Ferry to work on the gardens at the Tresanton Hotel. They walk over the road and find his van, which has seen better days. The ferry ride takes them about 45 minutes to arrive. Colin wonders if he is going to be paid for travel time.

For the whole day, he takes his lead from Rod and just does what he is told to do. For lunch, they go to a nearby cafe. He has a Full English Breakfast and coffee.

They do not finish work until after 6. They get back just before 7. Rod says, 'A good day's work, I think we are going to be good together. Tomorrow more work as I have a couple of private houses. We should be finished earlier than today, but I will see you at 9 again.'

Colin gets back and wonders if he should knock on Jasmine's door, but decides against it. He gets back in his bed, sits and opens a beer. He then realises that he has nothing for dinner. It will have to be Burger King again, and he sets off.

He is back at Rod's at 9, and they take a short drive to the Roseland and arrive at a large, imposing house which looks like it has a massive garden. Rod tells him that he will do the lawns, and Rod will do other jobs. They go to a garage, and there is a ride-on mower. Rod asks him if he has a licence for a ride on. He replies he is not sure - only joking. Rod tells him that after he has done the ride on, he will have to do the smaller lawns with the petrol mower. It takes him about three hours. Rod finds him as he is putting away the machine and says, 'All done.' They go to a nearby pub. He just has a sandwich and a glass of tap water. Rod has a Ploughman's and a pint of Guinness. They take a short drive to another large house, but with a smaller garden and no ride on. His job is lawn mowing again, and it takes only 90 minutes. They get back to base at around 4.

Rod says, 'This is great. It normally takes me the whole day to do the first place, and I have to do the second on Sunday, and now I can have a day off for a change. I think you did a really good job on the lawns for a man without a license. Time for money. I think we were away for 10 hours yesterday and another 7 today. I have only got £20 notes, so here is £180. The first thing you should go and do is buy a proper pair of boots to protect your feet. See you on Monday at 9 as usual.

Colin is feeling chuffed, and he has £180 in his pocket. He finds a likely looking shop and buys a pair of Doc Martens for £49.99. Then to Marks, where he buys 7 microwave meals, mostly pasta and stocks up on OJ and milk and buys a few more beers.

He gets home just before 6. He decides to ignore Jasmine and has a quiet evening with a couple of beers and a microwave. Nothing on the TV, so he just reads a book.

He gets into bed in a reflective mood. He has made his TURN and in 6 days he has found an okay place to live, got a job and is earning enough to keep him living without having to go into his float and best of all, met a pretty girl without a boyfriend. What could be better?

It is not so good for the other two women in his life.

Karen is perplexed. However hard she tries, she cannot find out the offence for which he has been charged and is out on bail, from which he seems to have absconded. Why did he not tell her? She would have understood whatever it was and helped him get through it, but instead he has run away? She will have to have a look at the finances. Has he run away with all the money? She finds that there is still quite a lot in the savings account, but not quite as much as she had expected. She finds a £12,000 transfer to somebody called Olliers and wonders what that is all about, and then starts to see a pattern of £500 daily Cash withdrawals, which he was doing even when they were in Southwold, and it all adds up to around £8,000. So he had been planning this for some time, even when they were away on a supposed holiday. Why did they go away? He had lost his job and needed a way to spend his days. It doesn't add up. And now he has abandoned me and our son. How could he have done that? I thought he loved us both dearly; it must have been very serious. She decides to now check the investments, which are all with Hargreaves Lansdown. She logs on and finds most of them are intact. At least he had only taken about £20,000, which will leave her plenty for the time being. When Jonathan is at school, she can always go back to work as a solicitor. She then thinks about living arrangements. This had been her home

with him, and now he has gone. She decides that she will have to leave and find a new place, perhaps a little cheaper and maybe out of London, which is what she has always wanted. She hunts out the lease. Luckily, Colin was methodical, and it was easy to find. The lease requires three months' notice, and there are various clauses about the state of repair, utilities, etc. She phones up the office and tries to give notice, but is told it has to be in writing. She writes it out, seals the envelope, and hand-delivers it to the office. Jonathan keeps asking where Daddy is, and she has no real reply.

On Friday, an official-looking letter arrives, which she opens. Mr Colin Bucket (no second name) is to appear at the Old Bailey on 6 October. The Old Bailey - it must be serious, but she is no clearer about the offence, as it is not specified.

Meanwhile, Penny is enjoying her new position. It is a bit of a drag because she has not been formally appointed in Colin's position. Late on Thursday, she is called into Personnel. She is told that she has been doing an excellent job under the circumstances, but the Board recognises the importance of the role and will be advertising the position next week. The Board would be more than happy for Penny to apply for the position.

Penny is dumbstruck and can only reply that she will be applying. Back in her office, she is not in the best of moods. She thought that the job would be hers no problem, but now they are looking for another. What happens if she gets a new boss? She will not be able to play the Colin trick again. A new boss could be so difficult to get rid of. The best-laid plans seem to be going awry.

The next thing that happens on Friday is that she gets a call from the police. Colin has breached his bail conditions and not undertaken his weekly report. His wife has reported him missing. To all intents and purposes, it appears that he has absconded. At the present time, he has only breached bail conditions, and in these circumstances, it is not possible to issue a warrant for his arrest as it is a minor infringement. However, nationally police forces have a full description of Colin and have been asked to arrest him if he comes to their notice. The trial is to be at the Old Bailey in October, and he has been sent the relevant notice. If he fails to appear on the said date, a full arrest warrant will be issued. Penny mulls this over. If he fails to appear, there will be no trial. What does that mean for her? Not a lot, he has gone, which was the point of the whole exercise, but she hasn't got his job, which in some ways makes it all a waste of time. Supposedly, she gets a new boss, should she go to the police and tell them the true story so he gets off because she dislikes him, as she did he did not really deserve all this. Don't be silly, you will find yourself in jail. Best to keep mum.

Chapter 9

Back to Colin. On Sunday, he goes to buy himself the Sunday Times and goes with it into the garden. Nobody is there. He wonders about the tenants in the other two bedsits who have never seen. He has not made the news, which is not surprising. The other news is pretty dull. There is no football, which is his main interest, and now that he is a gardener, he has little interest in business. He looks at the TV listings for the coming week, and there seem to be no good movies on the terrestrial channels, but SKY has some good ones, which he no longer has. He has noticed the Plaza cinema just down the road. He should check out whether they have anything good and get a sandwich for lunch. He does this, but there is nothing worth seeing.

He takes his sandwich, a glass of tap water and his book, which he has nearly finished, back into the garden. Still no sign of anybody. He finishes his book and decides he had better go and get another. He comes back from Waterstones with 3 books which will keep him going for a time. Back into the garden, and there is Jasmine in a full bikini today as the weather is sunny and warm. She gives him a big smile. Looks like she likes me or something.

She asks about the job, and he manages to sound positive. Her job is just like it has always been. They chatter away for a long time about nothing in particular. He is rather glad that she is not quizzing him about his old life. He doesn't want to build a web of lies. He just wants to be a nobody. A large, dark cloud covers the sun, and she says she had better be getting in. He wonders about asking her out for a drink, but she beats him to it by suggesting another trip to the Thomas Daniel. Surely it cannot do any harm, and he agrees to give her a knock at 8.

After a boring microwave dinner, this is what he does. She is still all smiles and asks him about his microwave dinner. She tells him that in her bedsit, she has full cooking facilities. Next weekend, she will invite him over to experience her culinary delights. What was that all about? It is quite a pleasant evening, and she has two espresso martinis and he has a couple of beers. The chat is similar to the afternoon, and they head back. She says to him, 'Have a good week at work, dinner on me next Saturday, and bring a decent bottle of wine. Maybe see you in the week sometime. And gives him yet another peck on the cheek.

Into bed, and he cannot truly make this out. It seems like she is coming onto him, all those smiles and invitations to dinner, but is she just playing? He has to admit he has no idea. He decides to give her marks against the two other girls who have been in his life. Karen used to score relatively highly, some good times in bed, not a bad cook, seemingly a loving mother, but she blew it a bit with that trip to Southwold. Always moaning about Italy and Greece and sleeping with Jonathan every night. To be honest, he is not missing her. Then Penny. Well, she really was the business. He has to admit the sex was pretty good, but she was just scheming and didn't make him pay for it. He wishes that he had never met her. Now Jasmine. She is very pretty and has a nice body, and she showed most of it today in her bikini. She seems to be coming onto him, but past experience is making him nervous. Does she have another agenda which is going to get him in trouble, that he cannot answer? She cannot be after his money as he seems to have little, so what is her play? He decides that, for the time being, he will just see where it leads.

He has a reasonable week at work and enjoys wearing his Doc Martens. There are a lot of private houses, and Rod tells him that two are new, which he has been able to take on now that he has Colin. He seems to spend a lot of time mowing, and there are two with ride-ons, which he likes best. They are at the hotel again on Friday, which is a little different, and they work on Saturday too.

They finish work early-ish on Saturday, and Rod gives him £550 in cash for the week and tells him he has another day off tomorrow. He goes to Marks to stock up and buys a bottle of Nero D'Avola to take with him tonight for £12, which he hopes will make the grade.

He gets home and has a shower. What to wear? She is cooking him dinner, so he decides on chinos and a blue short-sleeved shirt, which looks relatively smart. He has not seen her in the week, and she didn't specify a time. It is now 7, and he decides to have a beer and knock around 8.

Which is what he does. She opens the door and gives him that lovely smile. She has a lot of make-up and is again wearing a short skirt and a halter top, which appears to be braless. She says, 'Where have you been. I thought you had stood me up, which would have been a real shame. That looks like a nice bottle of wine. Come in. 'Which is what he does. She has made a jug of Pimms, and they both have a glass. Dinner is nearly ready, and she busies herself in the kitchen. She opens the Nero D'Avola and says, 'This looks like it is going to be good.' She has a small table with two chairs, and they sit down. The starter is Gazpacho. 'Sorry, it is cold,' but she thought it would be perfect for a summer evening. Back to the going- nowhere chat. Now for the main course. It is Gnocchi with purple sprouting broccoli and blue cheese, and it is really delicious, and the wine is just right. He comments that he could not have done this with his microwave. She is all smiles and goes to get dessert, which is a lemon tart. He compliments her on the dinner, which he describes as fabulous. She leads him to her small settee and says in return, 'Now you can give me a fabulous kiss.' He kisses her, and it is all tongues. She gives him a great big smile and says that was very fantastic. 'I think we need some romantic music,' and goes over to her CD player and puts on Carole King's 'Tapestry' and is back for more kissing. After quite a lot of kissing, she takes his hand and puts it on her breast. It feels very nice indeed, and he is very tempted to go further. She does not make any move to stroke his penis, which is a bit of a relief. Around midnight, he thinks it is time to go. She says, 'What a great evening.

We need to do it again, and I suggest next Saturday you take me out to Piero's, my favourite local Italian. And maybe see you in the garden tomorrow.' They part with another long kiss.

Colin gets into bed and reflects that he really enjoyed the evening, she is a great cook and took the lead in kissing and breasts. It was very tempting to go further, but he is glad that he did not. To be honest, Penny has made him scared of girls because you never know if they have another agenda.

On Sunday, he still goes to buy the Sunday Times and a sandwich for lunch and goes into the garden for another lovely sunny day. No sign of anybody. He reads his paper, nothing to watch on TV again, eats his sandwich and goes to get his book. When he returns, Jasmine is on the bench in a different bikini and still looks to die for. The chat is a little more personal. She tells him that she loved kissing him, but does not mention breasts. He wants to tell her what great breasts she has, but thinks better of it. As it gets a little cooler, she says that she is so sorry, but he will have to be on his own tonight as she is meeting a girlfriend. He doesn't think this is suspicious, but then does wonder if it is another man and dismisses it. She says maybe see you in the week, but if not, knock for me at 7.15 next Saturday and I will book a table.

Colin has a boring Sunday night alone and cannot believe he watched Antiques Roadshow. What a bunch of losers pretending to be excited about something which is only worth £50.

His week at work is the same as the previous one, and they work a little longer, and he gets £600 on Saturday. Rod and he seem to be getting on fine. In all honesty, the work is not as exciting as his old job and is actually a bit mundane, but at least he is earning and making a new life and can afford to take Jasmine to an Italian restaurant tonight. He wonders if it will be expensive.

He dresses in his chinos again but in a different shirt. He realises that basically all his clothes are now dirty, and he will need to find a laundrette.

As directed, he knocks on Jasmine at 7.15. A big smile to go with her make-up, and she is wearing a very nice black dress - not sure if there is a bra. They take a short walk to Piero's. It is very crowded and pretty noisy, and they are shown to a table. Jasmine exchanges buenos serras with the waiter, whom she calls Maximilian, who seems to be Italian. She orders two Aperol Spritz, and they are given menus. She is suggesting they share a starter Sardinian Plate with meat and cheeses, and then share a main course Risotto Pescadora or fish. This sounds fine with him. She says they have a very good Sicilian wine, Frappato. It is all ordered through Max, as he is now called. The Aperol appears, and they toast each other in a rather meaningful way. The wine comes next, and it is reasonable. He did not see the wine list, so he does not know the price. The food arrives, and it is very good. He likes sharing, as it seems a little romantic. He never shared with Karen anything new. They decline dessert, but Jasmine asks for a duo of limoncello. He had had it before in Italy, and they toast each other again, and he enjoys the smallish glass. He asks for the bill, which is £71, not too bad. Jasmine says to leave a good tip, so he hands over £80. It has been a jolly good dinner, but it cost a lot more than the £12 bottle of wine last week.

They amble home arm in arm, and Jasmine says, 'Yours or mine?' They decide on her place. When they get in, she goes to her CD player and puts on James Taylor's ' Sweet Baby James ', which is one of his favourites and produces a bottle of wine and two glasses. They toast each other again and start kissing. She moves his hand to her breast and says, 'And tonight it is no bra again. I hope you enjoy' which he most certainly does. They spend a long time doing this. She then starts to stroke his thigh, and he wonders where this is going. And then she starts to stroke his penis. He is at a bit of a loss, wondering what to do. She takes his hand and puts it up her skirt to her knickers, and he starts to stroke her. His emotions are all over the place. Since Penny, he finds that he cannot trust a woman and reluctantly takes his leave.

In bed, he wonders if he is just being stupid. He should have had sex with her; she was leading all the way, but maybe that was just her game.

He gets up on Sunday and remembers the washing. Last night, Jasmine had told him where the laundrette was, just past Piero's. He puts all the dirtiest in his bag and sets off buying a paper on the way. It is closed on Sunday, so he has to take it all back, buying his obligatory sandwich on the way.

Into the garden and nobody again. He goes through the paper, reading and sandwich eating and wonders if Jasmine is going to turn up. As he is thinking this, a dark cloud comes over and it starts to rain, so he goes back inside. He is at a bit of a loss without his happy friend. But no matter, she might quiz him on his leaving the previous night, which could be tricky. He starts to consider how he might explain himself. He could say he is scared of girls, but that doesn't really add up because he has already told his St Mark's story. A better story is that he thinks she is amazing, and he could see himself falling in love with her and asking to live together and be rejected again and go through all the agonies that entail. A better story, and he can't think of anything else.

Whilst he is musing, there is a knock on the door. Jasmine is moaning about the weather, and can she come in? Yes.

He has no CD player to set the mood. They sit not very close on the settee and start some normal chatter. He is waiting for her to mention last night, but she seems to be ignoring it, which is good in a way. The afternoon is getting on, and she says she is meeting her girlfriend again tonight, but would he be up for her cooking dinner again next Saturday? He would be delighted, and she tells him to make it 7. Just then, he remembers the washing and explains his predicament. She will be more than happy to oblige. Only a peck on the cheek.

Back to work on Monday and another 6-day week, and on Saturday, he gets £600 again. He goes off and spends another £12 on a bottle of Nero D'Avola. He has not seen Jasmine in the week, and he needs his washing. He knocks on her door around 5. She opens the door wearing a pinny and no make-up but still looks desirable. She accuses him of being early, and he explains he only came for his washing as he will have nothing to wear later. She goes to get his bag and hands it over, and says, 'See you later.' He gets back to his place and takes the stuff out of the bag. It has all been ironed, even the socks. He thinks this is the best way of getting the washing done.

At just after 7, he knocks on his newly ironed shirt and the same chinos. She looks great in what looks like the same black dress and full make-up.

The weather is nice and she has made Pimms again. She thanks him for the wine, and he thanks her for the washing, which gets a laugh. The food is different tonight, Vichyssoise and a Crab Salad, but with no dessert.

She puts on some music which he does not recognise and leads him to the settee. She is soon kissing him with gusto, and he happily replies. She lays back and says she truly looks forward to these encounters. She hasn't had a boyfriend for ages, and she would really like him to be her boyfriend. Would he like her as his girlfriend? He says he has not had a girlfriend since his St Mark's incident, and he would love her to be his girlfriend. She gives him another kiss and stands up, and takes her dress off. She is only wearing a pair of brief white knickers. Her breasts look great, and she is so desirable. She tells him to take his clothes off and get into bed with her, and make love to her. She has thought of protection, so no worries there. He had not expected all this to happen so fast. For the reasons that we already know after the affair with Penny and her lies he is reluctant to commit. He is going to have to think up some excuse to get out of this.

She says, 'You are being very slow.' He can only reply, 'I am sorry for being slow, but it is my nature. We have only just become boyfriend and girlfriend, and you want us to sleep together. In the long term, I would love to sleep with you, but I think now is too soon. I think we need to let our relationship develop.' She does not look very pleased and mumbles something which he cannot make out. She puts her dress back on and goes to changes the CD and gets two glasses of wine from the table. She sits a little apart from him and says, 'I really fancy you and I was probably wrong to take the lead in the manner I did. I have to say that I respect what you are saying. In future, I will allow you to take the lead in our lovemaking. There are no hard feelings, and I hope you will invite me out to dinner next Saturday. He invites her to dinner, and she smiles and says 7.15 for Piero's again. They go back to kissing, but no more. He leaves just after midnight. Maybe see you in the garden tomorrow.

A normal Sunday with nice sunny weather. He gets his paper and sandwich, and after lunch, continues reading his book. No sign of Jasmine, and around 6, he decides to go inside. He is tempted to knock on her door, but doesn't. Perhaps she went to the beach on such a nice day. He realises that he doesn't even know if she has a car. He probably guesses yes, because of her job.

A boring Sunday night.

Back to Rod's on Monday morning. He is very excited and says he has some great news. On Sunday, he had a meeting with a new client. He is a famous author, John Le Carre, who has a place at St Buryan about one hour away, with 27 acres and a long piece of coast. He has no gardener and has employed Rod to undertake the upkeep for two days per week. Better, he wants Rod to build a kitchen garden to rival the best in the country, and he mentioned a particular garden at Raymond Blanc's Manoir au Quatre Saisons, which impressed him greatly, and he produces a number of photographs which look amazing. For the next three months, they will spend another two days per week creating the ultimate kitchen garden for John. The pay is very good, and Rod will be able to pay Colin £20 per hour on this job. The bad news is that this means that, for the time being, they will have to work 7 days a week, as Rod does not want to let down his valued customers.

They take the one-hour drive to St Buryan. They do not meet the author but are introduced to his wife, who is a little plain. It is decided that today and tomorrow they will start the routine work, but are not allowed to make a noise before 1pm, as John writes in the morning. On Wednesday and Thursday, they will start in the kitchen garden. They are offered coffee, which they politely refuse 'must get on.' They spend the morning clearing and at 12.30 go to a nearby pub for lunch, which they had noticed on the way. Back just after 1, and Colin gets on the ride and does the lawns. Rod continues clearing. They leave just after 6. Rod tells him that he will have earned £160 today. Not bad for a normal day's work. Back home just after 7.

Colin is pleased with this arrangement. He will be happy to work on Sunday as more money and anyway it is a boring day.

They spent the next three days. On Wednesday, they mark out the area for the kitchen garden and then bring the wife out for a consultation. She paces it all out and says they measured Raymond's

And it needs to be bigger and specify the size. Back to work to increase the size. She comes back, paces and says it is now fine. On Thursday, they start to dig. Hard work and they only achieve about one-third.

Friday is back at the hotel. Rod says that over the weekend, they will fit in all the other customers.

Saturday, they rush around and do not get back until 7. Colin has to have a quick shower and change, and is not knocking on her door until nearly 7.30. He apologises and they rush off to Piero's. They order an Aperol Spritz again. Colin tells her about John and the new job. He has not yet had the pleasure of meeting him. Yes, she did go to the beach last Sunday as it was such a nice day, and yes, she does have a car - a convertible Mini Cooper. She would love to take him to the beach, but worst luck he can't as he will be 7 days a week for the next three months, and then Summer will be over. The order the Frappato again and Sicilian Board, and Penne Arrabiata to eat.

They follow up with a limoncello. It costs him £80 again with a tip.

Back to her place again, and she puts on James Taylor again and gets them each a glass of red wine. During dinner, there had been no mention of the previous Saturday and judging from her attire tonight, she is not trying to be sexy. He knows that it is now up to him to take the lead, so he takes her in his arms and kisses her. She is as responsive as ever. After a reasonable time, he feels that it is in order to feel her breasts. She is wearing a bra, so she is obviously taking notice. Then he stops, and she lets out a big sigh and says that was nice. He decides to keep it at second base, and she makes no attempt to stroke his thigh. Nearly time to go. He will not see her tomorrow as he is working, and she invites him for dinner again next Saturday. They kiss goodnight.

Colin lays in bed thinking that it went quite well. I have a girlfriend who wants to sleep with me, which is good. I am earning well and will see how much tomorrow. All in all, running away was not such a bad thing. He wonders about Karen and Jonathan, but decides he doesn't really care; he is more than happy with his lot.

Sunday is the first time he has done a 7-day week. They just about manage to finish all the jobs and do not get back until after 8. He is feeling dog tired but cheers up when Rod gives him £1,000 for the week's work. This is pretty good. When he was on his high salary, he used to make around £6,000 per month after tax, national insurance and his pension contributions. Now he is making around two-thirds, but with only himself to support, it feels like a lot.

He sleeps very well.

Back to St Buryan on Monday morning, and they have a very large load of farmers' manure delivered, which is placed near the kitchen garden. Rod says they will have to re-dig what they have already done to introduce the manure. It seems like another hard week. They have to redesign the kitchen garden. By Thursday afternoon, it is about two-thirds done. John's wife (they still don't know her name) comes to inspect and seems very pleased. She says, 'And by the way, you must call me Valerie.' Valerie goes on to say that next week, when the digging is finished, they will have to work out a planting regime. They still have not met John.

It is soon Saturday, and after another 6 days of work here, he is knocking on Jasmine's door. She seems to have gone back to sexy dressing and looks very desirable as ever. Pimms again, and she asks him about his week. He feels that he sounds a bit boring when all he can say is very busy, but then he tells her a little about the kitchen garden which they are building. He tells her that all their dealings are with his wife Valerie, and he is yet to meet John, although he supposes Rod has. And he then says, 'Can you do me a favour. I would like to read some John Le Carre again now that I am working for him. If you are passing Waterstones or any other bookshop, would you mind popping in and getting me some reading?' She says she will certainly do that.

Even with all his work, he has managed to buy a bottle of Nero D'Avola, and she opens it. It is back to Gazpacho for starters, which he doesn't mind because it is pretty good. It is not pasta tonight but roast chicken with all the trimmings, and she boasts that she has made the bread sauce herself. This is a welcome change from his microwave meals. And for dessert, there is homemade rhubarb crumble with custard. She is certainly making an effort tonight, and then she produces an ice-cold bottle of limoncello and two not-so-small glasses. She pours them both a good measure, and they have a toast. He wonders where this is all leading and is expecting her to take some sort of lead, but she does not. He decides to lead her to the settee for some kissing. As ever, the kissing is very nice, but he is feeling jaded and does not want to go further. She looks like she is expecting him to make a move, but he does nothing. She gives him a long look and asks if he is tired, and he says he guesses he is. She suggests an early night as he will be up again early in the morning. She says there is a new place opened called Lemon Tree Bistro, which looks interesting and we he like to try it next Saturday. It is agreed, and she will book a table and call for her around 8.

He is in bed by 11.30. He is not that happy. She seems to have gone to a lot of trouble with dinner tonight, and was certainly sexily dressed, and she seemed to be wanting me to make a move, which I didn't. He feels concerned that she will just think of him as a dead loss and dump him for somebody else. But at the end of the day, he is right to be cautious.

Our story has been all about Colin and his work and love affair, or not, but we will not forget the other two women in his life.

After her meeting with personnel, Penny applies for Colin's job. She is told that filling the position is urgent, and interviews for all candidates will happen in the next week. Despite her best endeavours, she is unable to find out how many candidates. She has her interview on Wednesday afternoon. It is the Managing Director and Head of Personnel. She knows them both reasonably well, and the whole situation seems a bit odd. She is first asked to describe her job, and she makes it sound like she is really the boss, which to her ears sounds rather good. She is then asked what she would be doing if she were successful in her application. This is a little trickier, as she thought she had already acted as if she were the boss. She then has an idea. She says she will seek out raw talent and develop them for the firm's benefit. That did sound positive and makes her seem like a big person. One last question. The only reason we are here today is because you slept with your last boss. If we appoint another in his place, are you going to sleep with him and create more problems? She cannot quite believe the nature of the question. The whole story is that she did not sleep with Colin but he tied her up and raped her and to ask a question about sleep in with the boss is out of order. She replies, 'I am sorry, but I think your question is mistaken. I did not sleep with my boss, I was raped which is an entirely different scenario.' She hopes this will kill that one but she is wrong ' you say that, but the facts are you invited him to your flat and were alone with him and we only have your story that you were raped.' She feels like shouting out that they are all so wrong, but she keeps her composure and leaves the room. Back in her or Colin's old office, she wonders what is going on here. She thought the interview went very well. She truly seemed like a boss, although she has never been as such, and gave them positive feedback moving forward. And then they accuse her of having an affair with her boss. That is, of course, true, but she invented a story to get rid of him. What do they do, interview other people for what is her job and hers alone? She has worked so hard to get that job, and now they are going to take it away.

On Monday afternoon, she is called into Personnel and has the following conversation.

'Thank you for applying for the job. In total, there were 5 applicants and including yourself, all seemed excellent. The Managing Director has decided that the company needs new blood, and the position has been offered to one of the external candidates who has accepted and will be in the position in about 6 weeks. In the meantime, the Board has requested that you agree to continue managing the department. There will be no adjustment to your salary for this short time.'

She cannot really believe her ears. She says she agrees and looks forward to the new boss and working with him.

Karen, meanwhile, having handed in the 3-month notice on the flat, starts to wonder about where to live. She had always thought they would buy a nice country cottage with a mortgage and live happily ever after. Colin has run away, and now she has no man in her life. Savings are okay, but not enough to buy a house or even a flat in London, so it will have to be renting. She would like it to be outside London, but she will soon need to go back to work, and the jobs and pay are better in London. But London property is more expensive. A real quandary, London or the sticks.

She realises that she is too innocent to research all of this, as she has always left all the decision-making to Colin, but now it is she who has to make the decisions.

Where to start. She has no idea. She knows little of London and even less about the sticks. She doesn't have any friends to help her along the way, and in three months, she will be out of here.

The only thing she does know is that the current rent is £2,250 per month. Ideally, with just the two of them, she should be looking to reduce this to around £1,000 per month.

She still thinks of Colin and, in many ways, wishes he were still here to guide her. Also, she has no further information about his offence. He must have been guilty, or he would not have run away. If he were innocent, he would have stayed and gone to Court in October and cleared his name.

Chapter 10

We are going to stick with Karen and her house hunting for a time. She researches out of town and finds that Chesham in Bucks might be a good place. For jobs there are a number of solicitors and there is the Metropolitan line to London if she has to find work there. She goes on the internet and searches Rentals with her budget of £1,000 per month. The only property available is a studio which would be hopeless. She increases the budget to £1,500 per month and there is more choice. A couple of 2 bedroom flats which look okay at around £1,350 per month and a semi-detached two bedroom house for £1,400 per month. The details say they are all close to the town centre and train station. She thinks about her situation. She will know nobody in Chesham but there again she hardly knows anybody here so it will make no difference. She phones the agent and gets an appointment to view on Friday afternoon. He gives her directions to his office and says the property is close. She will be there at 2pm. At 1pm she goes to the Barbican station and buys tickets to Chesham. Jonathan is all together excited about being on a train and after about an hour they are in Chesham. They have trouble finding the agents and do not arrive until 14.30. The agent is a nice young man called Mark. He is wearing a short sleeved shirt and tie. It is about a 5 minute walk to the semi-detached. Good points - it has decent sized bedrooms and a garden with terrace and it is to be let unfurnished which will enable her to bring her own things. Bad points - the kitchen is a small galley. The bathroom only has a shower. The living room is tiny and there is hardly room for a dining table and certainly not their current table. She tells Mark she is not sure. He says this is the only house available in her price range but he could show her a couple of flats. They return to the office and he gets a couple of sets of keys. She does not like either of the apartments and neither has a garden. She apologises to Mark and says nothing is suitable. He tells her that he will keep her in mind and contact her with anything new. He takes note that she will require a garden. It will not surprise you to learn that she never hears from Mark again.

They are not in the train back until after 5. Karen ponders her situation. The properties she has seen today will never do. She could try alternative areas but she has no idea where to look. Then she has a mini brainwave. Why not stay in the Barbican but in a smaller place. They only need two bedrooms and surely there will be one for £1,500 per month or less. She will go to the office on Monday morning and check it out.

Which is what she does. There is a two bedroom in a low rise available at £1400 per month. She gets the guided tour. Because it is low rise it has no views like their current place but it is £850 per month cheaper. She says she will take it. She goes back to the office and there is a discussion about timing. It is decided that she will move in on Friday and her notice period on the existing place will be waived.

She is now having to be busy, arranging all the things which Colin would have done. She has to speak to about 4 companies before she finds one who is free on Friday. Friday comes and she moves. She gives away one bed and a couple of other things to the movers.

On Friday night she prepares dinner in their new place and sits down with Jonathan to eat. It is all questions - why did we have to move, why are we not going to that place on the train and most difficult where is Daddy. She has to admit she has no ready answers to these questions and is non-committal.

She wakes up early on Saturday morning and Jonathan is still sleeping soundly. The move does not seem to have disturbed him - just the unanswered questions. For the time being she will stay mum about Colin. But then she thinks - he has runaway and I am left without a man in my life - do I want another man in my life. She decides this is not really possible as she is a married woman but then she is a deserted married woman. Could that be grounds for divorce. He has been the only real man in her life so she decides against divorce for the time being. Perhaps he will come back for his Court appearance, no she decides this is silly because the notice came after he had run away and he cannot know. Thinking on she comes to the conclusion that actually she would like a man in her life. She wonders if Colin has another lady in his life and guesses probably so then it will be all right for her. Jonathan wakes up and she makes him breakfast.

They need some supplies so they go to the local corner shop. There is a man in the shop who she finds quite attractive and she smiles at him and he smiles back. She pays for her shopping and makes her way back to the new place. She opens the door and there is that same man. They go to the lift, and even though it is only one flight she does have a lot of shopping. They both want the same floor. They get out and find they are neighbours - what a nice coincidence. He starts to get chatty and asks if she is a single mother. What a strange question. She is not sure how to respond. Technically she supposes she is now a single mother, and to admit this to an attractive man could open doors so she admits that she is. He tells her he is a bachelor living alone and spends too much time working to have much of a social life. He would like to get to know her better. Would she be free for an early drink at his place this evening and the boy is certainly invited too. She thinks ' am I being picked up '. She likes the idea of being picked up and agrees to knock on his door at 6.

She gives Jonathan an early tea because she doesn't want him interrupting proceedings by being hungry. She has a quick bubble bath and does her make-up and thinks she looks pretty good. She decides on a mini skirt and revealing blouse. Jonathan has finished his tea and is watching tv. 'Time to go ' she says. He takes some notice of her and says she is looking very pretty which is good for her ego.

They knock on the door. She realises that she does not even notice his name. He is all smiles and they make introductions and she finds out he is Paul. Paul offers a variety of drinks and she goes for a gin and tonic with an OJ for Jonathan. He seems to have made an effort and apart from peanuts, crisps and olives there are nice looking smoked salmon blinis. Jonathan gets his OJ and starts digging into the crisps, a little young yet for olives she thinks. Her gin and tonic is in a very nice glass with just the right amount of ice.

They all just sit there and there is no conversation. She says the salmon looks nice and he says help yourself which she does and tries to eat it without making a mess which she just about achieves but not Jonathan who has not only got crisps all over the floor but then knocks his OJ onto a rather nice white rug under the coffee table. Paul rushes to the kitchen and comes back with a cloth and mops up. There is a horrible orange mark on the white carpet. Paul goes back to the kitchen with the glass and returns with it replenished and says ' no matter. It is usually red wine. But we know nothing about each other and have one just learnt each others names. As I have already said I am a bachelor living alone and working much too hard. I am a solicitor and a partner in a small city practice with only 8 other partners. Our offices are in Cheapside and I spend most of my time there. Before I became a partner I worked long hours and looked forward to becoming a partner and taking it easy but I now find myself working even longer hours. For relaxation I like to run and most nights if it is not too late I run down to Blackfriars's and along the embankment. I play tennis once a week on Sunday mornings. I hardly have any holidays but try to at least go skiing once a year. I managed 6 days in Switzerland in March this year. I have never been married or indeed engaged and presently I do not have a girlfriend. Oh and I am 35 years old

and an orphan and have no brothers or sisters and one uncle who I have not seen since my dearly departed mother. How about you.

Karen replies ' like you I trained as a solicitor. When I became pregnant I gave up my job and for the last three years have been a full time mother which I find very satisfying. I am a little younger than you at 30. ' She wonders if Paul will be a good contact when she has to go back to work.

Paul says ' thank you for that but I am afraid you have not really told me very much. I could have guessed your age and would have had no idea that you are a solicitor but there is a lot more to the story. I do not mean to pry but there are some obvious questions. Where did you live before you moved next door to me, does Jonathan have a father and is he still in the picture, have you ever been married or are you still married and if not divorced, do you have a boyfriend, what do you do for leisure you look like a netball player a good girls sport, when was your last holiday and what has been your favourite holiday ever and where have you never been but would like to go. '

Karen had not been expecting all these questions. She has only just met the guy and these are leading questions, to answer them truthfully would be bearing her soul and this she is not prepared to do.

Her reply is ' we have only just met and we hardly know each other and these are leading questions. At the present time all I can tell you is that my last holiday was in Southwold in Suffolk in early June and the weather was terrible. Jonathan hated the beach. If I could go anywhere I think it would be Kenya in the Mara going on game drives. ' not really much of an answer and he is surprised when he says

'I am so sorry for all the leading questions but you interest me and I would like to get to know you better. Without being forward may I suggest that next Saturday we have an early dinner with your son and see how we get on.' She thinks this is a fine idea and agrees. He will book somewhere and leave her a note with the arrangements.

They don't stay too long. Karen puts Jonathan to bed and sits down and thinks about Paul. He is the first man she has been able to show any interest in for a long long time. He is good looking and probably rich being a partner. Two plus points. She thought he handled the OJ incident admirably with his white carpet ruined. Will it be black on their next visit or will that be the only visit. But he has invited them to dinner which means he could be interested. We will go next Saturday and see what happens.

On Thursday evening she gets a note saying he has booked a table for three at 6pm at the Cote Barbican which is a short walk and will call for her at 5.45. All set then.

She has no idea what sort of restaurant Cote is but looks it up on the internet and finds it is a French Brasserie which sounds fun. She decides she will wear her favourite black dress.

He knocks at 5.45 and is dressed casually in chinos and a Ralph Lauren polo shirt and she notices no socks - casual then but quite fetching. They take a short stroll to Cote. Being early there are only two tables out of about 30 with customers so lacking in atmosphere. They both have a Kir to start and OJ for Jonathan. Menus are brought. Paul suggests they all share the Charcuterie to start which to her is agreeable. She orders duck for her main course. Jonathan wants chicken nuggets and chips - the waiter says he will see what he can do. Paul orders Steak Frites which he jokes is a grown up version of what Jonathan ordered and they all laugh. He also orders a bottle of Chateauneuf du Pape.

The Charcuterie is very good but Jonathan only eats a little. His Chicken Nuggets is sliced roast chicken but he tucks in and eats all his chips only leaving a bit. Karen enjoys her duck and Paul says the Steak is just like being in France. They decide to have cheese and the selection is amazing. Karen declines dessert as she is too full but Jonathan wants ice cream, a good selection but he wants vanilla. They finish the wine and Paul calls for the bill. Karen offers to pay two thirds but he says it is all on him. During dinner the conversation has been fairly bland. Paul has made a good effort to include Jonathan and asks if he went on the holiday to Southwold. Danger is he going to talk about his dad but luckily he doesn't it, he does mention building sandcastles as if he did it all himself. Clear then. Paul now seems to asking for an invite back to her place. What the hell she says 'the night is still young. Why don't we all go back to my place.' Paul seems pleased. They return and Karen tells Jonathan time for bed. To her utter astonishment Jonathan goes over to Paul and hugs his knees and says goodnight. Karen quickly finds a bottle of wine with screwtop not quite up to the earlier standard and gives it to Paul with two glasses. She puts Jonathan to bed.

On returning she finds Paul with a glass of wine in his hand looking relaxed. She is complimentary about the dinner and he says we must do it again. So far so good then. During the week Karen has been fretting about the leading questions and wondering how to respond. She has gone through all the pros and cons. At the end of the day she has no friends to discuss her situation with. Paul is a solicitor and must be sensible. She considers he would be good to have as a friend and confidant and will tell him the whole story.

She takes a glass and fills it and gives him a big smile.

' In the restaurant with Jonathan it was difficult to have a proper conversation but hanging in the air are your questions which I did not answer. In answer to your first question before here we lived in Lauderdale Tower in a three bedroom place with my husband. We had been what I thought was happily married for six years. Sometime in early June he didn't come home one night which had never happened and I was concerned. He didn't come home a second night and I reported the matter to the police. I spent a time at the station and eventually an Inspector informed me that my husband was on bail and it seemed that he had failed to make his weekly report and it must be taken that he has absconded. You can imagine my shock. My husband of six years is on bail and he has absconded. He never told me that he was in trouble. A short time later a Summons arrived in the post with a Court date in October but with no mention of the crime. I have thought long and hard about it and can only conclude that he must be guilty or he would nit have run away and stayed to prove his innocence. I looked into the finances and it looks like he took about £20,000 with him. In this situation I really do not know what to do. I have no close friends to discuss the matter with and you are the only person I have ever outlined the situation. '

Paul puts down his glass of wine and has a very serious expression.

' Your story feels like it came out of a book. In all my professional life I have never heard such a story. It really seems like you need help. I am not entirely sure that I would be the right person for you in this situation but let's give it a try. Firstly can you show me the Summons.' She finds it. He says Old Bailey must be serious. Can you give me a copy of this which she does. Secondly is his passport still here. She tells him that the police told her they had it. He says normal for people on bail. He then asks if he has used his credit card. She has to admit she hasn't looked. They get out her file of statements and check through. She is pretty sure that everything from early June is her. Paul asks if she has searched for anything which he may have left behind. She says no. They decide to search his drawers and clothing. They find his credit and debit cards and driving licence hidden in one of his suits.

Paul says ' It seems this was a planned exit. He knew that he could not use his cards as they could be traced and his driving licence gave him identity which he would not want. It seems most likely that he has run off somewhere in this country. Did he have friends or relations in out of the way places where he could have gone to hide. If not, he would need to work but without identity which means a cash job of some sort. The fact that he planned well will make it difficult for the police or indeed us to find him. I think our first task is to find out the alleged crime which may give us some clues. I do have some good contacts in the judicial system who may be of assistance in that matter. Also have you contacted his work who may be able to throw light on the matter. It would be helpful if you could give me the details of his employer. '

Karen says ' A planned exit. He must have been guilty. I know of no friends or relations but I think he had an address book which I could find to have a look. I did phone up his work to try to find out what was going on but I met a Personnel blank wall. '

Paul ' you must not think he is guilty. You are innocent until proven guilty. Let's have a look at the address book.'

They do and there are no likely suspects.

They have another glass of wine but no real conversation.

Paul says he will start working on all this on Monday and it will be pro bono so not to worry about the cost. As soon as he has anything he will let her know.

Time to leave. Karen thanks him for his interest and wishes him a good game of tennis.

After he is gone she feels relieved. At last she has somebody on her side to share her concerns.

Paul is back in his office on Monday morning and finds that he has as usual a lot to occupy him and it is not until lunch that he remembers Karen. After lunch he is going to makes some calls to try and find out about the offence. Problem number one he does not know the name of Karen's husband. He will get nowhere without that. On his way home he knocks on her door and ascertains his name - Colin Bucket what a stupid name. He also gets his business address and phone number.

A busy morning but after lunch he has a little free time. He makes some calls to Court officials but doesn't get anywhere trying to find the alleged offence. He will try his place of work. He will ask for the Managing Director. After a lot of prevarication he gets through to the Secretary and he manages to make an appointment with James Withers for the next afternoon.

He arrives at the office in good time. He has to wait in reception for over an hour but is eventually shown into a largish office. A large man in shirtsleeves and braces is sitting at a desk. He looks about 40 which is quite young for a MD. There are no smiles and he just says ' do you have a card '. Paul hands over his business card, he does not seem I impressed. ' what can I do you for. I am afraid my time is limited so I would like to make this quick'. Paul feels this is not a great start but here we go ' I have been employed by Mr Colin Bucket who is one of your employees to handle his defence in an upcoming trial. One thing we are missing in the defence is character witnesses and I was hoping your firm would be able to fill that gap'. Jim bursts out laughing but then controls himself. ' I can tell you right now that this firm will not be providing character witnesses. Furthermore we are aware that Mr Bucket appears to have skipped bail and has not reported to the police as required. There is a warrant for his arrest. From what you have said you are obviously in contact with him and as soon as you have left I will be informing the police of your contact and I am sure they will be very interested. Goodbye. ' Which is precisely what he does.

Paul feels this is not satisfactory and he is getting nowhere.

Early the next day he is in the office and is informed that two police officers want to interview him. What can this be all about. He shows them into a conference room. They introduce themselves as Inspector and Sergeant but he doesn't catch their names. They show ID. The Inspector says ' it has come to our attention that you are in contact with a Mr Colin Bucket who is a criminal who has failed to fulfil his bail conditions and there is a warrant out for his arrest. Such contact is illegal and we require you to tell us where this man is to be found. ' Paul cannot really believe this. His knowledge of criminal law is weak and could he be charged with an offence. Time to go on the defensive. He explains that he is an acquaintance of Mr Buckets wife. She reported him missing in the first place. She is totally in the dark and wants to know what is the offence for what he is accused. He is trying to help her ascertain this. To this end he went to the employer yesterday and pretended to be representing him asking for character witnesses. He has never met or spoken to Mr Bucket and like his wife has no idea of his whereabouts. The police do not seem overly happy with this response and ask a number of questions which he is able to deal with. He promises that he will let the police know if he has any contact. They take their leave.

Paul is relieved that they seem to believe him and he will not be prosecuted. He should have thought it through properly and just asked if they were aware of the offence. He can only think of fraud. Unlikely to be armed robbery. He decides to wait until Saturday to update Karen.

He has another busy week and has to work most of Saturday. But it is Saturday night again and he is looking forward to his date. Well not really a date with the boy in tow but they will have time alone later.

He has booked a table at the Fork, a Chinese place.

He knocks for Karen at 17.45. She is less dressy this week but still with a lot of make-up. He is wearing the same as last week but different colour polo, pink tonight. Only a short walk. He orders a beer as an aperitif and Karen follows. OJ for Jonathan. They look through the menus and decide to share. They order about six starters and two main courses. Paul looks at the wine list and suggests they stick to beer which she agrees. Jonathan likes the ribs and Peking duck in pancakes. For main course they have ordered King Prawn Chow Mien and Scallops and Noodles. Karen thinks it is great but Jonathan asks for chips which he gets. Paul is again quite good at trying to bring Jonathan into the conversation. They decline dessert but Jonathan has ice cream again. Paul again pays the bill but does agree that Karen can cook him dinner next Saturday. Karen feels that this is becoming a nice habit. Paul is a bit more laid back and just thinks better than being alone.

Back to her place. Wine this week has a cork and a lot better. Jonathan to bed. Paul compliments her on the wine. He then tells her about his lack of progress in determining the offence but tells her he thinks fraud is the most likely. He recounts his near arrest by the police which she does not find at all amusing and puts on a very serious face. ' why cant it be impossible to find out the offence '. They chat about this for a time but get nowhere, the conclusion is that they will have to wait for the Court date to find out. But that is a long way off, it is now only July and it is over two months to go.

It is still early and Paul feels it would be rude to leave. It is a long time since he went to bed with a girl but in these circumstances he finds it difficult to fancy her. She is a married woman whose husband has run away, she seems to be very fretful and sex would probably be the wrong thing and he has to be her rock not her lover. Karen on the other hand wants to get laid. Fuck Colin and let's have some fun. But she is not sure of the way forward. Should she take the lead and drag him to her bed. All these thoughts are going on and nothing happens. When he does eventually leave it is just a kiss on her cheek.

After he has left Karen feels disappointed. All he wanted to do was kiss my cheek, he must find me attractive as I am young and pretty. I will have to spend the week on my strategy.

For the next three weeks their only intercourse is eating and chatting. Karen is finding it all very frustrating.

In the 6 weeks that have gone by Penny has been doing Colin's job but there is not much action and she has little opportunity to prove herself. She spends a lot of time plotting the downfall of Colin's replacement but has to admit she is lacking ideas.

August 1 arrives, time for the replacement. The day before she took all her things out of his office and put them in her old place. The replacement basically has a telephone and two empty filing cabinets. Good luck with that. It gets to 10 and no sign. Shortly after Jim comes into the room with a busty blonde aged about 40. Must be his new Secretary she thinks. He has always liked them younger but maybe he is looking for experience. But it is not his new Secretary as he says

' I would like to introduce you all to Deborah who has been appointed to Colin's position. I am sure you will all want to help her settle in. I will leave you to it. ' There is a stunned silence in the room. Nobody had been expecting a woman boss. Okay Penny had been in charge for a few weeks but only temporary. Full time it cannot be. Penny cannot believe it. She will need new and completely different strategies.

There are only the original three from the story Penny, the male assistant and the secretary. Deborah addresses them a little formally

' I am very pleased to have taken this position. I am sure you all know that the circumstances of my appointment were not the most pleasant. (and she glares at Penny in such a way as to suggest she has already worked out that this was a devious plan) I in my previous position was undertaking a similar role to what I have been employed to do here. My previous team was much larger and I am sure you all appreciate that we are going to have to work jolly hard. I am afraid that late nights and weekends may become the norm. On practical matters Jim has brought me up to date. We have three investments which are ready or nearly ready for an IPO and that will be our number one priority. At the same time there are 5 new investments under consideration and I have the files here for these and the IPOs. For the next hour or so I will be with IT getting myself logged into the system and then I would like to spend some one to one time with each of you. Which will probably take us to lunch. I will have a sandwich at my desk. In the afternoon I will study all my files and may ask you some questions. Tomorrow we will start on the real work but I am sure you all have plenty to do to fill your day. Any questions ? ' There are none. The IT guy comes in with a tablet and a printer and goes into her office. Penny sees that she also has her own iPad.

Penny is not doing a lot of work but just observing her new boss. After about an hour the IT guy leaves and Penny is called into Deborah's office. No smiles just a serious look and she says

' it is nice to see another lady in a senior position. I suspect you are ambitious which I like. I know that you applied for the job and have been in charge for the last two months or so. I expect that you are disappointed that you did not get the job after all your hard work and I respect that. I think the reason that I got the position is that I have greater experience. As we will be working together I hope that I can bring you to a level which would make you my ideal replacement if I ever move on. My short term objective is to make it all happen and hopefully get promotion to the Board and I look forward to working with you to meet these objectives. '

Penny presumes she had better say something but she cannot think what to say. Deborah says ' don't be shy now '. Penny says ' yes I did apply for the job because I thought I was more than capable. I think for my two months in charge I have done an excellent job. I look forward to working with you and gaining the experience which I need. ' Not a bad answer she thinks and there has been no suggestion that she set up Colin although it is in the back of her mind.

Chapter 11

Colin has no idea what is happening in the lives of Karen and Penny. Karen always relied on him to do everything. He imagines she will still be in the flat in the Barbican. Will she be fretting over his absence, probably. Has she got herself a boyfriend, probably not. She had a reasonable amount of money and is she thinking about going back to work, will probably wait until Jonathan is at school. Penny after all her evil scheming has probably got his job. He doesn't think she is really up to it and won't last long. Serves her right.

Is he enjoying his new life. Yes and no. It is hard working 7 days a week but at the end of the day the remuneration is good. He has little free time to enjoy. It is good working for a famous author but he would like to meet him. The best thing is that he has a pretty girlfriend who seems sexy. She is there for the taking but after Penny he is nervous of taking it further. He feels that he is hiding everything from her. Should he tell her his story. This would make it easier to have sex and all that but it could also ruin his new life. Looking at it from his point of view. He has run away from Court and must now be a wanted man with his picture and description in every police station in the land. He is living here anonymously and nobody would ever guess the true story. He decides by far the best thing to do is to remain anonymous and see where life takes him.

He wonders if a summons for Court has arrived. If so Karen would have read it. Will it have specified the offence, he has no idea. If not she will still not know why he has run away.

Back to work on Monday at St Buryan. On Wednesday they finish digging the kitchen garden and report to Valerie. She comes to inspect and seems well pleased. Tomorrow morning they will plan the planting and she asks them to come to the house. On Thursday morning they knock on the door. Enter take their muddy boots off and are shown into a large kitchen/diner. They sit at the table while she makes espresso. She says ' I am very sorry but I forgot to tell you that we also want to create an orchard. We have determined the location and size and I will show you later. It will need some preparation. We intend to have a good selection of fruit - apples, pears, plums, cherries and damsons. It will be necessary to buy young trees. There is a nursery near Penzance which should provide the necessary and we will visit it together next week. Now onto the kitchen garden. We believe that the kitchen garden should not be a place where we buy plants and put them in the ground. We must wherever possible grow our own plants from seed. There is a reasonably large greenhouse where we can grow our seeds. I will make myself responsible for housekeeping the greenhouse and do all the watering and other necessities. Now to what we are going to grow. John is very keen on asparagus and artichokes which are a must. He is also very keen that we have a first class herb garden containing many varieties. Next is salads. We will need a number of lettuces to give us a choice. Tomatoes and chilli's are also important. Then we get to vegetables. Potatoes - jersey royal new potatoes and main crop Maris Piper and King Edward would be good. Others - we will need root vegetables, carrots, parsnips, swede etc and other vegetables peas, mange-tout, courgettes, broccoli, cauliflower etc and last but not least onions and garlic. Next are soft fruits - strawberries, raspberries, blueberries, greengage's etc. I know this seems like a very long list but our aim is to be self sufficient as far as possible. It is a shame that our climate is not good enough to grow oranges, lemons, limes, avocado, mango, banana and other exotic fruits but we will have to eliminate them from our diet or reluctantly go to the supermarket. John has freshly squeezed orange juice every morning which he loves. Will he do without who knows. That has been a long list. To help you I have itemised everything that we want and here are two copies of my list for you. I suggest we start today and you go off to the nursery, there is one just down the road and start buying seeds and come back and start putting into trays or whatever in the greenhouse. Here is £200 to get you going. I would appreciate a bill and change. '

That was a long and very detailed shopping list. Rod says we had better get going then and off they go to the nursery just down the road. It only has about half of what they need but they still spend £80. They return to Valerie and give her the bill and change. She gives them another £200 and suggests they go to Penzance on Monday morning to get the rest and have a look at the trees. They spend the rest of the day potting seeds and report such to Valerie. She comes with them to the greenhouse and again seems well pleased.

Friday and Saturday is back to normal work. At long last it is Saturday night and Colin is knocking on Jasmine's door. Tonight she looks pretty as ever but is plainly dressed in jeans and a sweater. It has got a little colder. Colin is pleased that she is not trying to look sexy.

They wander down to the Lemon Tree. They have a cocktail menu and they both order a martini espresso. Jasmine says not as good as Thomas Daniel. A short wine list and they order the cheapest a French Merlot which is quite good. They decide to share scallops to start. A little small with only three scallops. She is going to have fish and chips and he goes for a sirloin steak - rare please. The main courses are okay. The limoncello is £4.95 a shot which they decline and do not have desserts. Gosh the bill is £91 and with a tip it comes to £100 which Colin pays.

Back to Jasmine and she puts on James Taylor again and gets out her bottle of limoncello and pours them each a good hearty glass.

On the settee and they are soon kissing - as passionate as ever. Colin is not going to take it any further tonight. It is nearly time to go and he is wondering if she is going to propose cooking him dinner next week. She doesn't. So he better make a proposal. He asks if she would like to go back to Piero's next week. Yes she would and she will book a table. Home.

Colin lays in bed and wonders what is going on. He had expected her to offer him dinner next week but she didn't. She accepted his Piero invitation. Is she pissed off with him because he is not making any moves for her body. Probably but he just does not know how to move forward.

On Sunday Colin gets another £1,000 from Rod for his weeks work. He has no food and the supermarkets are shut. He goes back alone to Burger King and then to the pub for a beer, still carefully avoiding anything social. He muses over his pint. At the moment I have only two people that I am interacting with. It would be nice to meet others but I have to be so careful. I know I have a story but it is all a lie and you can get tripped up. Better to leave it at that.

Monday morning. No breakfast. He is famished with only a cup of coffee. They go first to the larger nursery at Penzance and manage to buy more seeds. They also have a look at the fruit trees of which there is a good selection. He asks Rod if there is time for a quick visit to the attached cafe. He has a bacon buttie to relieve his hunger. Rod agrees they will stop at a supermarket on the way home as he too needs to stock up on essentials.

They report to Valerie on their purchases. They have spent another £120 and Rod hands over the receipt and the change. They tell Valerie about the fruit trees. She says she will see if John would like to have a look maybe this afternoon. They retire to the greenhouse to continue with the potting. They are just about to go and get some lunch when Valerie appears and says John is ready to go now. They will drive separately and she them there.

Colin does now meet John. He is quite old and very serious and not particularly talkative. They end up selecting about twenty five trees including two smallish olive trees. No bananas. It is all paid for and delivery will be on Thursday afternoon.

When they get back they go and inspect the area which has been chosen for the orchard and have a discussion about the necessary preparatory work.

As promised they do a supermarket shop on the way home. Colin gets a selection of microwave meals, breakfast staples and beer and wine.

It is another busy week. Not much sign of anything growing in the greenhouse, but it is early days. All too soon it is Saturday again and Colin is looking forward to seeing Jasmine. She is all smiles but dressed similarly to last week. Into Piero's and an Aperol Spritz to start. They order the Sardinian board and a vegetarian risotto along with a bottle of Frappati. It is as noisy as ever. Jasmine leans close to him and says

' You remain a mystery to me. I am a simple girl who grew up around here, left school and went to work for my father, not much to tell. I know you used to live and work in London in an office. I know that you proposed marriage to a girl and she rejected you but that is about all. I would like to know more. Where were you born. Are your parents still alive. Do you have brothers or sisters. Where did you go to school. Did you do A levels, which and what grades. Did you go to University. When did you loose your virginity. Have you had a lot of girlfriends. Have you travelled a lot on holiday or for business. Are you still in touch with any old girlfriends or colleagues from work. What do they think about your being down here and your life changes. On that the week after next I am going to have a well earned holiday and thinking of jumping on a plane at Exeter airport and going to Greece and I would love you to come with me. '

Colin is not too keen on this. The reality is he wants to remain a mystery and anything he says could in time trip him up. If he is going to answer he will have to think clearly and not lay any traps so he replies

' Thanks for the offer of a plane trip to Greece. I would love to come but I am afraid that I cannot let down Rod. He has got me working seven days a week and we are doing important work at the authors house. (the truth is of course, I cannot fly to Greece because the police have my passport but he is never going to tell her that)

The starters arrive and he wonders if this is a let off. He concentrates on eating. When they have finished she says ' now you can answer my questions '. He thought he had got away with it but he supposes he better say something but be careful.

' In answer to the many questions. I was born in the London hospital by Caesarian. My parents were from Essex which is where I lived until I was 23 and moved to London. My parents are deceased and I have no brothers or sisters. (This is a complete lie. Both his parents are still alive and he has a younger sister who is married and lives in London. He wonders what has been their attitude to his disappearance. He has not thought about them once since he left for Cornwall. Their memory makes him a little sad because in all honesty he does miss them a bit) I went to a Junior School until I was eleven and then to a large school, Brentwood School which was near where we lived, cycling distance. I took my A levels there and passed in Geography, Medieval History and Maths. I had a place at Manchester University but didn't really fancy it much so trained instead to be a Chartered Accountant and passed my exams to become an ACA which enabled me to get a good job paying a good salary. ' At this point the main course arrives and the eating is the main thing. He feels that he has not given too much away and nothing he has said could come back to haunt him. They finish eating and she says ' this is all getting very interesting, please continue. '

He does ' I think your next question was girlfriends. (it was actually virginity but he would like to avoid that) Over the years I have enjoyed a lot of female company. Until the girl I wanted to marry they were mostly short term flings and I don't think I was ever in love until I met her. Since I have been down here I have been too busy to make contact with anybody from my past. (actually he can make contact with nobody as he has run away) You asked about travel. Over the years I have travelled on holiday a lot mostly to Europe but I have been to Barbados a couple of times for winter sun. (He nearly completely blew it by saying that he went to California for his honeymoon but didn't) I have also travelled on business to Europe, USA and once to Australia. I think that about covers all your questions and I hope you will not see me as such a mystery. '

The limoncello arrives. She nods ' I still not think you are telling me everything (too true he thinks) and you still seem mysterious. It seems to me that you have totally left behind your old life as if it had never existed. I wonder why that should be. I wonder if there was something which you are running away from and will not admit. I am sure that if say for example I moved to London I would still stay in contact firstly with my father and all my old friends too. '

Colin is finding this hard because she is basically accusing him of running away which in essence is correct. How is he to reply to this. All he can say is

' I am not trying to be mysterious and I am certainly not running away. As far as I am concerned I am happy in my new life and have no desire to visit the past. '

She is not going to be put off and says

' and what about the girl you wanted to marry. Were you still in touch with her before you came down here. ' He tells her no. The only good thing about this is she has forgotten the virginity question but he is worried that she is raising these doubts. He is not sure how to deal with it.

Time to pay the bill and walk back.

She does invite him back to her place and gives him a glass of wine but does not put on any music. She says that she will not be able to see him for the next two Saturdays because tomorrow she will book her holiday with Saturday flights. In some ways he is happy as he will not have to deal with her suspicions but it will be a drag.

They do a bit of kissing but nothing more and he goes off to bed. They have not made any arrangements to meet on her return.

As far as Colin is concerned it is business as usual for the next two weeks. At Johns place they prepare the orchard and Valerie had produced some asparagus spears for planting out. The greenhouse pots are starting to show life.

It is Sunday two weeks on and Colin gets back from work around 7. He contemplates knocking on Jasmine's door as she must be back by now. He decides to do so. There is no reply. She must have gone out with her girlfriend. He goes back to his place and writes her a short welcome back note with a couple of XX and puts it in her letterbox.

The next evening there is a letter in his letterbox unstamped. This is the first time there has been anything in that box. He opens the envelope. A whole page of writing.

Dear Colin

Thanks for the Welcome back note.

Greece was great and it would have been so nice to have you there.

I found I really missed you.

I spent a lot of time in the sea which was a lot warmer than here.

I got a jolly good suntan.

Lots of nice Greek food and I really enjoyed the small fish Gavros.

For some reason I just remembered I promised to get you Le Carre books. I will do it this week and give them to you on Saturday.

You are invited for a Greek dinner at my place 8 o'clock

Hopefully see you then

XXX - one more kiss than you gave me.

Colin is taken with the note. It seems very friendly and there is none of her mysterious worries. It seems like she really wants to see me.

He wonders if on his next supermarket visit he will be able to find any Greek wine and will it be any good. He does in fact find a bottle of Gran Riserva which he will take on Saturday.

On Saturday night he is at her door at 8 with his bottle of Gran Riserva. Jasmine is looking tanned and is showing it off with her sleeveless top looking very sexy which she has not done the last few times. She compliments him on the Greek wine. She hands over two Le Carre books - The Night Manager and The Constant Gardener and he thanks her. She has got Pink Floyd Dark Side of the Moon on her CD player. The drink tonight is ouzo served neat with ice. It is going to be Greek tonight.

They start with Tzatziki and Whitebait (English gavros) which is nice. Main course is Kleftiko (lamb, cheese and tomatoes in filo packets). It is all very delicious and she has made a supreme effort. He compliments her. She compliments him on the wine which is not that bad considering it is Greek. More Pink Floyd on the CD.

It all seems very relaxed and his enjoying her company after the break. She does not talk about him being mysterious and there is a lot of chatter about her holiday but then she drops her bombshell. She has been worrying about his mystery.

' On leaving school I wanted to go into the police force and become a detective solving crimes. I spend a lot of time watching detectives on tv - Morse is the best but I also like Endeavour and Midsummer Murders. When I was away I was bored one night and decided to dig into your past. First of all I found the old boys website for Brentwood School which lists all the old boys and there dates at the school. There is no mention of John Sparrow for the dates you would have been there. I took a sample of three of your contemparies and emailed them asking about John Sparrow. None of them had ever heard of John Sparrow. Not put off I went onto the Institute of Chartered Accountants website and searched John Sparrow. Nothing. My detective conclusion is that you are a runaway using for some reason a false name. Would you like to tell me what this is all about.'

Colin can hardly believe what she is saying. He thought she was his girlfriend to be trusted but now she is playing detective and wanting to know his story. She seems convinced that he is a runaway with something to hide. Well in that respect she is right but he cannot imagine why she should have gone to so much trouble. Of course, she wants to be a detective. There are two ways out of this predicament. To deny everything or tell her the truth. If he denies everything he can foresee problems. She may not believe his denials and being the detective ask for proof. His passport, driving licence bank statements or credit cards to prove his name. He knows that he can provide no proof for John Sparrow. On the other hand he can tell her the truth about how he was set up by an ambitious assistant. His legal advice that he was going to prison for a long time as an innocent man and how the only way out was to runaway. There are a lot of dangers in this approach and it may go further and end up with him having to admit to a wife and son which would further complicate matters. What to do ?

She is obviously impatient with him and says ' it cannot take so long to answer a simple question, are you a runaway '.

He knows that he has to answer and goes for the denial

' I do not know why you think I am a runaway. I most certainly am not. When I left school I did not join the old boys as in reality I hated school and could see no point. When I was at school I kept pretty much to myself, did not socialise with my classmates or play much sport. I was basically a loner. You have contacted three people who do not remember me. Only three and is hardly surprising that I was not remembered. I never wanted to be remembered. As to the Institute I am surprised again that you could find no record of me. I pay my

94

subscription every year and lastly paid it last January by standing order. In my new life I may not renew my membership. At the present time I think I am more happy with my life than ever. I love the gardening work and find it very refreshing to be out in the open air rather than in an office and I am making good money. I do not have to pay tax or national insurance which was always a drag on the finances. And most importantly I have met you. I think you are wonderful and I very much look forward to seeing you and regret hard work is diminishing the opportunity to spend more time with you. I say it again I am not a runaway and I have nothing to hide and I would dearly like you to take me as I am. '

He thinks that sounded pretty good but will she be impressed.

NO

' I hear you but I am not impressed. My researches are showing me that you are most certainly a runaway. I do not know or indeed care why you are running away but you must be guilty of some wrongdoing. I used to like you a lot and as you know wanted to go to bed with you. I now find that I cannot trust you in any way. I think you should leave now. I will not be able to go out with you again given this situation. '

Colin is taken aback by this statement. The detective in her has found him guilty and it seems she is dumping him. He is guilty of nothing. All he can say is

' I am guilty of nothing '

He leaves her bedsit.

He lays in bed thinking that didn't go very well. I have lost her trust. I wonder if she is going to kick me out of this place.

Chapter 12

As this was all happening, things were happening to Karen and Penny.

Colin's parents had not heard from him for a few weeks which was unusual as he was normally very insistent on phoning them to check they were all right. One Sunday afternoon Colin's mother calls. It is answered by a foreign lady who says she has just moved into the apartment with her family. The previous occupants have left. She has no forwarding address or phone number for them. Colin's mother cannot really believe what she is hearing. She phones her daughter, his sister. She has heard nothing from him for sometime, they were not very close and he didn't like her husband that much. What to do. She decides she better write a letter but will they get it if they have moved away. She does not know it but Karen has had the post redirected for one year in case Colin tries to get in touch. She writes

Dear Colin and Karen

I tried to phone you this afternoon but could only get through to a foreign lady who said she had just moved into your apartment.

This is a bit of a shock. I know you had thought about moving out of town but I would have expected you to let us know your new contact details.

Hoping everything is all right. Look forward to hearing from you.

Love

Mum and Dad

Short and to the point.

The letter arrives a couple of days later and Karen opens and reads.

She had forgotten all about them and it seems natural for them to be concerned. Lucky she had the post redirected. She has to go and find their number and dials. Colin's mother picks up the phone and recites the number

Karen says ' Hello Margaret. It is your daughter-in-law Karen. (no reaction from the other end) I got your letter this morning and thought it best to give you a call. Everything is not all right. Colin has been charged with an offence which I have been unable to determine but was given bail. Without a word to me about his problems he just disappeared and the police are looking for him. I had to move out of the apartment because it was too expensive and now have a smaller cheaper place in the Barbican quite close to our old place. I am very sorry that I did not let you know what was going on and you had to write that letter. '

Margaret had not expected this. Her son a runaway. Impossible. She catches her breath and says

' This is all very dramatic. I cannot believe that Colin would have got himself in trouble and have to run away. This must be terrible for you and how is Jonathan taking it all. He must miss his dad. I have no idea what to do in this situation. I think we need a family conference to decide what to do. Could you come over on Saturday for lunch so we can talk it all through. '

Karen feels it will be good to share her feelings with family and agrees to Saturday lunch.

She catches the train to Shenfield on Saturday. Her father-in-law, Eric meets her at the station and takes the short drive to their house. ' Rum business ' is all he says. They arrive and there is another flash car parked in the driveway. On entering she encounters Jane, Colin's sister and her husband Rob and two boys about Jonathan's age. The three are sent into the garden.

It is going to be a proper family conference then. Eric starts ' tell us what is going on then '.

Karen repeats what she has already told Margaret. Rob asks what was the offence. Karen explains that she has no idea and tells them about Paul's failed efforts to find out. Rob says the fact that he has skipped bail must mean that he is guilty and Eric appears to agree with him. Karen finds this difficult to bear as she has no idea whether he is innocent or guilty. This is supposed to be a family conference to do something positive. She explains that the police have his passport so he must still be in the country and tells about finding his driving licence and credit and debit cards hidden and her estimate that he left with £20,000. They all agree that will keep him going for a time. They then try to think where he might have gone. There most likely scenario is Southwold where he took Karen recently. They then decide they should employ a private detective to try and track him down. Between them they agree this will be very difficult as he seems to have moved to the cash economy, has no traceable phone etc. They do agree that he has probably left London by train or coach. A private detective could visit all the mainline stations and coach depots with Colin's picture and see if they can find any trace of his destination. Rob agrees that he will find a suitable private detective.

They have a boring salad lunch with no alcohol. Eric drives Karen back to the station. On the way back she reflects that at least we are going to do something which is more than I was able to achieve on my own.

When she gets home Karen emails the latest picture she has of Colin to Rob.

Rob gets busy and employs PTInvestigstions at a cost of £75 per hour to do the railway and coach checks.

Remarkably after 4 days they report that they have a positive ID about the time Colin disappeared of a punter buying a ticket in Paddington to go to Truro. Even better they have produced CCTV of the purchaser. It is not that clear but certainly looks like Colin. Rob employs PT to go to Truro and dig further. Another week goes by and they get a report that Colin spent 2 nights at the Townhouse when he first arrived in Truro. Rob agrees that PT should spend another week in Truro trying to track him down. There is no real news in the second week except he may have been spotted a couple of times in a pub drinking Doombar. He was unsociable and kept himself to himself and did not appear to talk or socialise with anybody. Rob thinks it is worth another week. In the next week there is no new information. PT have checked all the employers paying cash but have found nothing. From their point of view it is a shame that the Thomas Daniel revealed nothing as that could have led them to Rod and bingo. They seem to be drawing a blank but Rob agrees to another week. Another blank. Again Piero's could have revealed Jasmine. The last chance is to take their findings to the police. The police are very grateful for the information. They will circulate the picture of Colin to all their officers and ask them to be on the alert.

Colin is unaware that his presence in Truro has been identified and is unlikely to take precautionary action. But he is in luck as after his falling out with Jasmine his only visible presence is the short walk he takes to and from Rod everyday.

But Colin had not counted on his being identified in Truro and a young keen inspector in the station. He wants to make his mark and he reckons that finding the runaway can do his career no harm.

The next day he calls all the officers into the meeting room. There is a large blown up picture of Colin on the wall and he gives each of them a smaller picture of Colin.

He says this man is a dangerous runaway who has been tracked to Truro. He tells them about the Townhouse and the pub where he has been positively identified. He says

' We are going to find this man. He must be staying somewhere. It seems likely that he will not have a lot of money so he is probably living somewhere cheap. I have got here three lists - cheap downmarket hotels, B&B and bedsits. I want an officer to check out each of these any volunteers. Three officers put their hands up and are each given a list. Next it is obvious he likes pubs. The pub where he was identified will need careful watching. I want one officer in that pub every night from 8 to 10 looking for him. I will provide a rota of responsibility. Lastly he may go to other pubs probably in Truro. I want every officer if he is not on duty to make it a point of visiting other Truro pubs and showing his picture and looking out for him. Any questions ?' Is he dangerous. Probably not and is unlikely to be armed. Will he be using a false name ? Don't know. What do we do if we spot him ? Call for back-up and then try to arrest him.

The three police officers diligently due their duty asking for Colin Bucket and showing his picture at the cheap hotels, B&B's and Bedsits. They do actually interview Jasmines father. He has never seen Colin so cannot identify his picture. He checks through the tenants and there is no Colin Bucket. He is left in peace. They interviewed the wrong person and in reality they should have been much more specific in their search looking for people who had moved in on a certain date which would have narrowed the field.

Penny is not having a good time either. Deborah is very demanding and most days they do not leave the office until after 9. Deborah does not consult her on anything and she feels that she is learning nothing and being treated little better than a filing clerk. She should of been in her position and to be truthful she liked working with Colin a lot better than Deborah. The best laid plans have gone up in smoke. In a way she feels sorry for Colin. What she did was entirely wrong but she cannot change her story because that would probably mean going to prison herself. She will just have to stick with it and work out a clever plan to screw Deborah. But the problem is she has no plan and cannot think of anything to advance her career.

On Friday evening Deborah says at 6 it is time for the weekend which is a first. Penny feels a bit brighter but then Deborah suggests they go to a local wine bar for a drink to get to know each other a little better. She doesn't really want to go but agrees. They go to the nearest and find a table away from the bar. Deborah orders a bottle of Pinot Noir. This is going to be a long one then. Deborah starts talking and says her main enjoyment is her horses of which she has two and keeps them in a stables near Hampstead. Every Saturday and Sunday she spends with her horses and from time to time enters events. Over the years she has won quite a lot of rosettes which she treasures. With the long hours and her weekends with her horses that does not leave much time for men and to be honest she thinks that for the most part they are a waste of time. What is this leading up to ? She is about to find out. Deborah says

' You must excuse my questioning but Jim has to told me why I am here. I understand that you had a dreadful experience with your previous boss. I do not need you to tell me all about it but if you do I will try to be sympathetic. '

So that is what this is all about. I do wonder if she thinks I set him up but I am going to avoid going into any details and she replies

' you are right it was dreadful. I do not want to talk about it and you have now brought it all back. I think I would like to leave now. ' Which she does.

On the way home she is very annoyed that Deborah thought it appropriate to raise the issue.

Chapter 13

Over the next few weeks, Colin does not know that he is being hunted by an enthusiastic young Inspector. The search for lodgings has revealed nothing. The Inspector is frustrated by not finding him. It should have been straightforward. His only conclusion is that he has changed his name, which makes it all the more difficult. The visits to pubs have been to no avail, but he keeps his team at it. Has he changed his appearance? Changed hair colour or grown a beard, who knows?

Colin has basically gone to ground. He is working 7 days a week and only eats and drinks at home, so as far as the police are concerned, he has gone off the radar.

His finances are quite good. He is making £1,000 a week and only spending about £150 on food and drink. After he has paid his rent, he is about £2,800 better off each month. Since that evening, he has not seen Jasmine once. Every month, he puts £600 in an envelope and puts it in her letterbox. In a way, he misses her company, but he does not miss the sexual side. She wanted to sleep with him, and after Penny, he was scared of the consequences. He is happy with his work. They have planted the orchard. The herb garden is finished and is looking great. They have planted out the asparagus and some of the vegetables for Autumn and Winter. It will not be until next Summer that the full potential of the kitchen garden will be realised. Valerie seems to like what they are doing very much, which makes it all the easier.

It is the first of October. What he doesn't know is that his Court case is coming up in 5 days. Karen knows, and she is wondering who should be in Court. Her, obviously, and she would like Paul to be there. He remains helpful, but nothing has happened in their relationship. She thinks Colin's parents should be there too. Up to now, she has not told her mother what is going on. Her father died a couple of years ago, and she had always been much closer to him than her mother. Her mother now seems to live in a fantasy land and is forever going off on cruises and other holidays, and seems to have no time or interest in her daughter. They have stilted conversations about once a week when she is not away. In some ways, she thinks she should tell her what is going on, but she is unlikely to be a shoulder to cry on as she is so wrapped up in her fantasies. On the first, she decides to come clean and rings her.

'Hi, Mother. I want you to listen very carefully.' Mother immediately interrupts, 'Why has something terrible happened?' She knew it was going to be like this. There is no awful accident or death, but something terrible has happened.' Mother, something terrible has happened. Colin has been accused of an offence and given bail. I do not know the offence. He skipped bail a few months ago and is due to appear in Court in five days. It seems unlikely that he will turn up, and there will be a warrant for his arrest. My life has been in tatters, and I do not know what I am going to do. 'There is silence,' says something, Mother.' I always knew there was something wrong with that boy. I am here to help. I will come to Court with you for support. I am not going away for a while, so I will come to you the day before and always be there for you. 'She has never been for me, and where did that come from about Colin? I always thought she liked him, or at least thought he was okay. She gives her mother her new address, and she will be there the evening of the 4th.'

It turns out not to be a great night. Over dinner, her mother is asking too many questions which she doesn't want Jonathan to hear. And she demands the bed, and Karen has to sleep not very well on the sofa.

She gets to the Old Bailey a lot disgruntled. Her team of Paul, his parents and her mother are all there. There is another person hanging around whom she sort of recognises but cannot place her. She is racking her brains and then remembers her as a girl from the office whom she may have seen once. What is she doing here? They are invited into the Court, but the girl remains behind.

It all looks very busy with two barristers and some aides in front of the judge's bench. The Judge comes in and looks fairly stupid in his wig and robes, but he does not have a kindly face. A jury is sworn in and takes their places.

The Prosecutor is invited to read out the charges. 'On 2 May 2024, Mr Colin Bucket, who is the defendant in this case, was invited to the apartment of Miss Penny Weathers. There he tied her up on her bed and then proceeded to insert his penis in her vagina against her protestations. The Crown considers this to be aggravated rape and he is so charged.' Clear and concise. The Judge says, 'And now the defendant can plead guilty or not guilty.' The other barrister, who assumes is the Defence, says that the defendant is unable to attend but pleads not guilty. There is a lot of legal talk that she cannot understand, but the upshot is that the police are directed to bring the defendant to Court.

Karen is astounded. Colin accused of rape it cannot be. In their huddle, they decide to leave the Court and find somewhere for a Council of War, which is a pub over the road. Nobody wants alcohol, and they just order coffee.

Paul opens the dialogue. 'The charge of aggravated rape is very serious. The defence counsel did manage somehow to enter a plea of not guilty, but Colin not being in Court will be a major hurdle in his defence if there is ever indeed a trial. This situation is difficult for me as I am a commercial lawyer and have little experience in these matters. We should have asked the defence counsel to join us, but we overlooked it.' Karen thinks that was not much help. Everybody seems to have different opinions, but at the end of the day, it is decided that they need to consult with defence counsel. Paul gets out his phone and reports they have a meeting in Chambers at 4.

They all turn up at 4, and Chuck the solicitor is there. He opens the conversation, 'When this situation first arose, Colin came to my firm seeking legal advice. He maintained that he was completely innocent and had been set up by the lady who was ambitious and wanted his job. If he was innocent, then it was a perfect set-up. He paid for us to hire a private investigator who only found one thing. That she had had an abortion. In reality, it proved nothing, solely that at some point she had unprotected sex. Our advice to him was that the evidence, whether set up or not, was very strong. His chances of persuading a jury he was innocent were very meagre. In all likelihood, he was facing a long prison sentence. My take on this is that as an innocent man, he could not face prison, which is why he has absconded.' There is a lot of chatter around the table. Karen raises the point about the girl they had seen in Court. It is surmised that she was the victim and could not go into court as she was to be the primary witness for the prosecution. They agree that this is therefore work-related. There is a lot of discussion about his professing to be innocent. His parents and Karen are sure that he is innocent, but the legal guys seem less sure. 'What can they do? Not a lot, it seems.'

To sum up, the legal guys believe that at some point he will be apprehended, denied bail and be taken to Court where, in all probability, he will be found guilty and go to prison for an extended term which will be all the more severe because he absconded. It is agreed that nobody here has any means of contacting him. 'What happens if one or the other makes some contact with him? The proper legal advice is that he should give himself up.' To Karen, this does not seem at all helpful.

She returns to her flat with Paul, feeling pretty down, and says to him,

'This is a nightmare. My dear husband has been accused of rape and to make matters worse the accusation is that he tied her up and then raped her. I cannot believe that he would do that. What makes it worse for me is that even if he did not rape her, he still went to her apartment and had sex with an employee. This is very low. Even if he was found innocent, I am not sure I would be able to get over my husband deliberately sleeping with another woman. I would never dream of sleeping with another man, and to my mind, he has killed our relationship entirely. Was he set up? That we will never know. But even if he was set up, as a married man with a son, he should not be sleeping around, and in that context, he deserves whatever is coming to him. It then raises another question. Were there others? Did I have a faithless husband? So many questions, my mind is a complete jumble.'

Paul feels a great sympathy for her, but what can he say?

'I do not know what to say. This whole situation is obviously very hurtful to you. I cannot think of anything to say to help you in your need. It seems to me that the only way out is to somehow make contact with him and find out the true story. I have to say that pleading innocence and a set-up to Chuck seems very convenient. You are always going to tell your solicitor you are innocent and plan your defence on that basis. You have told me that your brother-in-law employed a private detective who had traced him to Cornwall and confirmed he was there. The police have been notified. Right now, they will be looking for him and may well be successful. It would be good if he could be found.'

Karen has nothing much more to say, and Paul takes his leave.

Karen is all alone now, and all she can do is cry. It feels as if her whole world has come to an end. Can she believe he is innocent? She would like to. If he has been set up, it is a dreadful thing. What she would really like to do is talk to Penny. She knows that she would be able to tell her motives. But in reality, the chances of being able to do that seem minimal. She needs a strategy to make it happen. Next time she sees Paul, she will ask his advice about how to go about it. He is a man of the world and will come up trumps.

Colin, of course, has no idea about the Court and what is going on. He does not know that Karen now knows that he slept with Penny and what she has accused him of. If he did know that, he would also realise that his relationship with her is over.

Is this what Karen is thinking? We will find out.

Karen has arranged for Jonathan to be looked after by his nursery while she is indisposed. She goes to collect him. He has already had tea, so she puts him to bed.

She opens a bottle of wine and thinks about her position. She was married, but she had a husband who slept with another woman, and for all she knows, could have been sleeping around. He has deserted her and her son. She is not an expert in divorce, but she guesses she could divorce him. There is something tempting in this, but she does not want to admit defeat. Maybe he will return and prove his innocence, and we could start again and try to repair the damage. On balance, she decides not to get a divorce for the time being.

Chapter 14

From October until Christmas, Colin continues working 7 days a week. He is making plenty of money and now has nearly £20,000 in cash.

Rod has agreed with Valerie that in the New Year, they will reduce their time at St Buryan to two days per week, less money but time off.

He is not looking forward to time off. In the last three months, he has not been into town once, as he just walks to Rod every day, and they get their supplies at local supermarkets. He has moved from microwave pasta to microwave curry, which he finds more satisfying. He always has a good stock of beer and wine, so he does not need to go to the pub. To be honest, he always felt a little uncomfortable being out as he thought he was an obvious runaway.

It is lucky for him that he has become a hermit. The inspector has used all his powers to locate him and is frustrated that all his enquiries at the accommodation and overtime hours spent checking the pub where he was seen and other pubs have come to nothing. He is convinced that he is using a false name and has adopted some form of disguise, beard or otherwise, which is making it so difficult. He reads up on police manuals for finding wanted people. He thinks he has done all the right things, and nothing further suggests itself.

As Christmas is approaching, Colin realises he is going to be alone. The first time ever. He has always enjoyed Christmas. He loves turkey, and if he were with Karen always did the stuffing using a Terence Conran recipe and made proper bread sauce rather than using a packet. And he liked buying and receiving presents. He was fairly good at buying for Karen, and she was equally good at buying for him.

There will be none of that this year. Rod is going to spend Christmas with his sister and husband, and his nephews and nieces in Falmouth. There is no invite for him, and he is a little jealous. For him, it will be microwave curry with no Christmas pudding or brandy butter. He will treat himself to mince pies and maybe a bottle of champagne to drink all by himself. But he is not feeling very celebratory. He guesses Jasmine will be spending it with her father. He decides better to not make contact. Then he wonders if he should buy her a present. Better not. Jasmine has been wondering about Colin and his running away. She is certain that she is right. Should she report the matter to the police, it might be important. She decides against it as it would all be too much hassle, and she doesn't want the police looking into her affairs. She has got a new boyfriend and is sleeping with him. She is getting the sex that was lacking with Colin, but at the end of the day, it is all a bit dull.

Colin does not get up until late on Christmas Day. He doesn't turn the television on because he does not want to see people having fun and wishing him a very Merry Christmas. He is not merry. In fact, all in all, it is the worst day of his life, even with champagne. At one time, his life seemed pretty good; he enjoyed working outside and had a nice girlfriend. Now he is all alone. In the New Year, he will probably only be working 5 days a week, making less money, and what is he going to do at weekends with no friends and nobody to talk to? This was not quite how he imagined his life developing. What can I do to make it better? Finding a new girlfriend would be a start. How do I go about that? He has to admit he has no idea. He pinches himself and says, 'Stop feeling sorry for yourself. If you had stayed in your old life, you would be in prison for a long time and would probably lose your wife and family. You made the decision to do this, and you have to make it work. 'He feels a bit better, yes, he is going to make it work. In all this musing, for some reason, he decides that he will grow a beard. He has never had a beard. He needs to be a new man.

Karen's mother is going on a Caribbean cruise for Christmas. She probably wouldn't have invited her anyway, and spending Christmas with her mother is not her idea of fun. She is a little surprised to get an invitation to spend Christmas with Colin's parents. They would very much like to see their grandson, and she would be most welcome.

She agrees, so go down on Christmas Eve and spend three nights. She does arrive on Christmas Eve. To their house, and she takes their suitcase up to the room. Two single beds so Jonathan can spend the night with her. Just like Southwold, she thinks. She comes down, and Eric is opening a bottle of champagne. They toast each other and have idle chatter. She is surprised that C was not mentioned. They have an okay dinner with more idle chatter, and Jonathan is put to bed. She comes down, and they all watch TV. She retires. Before she goes to sleep, she realises that Colin has not been mentioned once.

On Christmas morning and they open presents. Margaret is then busy in the kitchen. It is a nice sunny day, so Eric, Karen and Jonathan take a short walk. Nothing to write home about. They just walk by endless houses with the same front lawns and borders, which at this time of the year are bare with no flowers. They return, and Eric opens another bottle of champagne. She supposes that in the circumstances, he is trying to provide Christmas cheer. The lunch is as expected. They drink what Eric says is an expensive bottle of claret. She is feeling a little tipsy. Would she like to play a game? Eric suggests Monopoly, as Jonathan can join in. They play. Jonathan is not really into it, and halfway through, she takes him for a nap. The game seems to go on for an eternity, but eventually Eric wins. She thinks glad that is over with, I wonder what the amusement will be tomorrow. This is partially answered by Eric, who says tomorrow he will be playing golf all day in the Thorndon Park Boxing Day competition, which is a tradition. No, him then, guess she will be stuck with Margaret for the whole day. They have turkey sandwiches for a late tea, but no alcohol, for which she is grateful. Jonathan is put to bed. She rejoins them.

His mother says, 'I wonder if Colin had champagne and turkey with all the trimmings today.' Here we go, thinks Karen. She had thought Colin would be a taboo subject at this festive time - it seems like it is not so. Before she can reply, she carries on 'Colin always seemed on top of everything. He did well at school, qualified as a Chartered Accountant, married a lovely girl whom I tell you we both adore and had an excellent grandson. It seems that he had everything anybody could have wanted. Then he sleeps with his assistant and she accuses him of tying her up and raping her. To my mind, this does not add up. Maybe he did sleep with her and then she accused him of rape. He claimed to his solicitor that he was innocent. I imagine that she went to the police with marks on her wrists. She says he did it, he says she did it, and it was self-inflicted. Even though he professes his innocence, it seems that he is not prepared to go to Court and try the matter before a jury. It would be for the jury to determine the facts. His absconding looks very bad for him. His family and parents are just left wondering what the truth is, and I am sure you have many sleepless nights considering every element.'

Karen has no idea how to respond; there is a little warmth in his mother's speech, but not much. It's Christmas, and the last thing she wants to do is get into a long discussion about Colin and his actions. She just smiles and says, 'Time for bed.' His mother is pissed off because ever since the Court, Colin running way is all she can think of. She has nobody to talk to about it except her husband, and he is not much help. She wanted to find out more from Karen - the state of their marriage, was there still love, did she suspect him of other affairs, and so much else.

Boxing Day is not very pleasant. There is little conversation between Karen and Margaret. Eric gets back around 5 and senses the mood. He tells them how he played badly and was nearly bottom of the leader board, and makes a couple of golf jokes. Two blank faces. They have a turkey curry for supper, which Jonathan does not take to. He is put to bed, and they spend the rest of the evening watching TV. She can't wait to get away the next day. It looks like Colin and Karen both had a disappointing Christmas.

Colin mooches around on the days after Christmas. He goes to Marks and buys some supplies and a newspaper. There is a story about a murder in the Roseland. An elderly lady was walking her dog on Boxing Day. The dog returned alone, and she failed to show up. Her husband alerted the police. Two days later, her body was found in a ditch. There is a full police investigation. He notes that it is close by and also that he and Rod visit the Roseland every week. As far as the search for Colin is concerned, this means that all the police resources are now focused on the murder. He had been thinking about going to the pub on New Year's Eve, but decided against it and had a boring night at home. The police were too busy to be pub watching in any case, and Colin looks a lot different with his beard and longer hair, which has not been cut for over 6 months.

After nearly two weeks, it is time to go back to work, and he is grateful to be earning and out in the fresh air. Rod seems very cheerful. He had a most enjoyable time with his sister and family and was there for over a week. How was Colin's Christmas? What can he say? Rod had a great New Year, and they had a party at his sister's. Colin wishes he had been to a party. It seems in his new life, parties are off the menu. Looking forward, he is going to have to try to find a way to change this. Next Christmas, he is going to have turkey and all the trimmings, and party on New Year's Eve and have a beautiful girl to sleep with. Shouldn't be too hard?

They spend the first couple of days back in St Buryan.

On Wednesday, Rod is looking very serious 'Did you hear about the murder on the Roseland' Colin decides to plead ignorance. 'Well, anyway, a witness reported a white van near the crime scene. The police have contacted me as they have a list of all the white vans in the area. They have DNA evidence, and I have been asked to attend the police station and give a DNA sample. Not too worried as nowhere near as with my sister over Christmas.'

A normal day's work. On Thursday morning, Colin asks about the DNA test, and Rod says

'Almost forgot. They asked me if I had any other people in my van. I had to give them your name and address, and they asked me to contact you and get you to go in for a DNA test. I will drop you off on the way back tonight.'

Colin spends the whole day concerned about these events. He most certainly is not a murderer but if he gives a DNA test, they already have his DNA and will link him to the alleged rape. They have his address, and if he does not provide DNA will come after him. It is a murder enquiry, and he feels sure they will be very thorough, with not a lot to go on. It is clear to him that he cannot give the DNA test.

At the end of the day, Rod drops him off almost opposite the police station. He has no intention of going in. He gives Rod a wave and a thumbs up and watches him drive away. He walks quickly back to his bedsit and packs his bag. He leaves the key on the table and makes for the bus station.

This is going to be TURN 2.

Chapter 15

At this stage in the story, we are going to explain what happened when Colin ran away again. He was on the police system as a possible suspect. As we know, he didn't show up for the DNA. The system was very slow, and after two weeks, the police were getting nowhere. No DNA matches had been found, and apart from this, there were no clues to pursue. A sergeant is given the job of reviewing the DNA. He compiles a list of people identified for DNA and realises there are three people on the list who have not complied with the DNA test. He has a name and address for each. One evening, he visits the first two and takes DNA. He then makes his way to Colin's address. It is four bedsits, but he does not have the full address. He starts knocking on doors, and the first reply he gets is from Jasmine. Does John Sparrow live here? Yes, he does in number 4. They knock on his door, and there is no answer. Jasmine tells the sergeant that she is in charge and has a master key, and will let him in. The first thing they see is the keys on the table. They check further. The fridge has things which are two weeks or more out of date. There are no personal possessions. It is a fairly easy conclusion that John Sparrow has run away. The sergeant returns to the station and reports the matter to the Inspector who is in charge of the investigation. The inspector is thinking positively, at last, some sort of breakthrough. They need a description of John. The sergeant is tasked with bringing Jasmine into the station, which she does the next evening with some reluctance. She is taken into an interview room and asked to describe John. Her description is pretty vague, which the sergeant finds frustrating. He decides to try some mug shots, but there is no recognition. He tries to think outside the box a little. He goes back to his office and finds the picture of Colin, which had been used when they were trying to track him down as a runaway. Jasmine looks at the picture and says that it is him. The sergeant feels it is better not to tell her that their records give him a different name, and goes to get the Inspector. The inspector introduces himself and tells her that the picture is of a gentleman who has absconded from bail and run away. Jasmine immediately tells them of her suspicions. They ask her a lot of questions about him and seem convinced that it is him. They then ask her if she had ever been interviewed by the police about her tenants. She replies in the negative and guesses they may have contacted her father, who, in reality, knew nothing about the tenants. She is permitted to leave.

The Inspector calls a conference of all the officers involved in the case who are presently in the station.

'I think we are making headway. The sergeant identified three people who were on our database for DNA testing and had not come forward. He was able to obtain two samples, but when he visited the third, he found that the person had vacated their bedsit. We needed a description of the man who called himself John Sparrow. As luck would have it, we identified Colin Bucket, whom we had been searching for as a bail absconder. Mr Bucket was accused of aggravated rape so prima facie is a villain. In the case of the murder of the lady on the Roseland, the preliminary autopsy did not indicate anything of a sexual nature. The body is still in the mortuary, and I have now asked for further tests to be undertaken to make sure there was no sexual interference. Against this background, there are a number of questions. Why did Mr Bucket not show for his DNA? I have to deduct that he had already given DNA prior to his bail and would have been concerned that the murder DNA would have identified him as a runaway. Even so, at this time we have no suspects for the crime, and his lack of DNA puts him in the frame and for the time being, I want him to be our prime target. I will be circulating his picture to all the police stations in Devon and Cornwall as we want the net to be as wide as possible. Any questions. 'There are none.

The Inspector is still a little worried. When they had the search area in Truro alone, they were unable to apprehend him. He may well have changed his appearance, and to be honest, he could be anywhere, not just Devon and Cornwall. They will have to restart the process with friends and family.

Over the next week or so, they interview Karen and his parents. Nobody has heard a whisper from him, and there are no ideas as to where he may be hanging out.

Back to Colin. He walks down to the bus station, wondering where to go. He looks at the bus timetables. A lot of places he could go. He decides on Newquay because it is a transient place with a lot of tourists, but he doesn't think many at this time of year. What can be his story? He must have a story. He needs to have come from somewhere. London does not seem right. He should avoid Truro as too close to the truth. He decides he has come from Plymouth to be closer to the sea. Not as great as Plymouth is by the sea. He is a gardener by profession. Well, he has been a gardener for the last six months or so. Where is he to find a gardening job in Newquay - who knows?

The bus to Newquay has taken over an hour, and it is nearly 8 o'clock. He must find a bed for the night. He gets off the bus and starts to walk along Cliff Road. The hotels all look a bit expensive. He turns right onto Berry Road and spots a place called Invernook, which looks downmarket. It is now nearly 9. He knocks on the door, which is opened by an old lady. He tells her a story about no lodgings, which doesn't sound truly believable. It is the off-season and she can offer him a room for £25 per night, breakfast included. Not too bad. He books for 4 nights and gives her £100 cash. He is feeling quite hungry. He asks the lady where he might get dinner. She has no idea but will make him bacon and eggs, which he has with a cup of tea. His room is not too bad.

Down to breakfast and more bacon and eggs, and tea. He seems to be the only guest, so he starts chatting to her. Her husband of over 40 years died of cancer last year, and she is left all alone. It is quiet at this time of year, but from Easter, if they are lucky, to September, there are a lot of tourists, and she has clientele who come every year. She is thinking of retiring, but selling will be a drag, and then she will have to find a place to live. She was born in Newquay and has lived here all her life. She does talk a lot. But what about him?

He tells her that he has come from Plymouth, where he was born and brought up. All his working life, he has been a gardener. He married his childhood sweetheart and had 12 happy years together and a son. He got home from work one day and found a note on the table saying she had left him and was now living with his best friend. Sorry and all that. He divorced her and has just sold the house - he had to give her half the profit, which seems so unfair as she was the one who left. He considered his options. He had no wife or best friend, and all the good things in Plymouth were out of the window. He decided to move away, and Newquay seemed a good choice. His story does seem believable, and the old lady, who has now asked him to call her Maude, is almost in tears and starts talking about her happy marriage. They had three children who now all live a long way away in London, Kent and New Zealand. She has 5 grandchildren, but she rarely sees them. Last Christmas, she was all on her own. John, as he has identified himself, commiserates with her. As he is doing this, he thinks about his name. The police will be looking for Colin Bucket, also known as John Sparrow. He is stuck with John, so he better change his name to Wright. She hasn't asked his surname, but if it is ever needed, that will be it.

He wonders if the police have noticed yet that he did not appear for his DNA. He thinks they are probably incompetent, and his name will still be sloshing around in the files. How wrong can you be - what he does not know is that he is now a prime suspect in a murder. It is lucky he has grown a beard, as it will make it all the harder to find him. The police were remiss in not reinterviewing Rod because then they would have known about the beard and made it more likely to find him.

When Colin does not turn up for work Rod is a little pissed off. He knows where he lives but does not know the number of his place. Perhaps he is unwell. Maybe he will be back tomorrow. He does the work on his own that day. The next day, he again fails to appear. He then remembers he dropped him off at the police station. Perhaps he has been arrested - unlikely as DNA would take a while. Perhaps he did not want to take the DNA test. Why not? Surely he is not a murderer such a quiet and unassuming manner, then maybe he is on the DNA database for something else and did not want to be identified. The most likely, and thinking about it, he was always a little mysterious about his past - that will be it. The police are negligent because they do not follow up with Rod, and he has no intention of making contact with them.

Back to Colin or John, as we are now going to call him, as he has changed identity. He has a Maude breakfast and decides it is time to explore. He goes back to Cliff Road and looks at the sea, which he finds uplifting. But he has tasks. To find a permanent place to live, to find a job and to find places for dinner. He buys a local paper. The price of a bedsit here is more like £200 per week, which is more than the £150 he was paying in Truro. Staying with Maude would be cheaper, and her breakfasts are pretty good - perhaps he will extend his stay with her. He looks at the jobs. There are no gardening jobs advertised, and most of the jobs seem to be in catering. He is not sure he is cut out for that, and it would be higher profile, and he would be visible. Also, he is not sure that they would be cash jobs, and he would probably need proper ID and pay tax and NHI, which he does not want to do. Perhaps Maude may have contacts which could be useful.

Time to look for somewhere for dinner. He notices a place called 'Secret Garden.' He wanders in and it is empty, being just after midday. A very pretty blonde girl gives him a lovely smile and asks if he is looking for lunch. He replies yes, and she brings menus. It is nearly all pizza. The pizzas are mostly under £10, and he orders a margarita at £8.50 and a glass of tap water. He finishes it, and it is pretty good. He is still the only person in the place, and the blond girl comes and sits at his table and starts chatting. She owns this place with an Italian girlfriend who is in the kitchen. Not very busy at this time of year, but you should see it in the Summer. Full up from around noon to ten at night when they close. At this time of year, she is the only waitress, but it gets a bit rushed on Friday and Saturday night, but she can cope. In the summer, they employ a couple of local guys as waiters. What about him? What brings him here? He does not like it when people ask him these kinds of questions. He is a man on the run and has to have a plausible story. He decides the Plymouth story he told Maude last night sounded pretty good, and so that is what he tells her. She looks very downcast and almost as if she is about to cry, and says What a terrible story, and she feels so sorry for him. He shrugs his shoulders and says No matter. Does she know any gardeners who might need a hand? She doesn't. Worth a try. He asks for the bill. He gives her £10 and says, Keep the change. A £1.50 seems to delight her. As he is leaving, she says, 'Hopefully see you again.' He has been the only customer.

He wanders around the town and finds Bunters Cafe. It has a menu outside which looks cheap with fry-ups and fish and chips, and is not far from Maude. He will try it tonight. He notices that there are a lot of fast food places, including his least favourite, Burger King. He will be giving that a miss.

He gets back to Maude at around 4pm. He is still the only guest, and she makes him a cup of tea. They retire to her sitting room and start chatting. Maude tells him that she has been busy today. After their chat last night, she realised that it really was time to sell up and move on. She would get herself a small flat here because this is her roots, but she spends most of her time visiting family. She does not even have a passport and has never been abroad. She can go to New Zealand and get to know one of her grandchildren, preferably in our winter and also visit her kids in London and Kent. It would be a happy life. She has phoned two estate agents and they are coming to view tomorrow. John applauds her and says he is sure she is doing the right thing, and family is very important, and it will be a joy to spend time with them. He tells her about his day. She has never been to the Secret Garden but has heard good things. She has been to Bunters, which she enjoys. John tells her that he is thinking of having dinner there tonight. She asks if she could join him. Is this an invitation to a date? He has never dated an older woman, and a widow at that. Will she be expecting and wanting sex - who knows? He says certainly he would be delighted to have her company, and they agree to leave at 7.

He goes to his room and has a shower, and changes. Still a bit early, so he spends a little time reading. Time to go. Maude is standing by the front door, looking like a completely different lady. She has applied make-up and is wearing a black dress and high heels. She puts on a smart-looking coat and a nice scarf. He wonders if he is being set up. They arrive at Bunters, which, being a Friday night, is a little busy, but get a table at the window, and all they can see is the black night. They consult the menus and both decide on fish and chips. What to drink. Wine naturally. They both prefer red and order a bottle. They only have House Red and House White, which is not a very sophisticated place.

John decides to talk about looking for a gardening job. Maude has nothing to offer in this regard. The fish and chips arrive, and they both tuck in. Not much conversation while they are eating, but Maude is tucking into the wine. In fact, Maude seems to be getting a little tipsy, probably because she does not drink a lot. Neither of them wants dessert, and they ask for the bill. With the wine and service charge, it comes to £50 or so. Maude says she will pay as she invited herself. John refuses and offers to pay himself as he has had such a great time. Eventually, they agree to split the bill.

They return home and go into the sitting room. Maude says she doesn't keep wine, but will Scotch do? Off she goes and returns with two glasses and the bottle, and pours them each a generous measure. This is her normal nightcap. By this time is very chatty. Most of it goes I one ear and out the other with John. But she is lying back on the settee and showing a lot of leg. Is she going to seduce him? He is certainly not going to try to seduce her. At long last, she finishes her drink and says, 'Time for bed.' This puts him on the alert, but it was needless as she retires to her own bed and he to his. Going up, she blows him a kiss. Got to be careful.

The next morning, another good breakfast and Maude says how much she enjoyed the evening. He does not offer a repeat invitation.

He leaves the house and spends the day wandering about aimlessly. He has a sandwich for lunch in a cafe, which is not great. At least it is not raining.

Back again at 4pm, and Maude offers tea, which he accepts. He has decided to go back to the Secret Garden for dinner because the waitress was attractive and he needs something like that in his life, but he will not mention it to Maude.

She is all chatter again, but then asks, 'When you arrived here, you only had a small hold-all. After owning a house and twelve years of marriage, I cannot believe that is the sum total of your possessions.' Good question. The hold-all is a sure sign of a runaway, and he needs to avoid any suspicion of that. So he answers, 'You are right. Back in Plymouth, I have all my old clothes, books and CDs, but I was not sure of my living arrangements here, so I put them all into storage. When I get a proper place, I will collect it and be a whole person again.' Not bad, and she seems to accept it.

He tells her he will be going out later to get some dinner, but she doesn't invite herself. Instead, she gives him an entry key in case she is in bed when he returns.

He goes to his room and has a shower and changes, and reads a little. In fact, he finishes The Constant Gardener. A great story, and he has met the author. He still has the other book to read, but he will buy others, of which there are a few.

He gets to the Secret Garden at about 7.30 and it is about half full. The blonde gives him her wondrous smile and sits him down. He decides on the seafood pizza and a glass of red wine. Most of the other customers seem to be leaving. By the time he is finished, he is the only customer, and the blonde again comes to sit with him 'all over for tonight.' He realises that he does not know her name. Jasmine. It cannot be. She asks him if he enjoyed the food, to which he replies enthusiastically. Time for the bill. Just over £20 and he gives her £25 and says Keep the change, which makes her very happy, and then she says,

'It is still early. You have not met my girlfriend, the cook (is she telling me she is gay ?), and as a regular (where did that come from?), You must. We live upstairs. Why not join us for another glass of wine and get to know each other a little better? This is an offer he cannot refuse. She locks the front door and takes him into the kitchen. He is introduced to Elena, who is dark-haired and equally attractive. John thinks Lucky me, I am spending Saturday night with two stunners. Elena has just about finished clearing the kitchen, and they take the stairs up to their place. It seems small, but he is given a whistle-stop tour and discovers they have a bedroom each, so probably not gay. Jasmine gets a bottle of red wine and three glasses. The girls sit on the settee and he in a chair. First question, 'What brings a young man like you here in the middle of Winter?' A leading question, so how is he to respond? His Maude story is quite good, but he is not sure he wants to tell two very attractive ladies that he was dumped by his wife for his best friend. Time to improvise

'A long story, and I will try not to bore you. I was born and raised in Plymouth. I was not that good at school, and my great love was gardening. When I left school, I went to college for a year and studied Horticulture, which I enjoyed a lot. I then got a job with a gardening firm where I worked for 11 years. Some of the work was menial labouring, but from time to time it was more interesting with planting kitchen gardens and orchards. About three months ago, my boss informed me that he had sold the company but that my job was safe. It was not safe. About a month ago, I was informed that I was to be made redundant. I think it was because I was well paid and the new owners could easily replace me with a cheaper version. My redundancy pay was not too bad. This all left a sour taste in my mouth, and I felt Plymouth had let me down and decided to move on. I chose Newquay because it had a vibrancy and soul which I thought would suit me. So here I am looking for gardening work. I have only been here three days and have not yet found anything. If you know any gardeners looking for help, then I am their man.'

The girls are nodding politely. Second question

'Are you married, do you have any children, did you leave a special girl behind in Plymouth who is going to join you later?'

A leading question, but the answer is easy: three no's. This seems to satisfy them. Time for him to ask questions. Tell me about yourself, then. Jasmine first

'Like you, I was no good at school. When I left school, the only job I could get was as a waitress, which I liked, interacting with the customers, etc. I worked at the Headland Hotel off Fistral, and it was year-round work. I met Elena there, who had been recruited from Rome to add flair to their food. About two years ago, I lost both my parents. I will not go into details. My father was moderately rich, and I inherited loads of money. I decided it was time to be independent and have my own business. This place came on the market and I bought it. I then enticed Elena to join me, and here we all are. The business is difficult. Firstly, in the winter months, we lose money. Our net profit does not cover the overheads, but in the Summer it is much better and over the year we make a reasonable profit. We close for the whole of February and head to Rome to spend time with Elena's family. The worst part of the business is the paperwork. There is so much from VAT returns to annual accounts and everything else. It is my responsibility, and I am still learning.'

Elena does not have much to add but talks about learning to cook from her grandmother, catering school and working in trattorias in Rome and then being seduced by Newquay, where she is very happy.

In answer to his question, he learns that neither of the girls has a man in her life. Good for him, but he can't decide which is the most desirable. The girl with the money or the cook. Difficult choice.

He leaves quite late, having drunk as they did lots of wine. He lets himself in with his key. No sign of Maude.

He comes down for a late breakfast. Maude says no problem and serves him up the usual. He would prefer coffee, but doesn't like to ask. Maude mentions that tonight will be his last night. After a short discussion, it is agreed that he will stay for another 8 nights, and he goes and gets her £200. She then says that she is roasting a chicken tonight. Would he like to join her for a Sunday roast? Yes, he would and he will bring the wine.

A pretty boring Sunday. What is a man in his position to do? Not a lot. He takes a walk along the coastal path as far as Watergate Bay - a good place to come in the Summer. On the way back, he buys a bottle of red wine. He gives Maude the bottle, and she says dinner will be at 7. He retires to his room and reads the second Le Carre for a time, and then makes his way to the kitchen. Maude is looking very busy. She has make-up again but a different blue dress, mostly hidden by her apron. She opens the wine and gives him a glass.

In due time, they sit down to eat. Maude asks him if he has been searching for his permanent place where he can bring all his stuff. He has to admit he has not really looked and has been without luck concentrating on employment. She has no idea in this respect. The food is pretty good, and they have an apple crumble and custard for dessert. Conversation has become a little stilted, but at some point she does tell him that he is welcome to stay as long as he wants - it is nice to have a handsome your man in the house to enjoy life's pleasures. What is that all about? He cannot imagine.

They retire to the sitting room and switch on the TV, and watch Antiques Roadshow. He had never seen it and considered it pathetic. They then start to channel hop and find nothing of any interest, and the TV is turned off. And they have finished the wine. Maude goes away and comes back with what looks like a new bottle of scotch and two glasses. As the other night, she seems a little tipsy but still pours them each a good measure. She is relaxing on the sofa and showing even more leg. Is this a come-on? They don't talk about much, and both end up with an early night.

Monday morning. John wonders what he is going to do to amuse himself. He thinks back to London when he was excluded from work. Apart from the visits to the solicitors, he did very little and frankly was bored. The thought of the week ahead is dreadful. Nothing to do. How can he fill his time? And the weather is terrible with dark clouds and a lot of rain.

After breakfast, he tells Maude not a very good day for going out. Is there anything he can do to help around the house? This is a bit of a stupid question, as he has never done any DIY in his life. His father handled it when he was younger and never tutored him in the art of DIY. Living in the Barbican, there was no need.

Thinking about his father, he wonders how his parents have taken his disappearance. It is likely that they will now know the accusation. Would they believe their son was a rapist? And if he was innocent, why did he run away? Thinking of his parents, his mind then comes back to Karen. To her, the same questions must be on her mind. Did they make contact with Chuck, and did he tell them that Colin, as he then was, had pleaded that he had been set up by an ambitious assistant? Even if they did, would they believe that he had been set up? If he was innocent, why did he not face the Court? They probably all think I am guilty. Is he missing them? Not his parents. Karen, maybe a little, but there are new opportunities with Jasmine or Elena which seem more exciting. In all this, he realises he has given very little thought to his abandoned son. He does not think he ever loved him. He just became an excuse for Karen not to work, and he became the only breadwinner. What is she doing without him? Is she still in the same flat? Has she got a new man in her life? Does she hate me? The answers are

She moved to another flat.

She has no new man in her life. But she is rather taken with Paul. However, since the Court, she has hardly seen him, and it is almost like he is steering clear of her. She thought they were building a good relationship, which might have some sort of happy ending. Colin is out of her life, and she does need a happy ending. She has not had sex for a long time, and her libido is telling her she needs it.

She doesn't hate Colin. It has all been an experience that she could have done without, but as far as she is concerned, he is yesterday's man. If he ever comes back, innocent or not, as far as she is concerned, it is over.

John spends the morning doing some odd jobs for Maude. He is not too proud of his work. At lunchtime, he goes out in the rain and buys an umbrella, and has a not-too-good sandwich. Maude has some more jobs for him in the afternoon. Same again.

At around 4, Maude gives him a cup of tea and a slice of homemade Victoria Sponge, which she has made this morning. She reports that an estate agent is coming tomorrow morning to value the house. He agrees that he will make himself scarce.

On Monday evening, he contemplates going back to the Secret Garden. Don't want to appear too keen, so ends up in Bunters again. Almost empty apart from one family. The waitress recognises him and asks where his girlfriend is. This is strangely unsettling that the waitress would have thought they were on a date - what does she take him for? He has fish and chips and a beer, and returns home and wishes Maude goodnight. Yes, he has remembered the estate agent is coming in the morning.

On Tuesday, it is still raining, so he goes out with his umbrella and ends up in Costa after buying a paper. He spends a long time over his one coffee and paper, but nobody seems to notice. He wanders around and has another sandwich lunch. I cannot do this every day. I have a reasonable amount of money, but I have to start earning again before it runs out and to relieve the boredom.

He gets back just after 2, and Maude is beaming. The estate agent came and gave her a very good indicative price. Is she going to tell me-no -. I have signed him up. He is coming back tomorrow with a photographer and his measuring stick, so I will have to ask you again to be out of the house. He says that I should not expect a quick sale as the market at this time of year is stagnant and nothing much will happen until Easter or later. John thanks her for the update and retires to his room to read.

Tonight, he will return to the Secret Garden, and he has an idea.

Jasmine gives him her normal beaming smile, and he notices he is the only customer. Why do they bother to open? He orders a margarita pizza and a glass of red wine. As usual, when he has finished, she comes and sits at his table.

'I have been thinking,' he says, 'The other night you were moaning about all the admin jobs. When I was a gardener, I did spend some time in the Office and did help with such things as VAT. As you know, I am currently looking for employment. Yesterday I spent the day doing DIY for my landlady, which is not really my forte. I have loads of spare time and wondered whether I might be of any use to you in your admin nightmare. I would be more than happy to do it for nothing.' Well, he couldn't have said I am a Chartered Accountant and at your disposal. She says that sounds great, and he agrees to come over the next morning.

He is invited up to their place again and has a pleasant time drinking wine with two of the prettiest girls who would put Karen in her place any day. He learns that they are both 24 years old, and he admits to being 30, which does not seem to be a problem. He wonders if he should do this, but why not? I have now been here 3 times and had 3 great pizzas. Elena is no doubt a talented cook, but the menu is limited to pizza and salad. I am sure that Elena is capable of a lot more. Have you considered adding more Italian things to your menu? Pasta, Risotto, Bruschetta and other things Italian. It would give you an extended catchment for clients. He is waiting to be shouted down. Elena replies that they had considered it. The benefit of their menu is that there is little waste, and extending the menu would mean waste. She would love to start her day making pasta in the kitchen, according to her grandmother's recipe. He may be right; they will rethink the whole thing.

He goes home and returns the next day after breakfast.

She says she is behind with VAT, can he help? She gives him a large file and another file with the previous returns. The VAT return should be simple because there are not many inputs, as food is zero-rated, and it should just be a matter of accounting for the receipts. The box file is a complete mess with a jumble of till receipts. Going back, he sees the date of the last return and retrieves the till receipts for the next period. This all takes him about two hours. He calls Jasmine over and tells her it is completed, and asks her to introduce a new system for filing the till receipts daily, to which she readily agrees. Is there anything he can help with? Not really.

They start chatting and Jasmine says that they have booked their flights for 1 February for their month in Rome, flying from Bristol, which is the nearest airport with flights to Rome. She had been talking with Elena and they would like to invite them to accompany them on their trip. He hasn't got a proper job and has time to spare. Elena's parents have a house with room to spare, so he would not have to pay for accommodation. And it would be so nice to all spend time together away from their restaurant. John, or Colin as he once would love to join them, but for the problem of his passport being with the police. He loves Italy and has been to Rome once and thought it was adorable. His favourite place was the Colosseum, which he loved. How to respond to this kind offer? 'I am very grateful for you asking me, but there is a slight problem. I have never been out of the country and do not have a passport. I think the passport process is complicated and there is no way I could get one in time. I will start the process, and maybe next year, if we are still friends, I can join you. Jasmine seems a little disappointed by this but does not pursue it. Elena comes to join them. When they get back from Rome, she is going to change the menu and make it more Italian and get some decent Chiantis and primitivos and limoncello to give the place a proper Italian feel. She will be very happy making pasta. Jasmine mentions his passport problems and that he will not be joining them.

Elena, too, seems disappointed. He had completely forgotten that they had told him of their February trip to Rome – god, it is going to be such a drag for the worst month of the year. Elena says, 'Lunchtime.' He just has a Caesar's salad and a glass of water. He goes by a bookstore on the way home and buys two more Le Carre books - Smiley's People and Tinker Tailor Soldier Spy. He goes back to Maude, who today gives him tea and cake, and back to Bunters to dinner. With the girls going away, he is going to have to find somewhere else.

On Thursday evening, Maude is very excited. There is to be a viewing of the house tomorrow at 11. He agrees to be out. This week, apart from doing the VAT which was a bit of a doddle, he has no progress whatsoever in finding a job. He has not had anybody to ask about gardening job opportunities and on Thursday, the local paper had nothing at all which might have been suitable. His whole life seems to be going nowhere. He is not even sure if he has a girlfriend - he has been to the flat of two girls three times, he was invited again on Wednesday night after dinner, but it is just the three of them chatting and drinking wine before he goes home to his own bed. It is difficult to see how this can progress to anything more unless they both want sex and suggest a threesome, which even in his wildest dreams seems unlikely.

He arrives home on Thursday afternoon. A very nice man came to view the property and he seemed to like it. She is not sure of his angle and whether he would continue to operate as a guest house, but the agent did tell her that he had been notified that he had the money, whatever that might mean. Maude serves him tea and cake again and then asks if they should go to Bunters again tomorrow night. Another date, but he has no reason to object and readily agrees. Only leaves one problem, where to go tonight.

He ends up at Oceans, which is just along the road from Bunters, which he does admit he prefers.

Another boring Friday. The weather is not too bad, so he takes the walk to Watergate Bay, which, as before, he finds very pleasant. The sandwich lunch is better here, but more expensive.

Dinner time and Maude is dressed up again with make-up.

Dinner is much the same as last time, and Maude is well into the wine. After they have finished eating, she says,

'You told me all about your marriage breakup up which nearly made me cry. You have moved here to Newquay to start a new life. I know that you have been here less than two weeks, but you are out and about a lot. I would guess that you must be looking for another woman or perhaps a girl in your life, and I wondered if you had found anyone. When my husband died, I missed the camaraderie and wanted a new man in my life, but then I looked in the mirror and thought, who would want me? Since he departed, I have had no dealings with any man until you came along. Over our short time together, I think I have grown very fond of you. You are a lovely, caring man, taking me to dinner and helping with jobs in the house and I couldn't ask for more. I assume that you are looking for somewhere permanent to live so that you can ship all your treasures from Plymouth and have your clothes, books and CDs. You have not mentioned whether you have looked anywhere. But I just wanted to say that until you find your desired place, I would be more than happy to have you living at my place.'

John isn't at all sure what's on her agenda. Is this her way of seducing him?.

'You are very kind. Firstly, I am so pleased to have found such a nice place to stay and you are a landlady to beat all others. Secondly, for some reason, I have not been looking for my permanent place. Part of me wants to be permanent, but another part of me does not want to bring everything from my old life back into the frame. I know I have paid you until Monday, but with your permission, I would like to extend my stay and over the weekend, I will pay you for at least another two weeks. And lastly (he wonders if he should tell her about Jasmine and Elena, but decides to leave them out of it), I would like to meet a girl, but I have met none and do not go anywhere that this might happen.'

Maude seems satisfied with his answers and the chat moves to her sale. It seems that she has set her mind on this happening and is looking forward to getting on an aeroplane and going to New Zealand. She tells him that she will be prepared to accept sensible offers, especially if the buyers are prepared to move quickly. That's it, then he thinks.

Back to Maude. She has not bought any wine, and neither has he, so it is back to the glasses of scotch. She is lying back on the settee and showing just a little more leg, and is all smiles. He is not sure if she is trying to seduce him, but his suspicions are aroused when she asks him to join her on the settee. He can hardly say no, so he moves over and takes a position as far from her as possible. He finds himself feeling a little uncomfortable. It has been a long time since he had proper sex, and his only recent adventures have been feeling the breasts of the first Jasmine and watching her remove her dress and revealing nearly all. To his dismay, he finds that he is getting an erection. This cannot be correct. He is with an old lady who is just a friend but there it is. Is she going to make a move? Yes, she is, she moves closer to him. 'Would you like to kiss me?' Even though he wondered if he was being seduced, he had not expected such a direct question. He can feel his erection getting larger. He wants to say no, but you can give me a hand job - but he doesn't. He leans over and gives her a friendly kiss on the cheek. 'That was very nice, but silly boy, I meant a proper kiss with tongues and all that, which I haven't done for ages.' John can feel his erection saying yes, but he cannot go with an old lady, even if there are some attractions. He just gives her another kiss on the cheek. She pours them both another large scotch. He stays on the settee.

'I am so sorry. I am just a stupid old woman. You are an attractive young man without a girlfriend. I used to like sex a lot, and since you have been here, I have had this fantasy about going to bed with you and enjoying each other's bodies. I can see that is not going to happen, as you are probably thinking there is not much to enjoy in my body. All I can say is sorry and hope that we can still be friends.' There is not much that John can say to this, so he just tells her she has nothing to be sorry about. They finish their drinks and retire to bed.

As John is lying in bed, he wonders if she is going to have one last try and come into his bedroom in her nightie or naked, but she doesn't.

All seems well at breakfast. Tonight, Maude had Roast Beef, and he agreed to join her and he will bring the wine.

It is sunny today, so he decides to take the Watergate Bay walk. A nice sandwich. On the way back, he gets to a bench, and there is a pretty girl sitting all alone. He wishes her a good afternoon, and she replies similarly. Would he like to have a rest and sit down, and have a chat? He takes notice of her. Nice blond hair and a pretty face wearing a dark blue coat and jeans, and proper walking boots. Yes, he would like to sit down. Well, what is he doing out here? Going for a walk. What is she doing out here? Surprise, going for a walk too. They agree they both like walking. Did she get to Watergate Bay? No, this is as far as she got. This chat seems to be going nowhere. They both ask each other whether they live in Newquay, to which the answer is yes. She then asks him, What is he doing tonight. Is she asking him for a date? He tells her that he will be having a Sunday Roast with his widowed mother. Why did he say that? Yes he does live with his mother. She has no idea what she will be doing tonight. Does he have a job? Yes, a gardener (not strictly true, but he was a gardener until recently). Does she have a job? Yes waitress at the Headland Hotel, where she lives in the staff quarters. She works Tuesday to Saturday double shifts and has Sunday and Monday off. He is just about to suggest they meet tomorrow, but then remembers he has a job. He asks her if she is doing anything tomorrow night. No, she isn't. Would she like to have dinner with him? Yes, she would. Now a bit difficult as he has only been here a short time and doesn't know anywhere, so he asks her if there is anywhere she would like to go. She says her favourite place around is the Boathouse, which has street food. They agree to meet there at about 8. He walks her back to the Headland and buys a bottle of claret to go with the beef in a convenience store, which is still open. He had almost forgotten, lucky he remembered.

Dinner with Maude is fine, and she makes great Yorkshire pudding. Dessert is sticky toffee pudding, which seems homemade. She enjoys her wine. They watch Antiques Roadshow again and then turn off the TV. A glass of scotch each, but no mention of kissing. Back to normal then.

John has another boring day on Monday, but is looking forward to the evening. We have not mentioned that Maude has taken on his washing.

So that evening, it is a newly pressed shirt and washed jumper and chinos and off to the Boathouse. No sign of the girl, but then he realises that he forgot to get her name. How does he start the evening? 'Hi Girl.' She turns up at 8.15, likes to keep a man waiting. They manage to exchange names, and she is Nicola. Not a lot of conversation as too busy eating. The food is varied and rather good - a new place for his evenings alone, and a young crowd which adds to the atmosphere. The only problem is no booze, so after they have eaten (she shared the bills, which seemed very good of her), they retire to a nearby pub. She asks for an Aperol Spritz, which is £10, and he has a pint of Doombar. They go to a quiet corner. She was brought up in Essex and was hopeless at school. When she left school at 16 with only one GCSE in Art, she had no idea what she wanted to do with her life. Her first job was working in a local boutique selling women's clothes, but she didn't like the owner too much, and the pay was terrible. She had always loved the sea and had been on holiday to Newquay, and so she decided to decamp. She came to Newquay just over 5 years ago after Christmas and got the job which she still has. Working as a waitress is better than a boutique. Pay is not too bad, and she gets a share of the tips—not much at this time of year, but good in the Summer—and her board is free. She loves the sea and her passion is surfing, and bring so close she has managed to get rather good. It is too cold at the moment but she will be back in the water in April. Doing the maths, she must be about 22. He better say something, but he must get his story straight. He was born and brought up in Newquay. Like her, he was hopeless at school but did get 3 GCSEs. (always good to be one or two better). A year at a horticultural college, and then he became a gardener. Has worked for a family firm ever since. Loves being outside, but also helps in the office. He doesn't mention his age. No talk on either side of girlfriends or boyfriends. They finish their drinks and she buys a second round. They chat away very happily but learn little about each other. They agree to repeat the evening next Monday as he is committed to family on Sunday evening, and who knows, might see on the Coast Path on Sunday. He walks her back to the Headland. She gives him a proper kiss but no tongues. Not a bad evening, all told.

As he walks home, something is nagging him. He has run away, and instead of sticking to his first story about unrequited love and Venice, he has now made up three more since he has been in Newquay. The wife who dumped him, losing his job, and always being a Newquay boy. Will this come back to haunt him? What he does not want to do is run into Nicola during the day when he should be working as a gardener. She will be working lunches and dinners, so he should be safe then. He will just have to avoid the town in the mornings and afternoons - shouldn't be too difficult, but be extra careful on Monday, which is her day off.

This scheming is all very well but there is one thing that he has overlooked. Nicola met Jasmine and Elena when they were all working at the Headland. They are not great mates, but she does from time to time, go and eat at their restaurant. The next Sunday is pretty dull and not a great day for a walk, so she decides to go and pay them a visit. She turns up at the Secret Garden just before 1, and it looks like she is going to be the only customer. Jasmine seems genuinely pleased to see her. She orders a margarita pizza and a jug of tap water. No point in spending too much. After she has finished, Jasmine comes to sit at her table, and shortly after, they are joined by Elena. She talks excitedly about their upcoming visit to Rome. They are flying next Sunday, so it is lucky she came today. Nicola says it looks like a good time to go with so little business, and she tells them how envious she is. She only gets two weeks' holiday a year, and for the last two years she has stayed in Newquay. Nice to have the surf but not the same as going away. She then asks them if they have boyfriends. They both reply in the negative. Too much work, no time for boys. They then ask her if she has got a man. 'Well girls, the answer is sort of yes and no. I had a very interesting date with quite a good-looking guy last Monday, and we are going to have the second date tomorrow evening. I am not sure if we are girlfriend and boyfriend yet, but it seems to be going in the right direction.' This makes Jasmine and Elena interested and they start to ask lots of questions. Nicola cannot really believe this interest, but she decides to play along.

'We went to dinner at the Boathouse. Then we went to a pub for a couple of drinks. He walked me home and gave me a sweet kiss at my door.' The girls want her to tell more. 'His name is John and he has average height and build with longish hair and a beard. He is a local boy and still lives with his mum. His day job is gardening. 'Elena says that it is strange. We have a customer called John who looks a lot like what you have described. But it can't be him because he has only just moved to Newquay and is looking for work, strangely as a gardener.

Our guy comes in here frequently, and we treat him to extra wine after dinner upstairs in our flat. It's funny that there should be two very similar guys in the same place.' They are all in agreement. Jasmine finds out that the second date tomorrow night is also going to be at the Boathouse.

John has dinner with Maude again on Sunday - roast lamb with him providing the wine. She doesn't make any advances, for which he is grateful. He is looking forward to seeing Nicola again tomorrow night. She seems like the kind of girl he would like to spend more time with. He is not sure how they would ever be alone, as he could not bring her back here. But maybe he could if he could persuade Maude to be his mum, but then getting her to stay would be difficult. That is only going to happen if he gets his own place, but at the moment, he is happy here. He reckons that her staff accommodation would certainly not be on offer. What he doesn't know is that Jasmine is intrigued by Nicola's man and she is going to spy on them.

John turns up on time, and Nicola, all apologies, is 20 minutes late. Jasmine and Elena have agreed that for one night only, Elena will be the chef and waitress - unlikely to be busy. But Jasmine will need some form of disguise. They put her hair into a turban, and Jasmine wears a pair of glasses. She normally wears contacts. They both agree that she is unrecognisable and in any case, she will stay a long way off. She gets there just after 8 and spots her John sitting alone. About 20 minutes later, Nicola arrives and joins him. So it is the same John. This is all a bit confusing. Their John has recently arrived from Plymouth and is looking for gardening work. Nicola's John was born and bred in Newquay and lives with his mum and has a gardening job already. Which is to be believed. She rushes her food and hot foot back to Elena. She is equally confused. They decide that next time John comes to their place, they will have it out with him. And should they tell Nicola?

John is totally unaware of all this and has never spotted Jasmine in the Boathouse. After they have eaten, they retire again to the pub and have a couple of drinks. He walks Nicola back to the Headland and they have an all tongues kiss. Yes, she would like to spend Sunday with him, and he will be here at noon, come rain or shine.

He gets home and tells Maude about Nicola and his evening. She has never been to the Boathouse, a bit too young and trendy for her. She tells him he is welcome to bring her over anytime. Is this when he admits to the falacy that Maude is his mum? He thinks not.

Tuesday is another boring day. He must try to find a way of getting work. His finances are still reasonable, and he is not spending a lot of money, but his funds will not last forever, and to be honest, he is fed up not having anything to do. He has always been hard-working, and he needs to find something. Maybe in the Summer, he could be a waiter under Jasmine. Thinking of her, he decides to go there for dinner - he needs a little brightness in his life.

He arrives just after 7.30. He is the only customer. He does not get the normal beaming smile. Have I upset her in some way? He chooses a different pizza with chilli and orders a glass of wine. The service certainly seems a bit off. When he is finished, he wonders if she will join him. In fact, they both join him. Jasmine says

'You have got some explaining to do. We are good friends with Nicola, whom we met at the Headland. She came here on Sunday for lunch and told us all about this guy she was dating called John. Her John sounded a lot like you. Last night I went in disguise, you wouldn't have seen me, and watched you having dinner with Nicola. You have told her that you are a local boy and live with your mum and work as a gardener. You told us that you are from Plymouth and lost your gardening job, and are currently looking for work, and indeed, you have tried to see if we knew of any opportunities. One of these stories must be true, or perhaps neither is true. If neither is true, then there must be some explanation as to why you are here. In our minds, there are many possibilities. We love to watch crime dramas from time to time, and our best guess is that you are a runaway. We have considered reporting you to the police in case they have any

interest in you. Slightly difficult as we do not know where you live.'
John is dumbstruck by this little speech. He had told himself it was
not a good idea to have multiple stories, and now it has come to bite
him. The most worrying is that they have declared their suspicion that
he is a runaway and are thinking of going to the police. If they did go
to the police, the search for him would be centred on Newquay, which
would be a drag. He is going to have to say something good. The best
form of defence is attack, and that is what he will do.

'I do not like being spied on. What you did was the lowest of the
low. As far as I am concerned, there is nothing to explain. I come to
your restaurant for food and a little chat. I am currently dating an old
friend of yours, and we eat, drink and chat. I have to admit that I live
in my own world of fantasy and try to be a different person in different
situations. I have no idea how you could have come to the conclusion
that I am a runaway because nothing could be further from the truth.
I suppose you want to know who the real me is. I have told you about
me and why I am here. I think we should just leave it at that.'

He is not sure this is very convincing, but let's see how they
respond. Jasmine: 'If I understand you correctly, you are saying that
what you have told us is the truth. You came here from Plymouth after
losing your gardening job and are currently looking for alternative
employment. What you have told Nicola about yourself is a total
fabrication. It is difficult for us to understand why you would lie to
her about your circumstances. And our conclusion is that it is all lies,
and you have something to hide.' This is all getting so difficult. He is
going to have to brazen it out. 'You are mistaken, I have nothing to
hide. Go to the police if you want, but you will just be wasting your
time and theirs. I am not sure that they would take too kindly to that,
and indeed, what you are proposing may be an offence. You know all
about me that you need to know. As far as Nicola is concerned, I did
not want to tell her that I didn't have a job, as that would have made
me look like a loser. So I decided to have a gardening job. At the same
time I did not want to tell her that I was living in cheap digs because
my funds were low. So I sort of pretended my landlady was my

mother. It is a bit like that. She gives me breakfast everyday, washes my clothes and gives me a roast on Sunday. That is what mothers do. I do not think Nicola will have come to any harm from not knowing the truth.' Well, that sounded pretty good, and hopefully I have put them off the police. Jasmine says not much else to say then, and he departs.

After he has left, the girls have a serious conversation. They decide they must inform Nicola of this conversation, as she is the one most at risk. Their instincts tell them that he really does have something to hide, but after what he said, they are nervous about going to the police. Also, they are going to Rome on Sunday, and they don't want anything to interfere with those plans. What if he comes back to the restaurant? Should they refuse to serve him? Hopefully, he won't. So the matter will not arise.

When John gets into bed, he is worried. Their threat of going to the police seemed very real. Did he say enough to put them off? But it is a threat. In his situation, he cannot afford threats. He thought he was happily out of the way in Newquay, and with his beard as a disguise, it was very unlikely he would be identified. That no longer seems such a given. He will spend the next day thinking it all through. If he has to leave his next place, he must stick to one story. Does he like Newquay - not much. The days seem endless. He used to enjoy socialising with Jasmine and Elena, but they will not be here for a month. To be honest, it seems unlikely that there will be any more social life with them. Nicola is nice, but it is very early days in their relationship.

Chapter 16

Nearly another month has gone by since we visited the other characters in our story.

There is not much to report about Karen. She has heard nothing from Paul and has made no attempt to contact him. She has basically become a stay-at-home mum and all her energies are directed at making a nice life as she can for Jonathan. She has had no opportunity to meet suitable younger men. She calls Colin's parents mostly on Sunday evenings. The conversation always seems to be the same - nobody has heard anything about Colin. It is only after these conversations that she thinks of him. In some ways, she still wishes he were still here because, to be honest, her life has become a nothing.

Penny, there is a lot more going on. To be honest, Deborah does not like her. She becomes more convinced by the day that Penny orchestrated the downfall of her old boss. She notices that in meetings she is always trying to take the lead, which she finds frustrating - she is, after all, the boss, but Penny seems to be refusing to recognise that.

After Christmas, they commence on another IPO. Vape One which is an interesting name. The Board have the highest hopes for a successful launch. The team get working. It is late nights and Saturday for all. Penny is given the job of bringing forward the profit forecast and works very hard at it. After about three weeks, she thinks she has undertaken all reasonable checks and signs off the document and passes it to Deborah.

Deborah is pleased as it is a key job, and it is good to get it done. She has had nothing to do with the Profit Forecast, concentrating on other matters. She decides to take a look. The top line figure shows profits nearly tripling next year from the audited £20 million in the previous year to just over £59 million. Not bad. There are management accounts for the first three months attached. This shows a profit of only £5.3 million in the first quarter. Where did the £59 million come from? Regarding Turnover - in the first quarter, turnover increased by 6%, but in the forecast, turnover for the year is up 80%. How can that be? Perhaps, they are intending to make a substantial increase in marketing expenditure. Not so the expenses are flat. All her instincts tell her that this forecast is pie in the sky. She calls Penny into her office. 'You have signed off the profit forecast as approved. As you know, the profit forecast will be an important part of the listing document. I have undertaken a preliminary analysis of the figures, and in my book, it does not add up. Turnover for the rest of the year is forecast to grow by 80% compared to 6% currently. You must have looked into this. What is the explanation?'

Penny had not expected Deborah to check her work. To be honest, she took the company figures at face value. Their Finance Director seemed very professional, and she was prepared to accept his figures without doing any real checking. All she can say is that the company provided the figures. I am sure that the readers do not want to get bogged down in numbers. Deborah took charge of the profit forecast and called the Managing Director and Finance Director into a meeting. At the end of the day, they were unable to offer any real explanation for the turnover increase. It was not through marketing but rather an increased presence in supermarkets and chain stores selling tobacco products. There is a lot of backwards and forwards but eventually the profit forecast is adjusted to show a profit forecast of £22 million. At this level, they will still be able to achieve a successful IPO, and their company will make a significant profit on their investment.

Deborah is not happy. If she had accepted the Penny approval for the profit forecast, the IPO would have no doubt been a success, but what would have happened when the results were finally published? Their company would lose all credibility and make future offerings so much more difficult. She takes her concerns to the MD. He cannot believe that Penny could have made such a dangerous error, and he praises Deborah for her thoroughness. But what to do about Penny? He is in no doubt that she has to go, as there can be no place for her here. And that is what happens. Penny is sacked and given 6 months' redundancy and has to sign an agreement not to seek employment for 3 months. Deborah is happy to be rid of her. She always had doubts about her actions and did not like the manner in which she tried to take over meetings.

Penny, on the other hand, is devastated. Okay, she should have been more robust in checking the forecast, and she did approve it, but for the life of her, she cannot see that this would be a sackable offence. When she got rid of Colin, she had such high hopes, but now it is all shattered. She contemplates her options. She could go to an employment lawyer to see about unfair dismissal, but that can wait for the time being - she is going to take a holiday.

It is nearly February, and the weather is dreadful. What see need is the Caribbean. She books business class flights to Antigua and a month at the upmarket Carlyon Bay.

Meanwhile, the police are becoming increasingly frustrated. They are making no progress with the murder case. They only have one suspect - the man who failed to show up for the DNA test. They have his picture, which has been circulated all over Devon and Cornwall, but no leads. He must be staying somewhere. It is decided that they will start the house-to-house enquiries again, going to all the cheap hotels, boarding houses and B&Bs. It will require a lot of manpower, but it has to be done.

Chapter 17

Now, back to John.

What he does not know is that the next day, Jasmine goes to see Nicola. She is serving lunch, but not that busy. When the lunch service is over, they find a quiet place to talk. Jasmine informs Nicola of all the circumstances surrounding John. Nicola is astounded. To her, he seemed like an honest salt-of-the-earth kind of fellow, and she had imagined their relationship developing. That can no longer be on the cards. They end up concluding that he is not to be believed. The conversation then gets onto the police. If he has something to hide, should they be informing them? Jasmine explains that she and Elena do not want to go to the police as they are travelling to Rome on Sunday and do not want to muck it up. Nicola says she will think about whether she should report him. She is upset enough to do so, but is not sure if she can really be bothered. She has little to gain from it. Her only decision is that she will not be around on Sunday when he comes to pick her up.

John spends the day inside thinking. To date, he has done a pretty good job of disappearing and as far as he is aware, the police have no idea of his whereabouts. How wrong can you be, as we know he has been tracked to Truro and his picture is with all the local forces. What good is a picture, because he now has long hair and a beard and would be hard to recognise. If the girls did go to the police, they would be unable to provide any address for him. He feels sure he never mentioned where he lived, as there had never been any need. The police would have to visit all the lodging places in Newquay. It is unlikely that Maude would give him away, but wait, if the police were clever, they would be asking about dates of arrival, and he would fit that. He might not be as safe as he thinks he is.

Around lunchtime, Maude comes to tell him she is just going out and does he need anything. No.

This is his big chance to escape.

Time for TURN 3.

John packs all his belongings into his single bag and puts the key on the bed. He leaves the house and heads to the bus station. He has no idea where he is going. Back to Truro does not seem like a good plan. He looks at the departure board. The choice seems to be between Redruth and Padstow. Redruth would be cheaper, but Padstow is by the sea, which he prefers. Padstow, it will be, and the next bus is leaving in 9 minutes.

Whilst he is waiting for his bus, Maude returns home and shouts her return. No reply. She spends the afternoon pottering around, and around 4, decides to make them both a cup of tea. She knocks on his door and says, 'tea's ready.' No reply. She opens the door, and the first thing she sees is the keys on the bed. Strange. For some reason, she then goes and looks in his cupboard. Nothing. It seems he has left her without a word. She thought they had a good relationship with dinners out, Sunday roasts and his washing. She may have gone a little far with the flirting, but that all seemed to have been forgotten. What could have made him want to leave so suddenly? It really is a mystery.

And as far as she is concerned, it remains a mystery for another week. Late one evening, there is a knock on the door, and a young man identifies himself as PC Swain and shows her an ID, which she doesn't really take in. He tells her that they are looking for an individual who may have come to Newquay in early January. This is his picture. Could I ask you to look closely at the photograph and tell me if you recognise him? She looks closely, and there is no recognition. He then asks if she has any guests at the moment. No. Has she had any guests since early January? Yes she had a young man called John who stayed for about 4 weeks, but he had long hair and a beard and looked nothing like your picture. You said about 4 weeks ago, when did he leave? Last Wednesday. Do you know where he went? Funny you should ask that, but no. He had paid rent for another week, but I went shopping one day, and he just disappeared. PC Swain wonders if he is onto something here. He thanks her for her time and says the police may be in touch. No, she is not going anywhere. PC Swain returns to his police station and phones Truro. The Inspector is still working. The PC goes through his conversation. The Inspector thinks there might be something here. Tomorrow you will return to the address with our artist, whom we will send over to you in the morning.

The next day, PC Swain and the artist return to Maude. She is surprised to see them. She is asked to describe John's hair and beard to the artist. Sitting at the table, he takes about 10 minutes to superimpose the hair and beard on the picture of Colin that they have. He shows it to Maude. She is not sure. The facial features seem to match, but she is not sure about the eyes. John had blue eyes. The artist gets out his mobile and phones the Inspector. Colour of the suspect's eyes, please. Will get back to you. The wheels of the police procedures creak. Surely we must know the colour of his eyes. Eventually, news comes back - yes, blue eyes. The artist is phoned and told blue eyes. It is determined that with Maude's assistance, John, her lodger, is probably Colin. They then have a discussion about his leaving. The most probable is between 12 and 1 last Wednesday. The artist phones the Inspector with their conclusions.

The Inspector is elated. It was on his insistence that they spent many hours going door to door in the many lodgings across the two counties, and now they have a result. The first thing to do is find where he went. He has probably left Newquay, which would mean the bus or the train. He immediately sets in motion getting the CCTV from the train station and the bus station for Wednesday between noon and 6pm.

It takes about 3 days to get to the train station. They carefully watch it all, but there is no sign of a man with long hair and a beard. In another couple of days and the bus station arrives. John or Colin, as they know him, can be seen boarding a bus going to Padstow. Next thing to check is did he arrived in Padstow or got off on the way. Another CCTV request for Padstow bus station. This comes the next day, and there he is getting off in Padstow.

The first thing to do is get the new picture of Colin with beard and hair, not only to Padstow but also all over Devon and Cornwall, in case he moves again. And now we know he is in Padstow, we will have to go through the process of checking all the lodgings. He telephones his counterpart in Padstow. He reluctantly agrees that his force will be full on in finding Colin.

This has all happened around two weeks after John arrived in Padstow, so he is safe for now, but does not know it.

He gets off the bus, and it is just after 3. It is refreshing to be in a new place, and it seems to have a buzz about it even though it is still the depths of Winter. Looks like more tourists here. Probably come for the food. In his old days, if he were here, he would no doubt have been eating at Rick Stein's. Not now, as too expensive, and he doesn't have the right clothes. To be honest, he is coming to look a bit like a vagrant. He decides to go to the back streets where lodging will be cheaper. In one of the backstreets, he sees a B&B and goes in. The cost is £37 per night. He decides to book two nights and hands over £80. They are mystified as all the world pays by card, and they do not have any change. Keep the change, then. The room is small and smelly, and he has to share a bathroom down the corridor. He will not be staying here long.

In fact, he finds that he does not like Padstow, and after his two nights, he decides to move on, which is lucky. The B&B gets a visit from the police and is able to confirm he stayed two nights but left no forwarding address. They mention he paid cash. The police have no idea whether he has stayed in Padstow. They report their findings back to Truro. The Inspector tells them to keep looking in Padstow as he does not think he will have moved along again so soon.

John does not really know where to go. He goes to the bus station in the early morning. There are buses to Wadebridge, which is where he goes. He has never heard of it and does not know what to expect.

There is a different atmosphere here. Looks like a real town, not just a place for holidaymakers like Newquay and Padstow. What is his story going to be here? Whatever it is, he must stick to it. His beard and his hair make him look a bit like a vagabond. He cannot be a tourist. What reason could he possibly have for being here? A sudden idea strikes him - he will be a writer. He used to live in London, but he found it impossible to find space for his creative writing. He needed to be in a place that was a lot less busy. He could write, but he also needs to find a job and earn some income. How is he to explain that? Easy - he is poor and needs to pay the rent and eat. From his experience in Truro, he thinks a bedsit will be best.

He goes into a newsagent and buys the West Briton and retires to a small coffeehouse. He likes it here - no Starbucks or Costa. There is nothing suitable in the ads. A pretty girl is serving, so he says to her, 'Excuse me. I have just arrived here from London and need a cheap place to stay for a while as I am writing a book. I just looked in the West Briton and there was nothing. You look like a local girl, and I don't suppose you know of any bedsits or similar that might be available.' She seems to be just staring at him, but then she says, 'I live in a bedsit just round the corner and I happen to know that there is currently one available. I do not know the price, but I pay £500 per week. If you like, I could give the landlord a ring and see if I can get you a viewing.' Which is what she does. She comes back and says the landlord is there now, and if you like, you can go round and view. She gives him directions, and off he goes.

It is quite a nice Edwardian house. The front door is open, so he enters and shouts out, 'Hello.' A middle-aged man appears, who is a little fat and bald and introduces himself as the landlord. No names.

John just says my name is John. The landlord says the available bedsit is on the top floor. They ascend two flights. No, he doesn't mind the stairs. They enter through a blue door. This is bigger than Truro and also has a cooker and a colour flat screen TV. Going up in the world, then. They take a while looking round. The landlord asks if he likes it. 'I am a writer who finds that he cannot write in London, so I decided to move away to allow my creative juices to flourish (where did that come from). Being up here in the eaves would be a perfect place for me to write. This is the first place I have seen, but I think it would be ideal. The question is how much?

The landlord replies that the normal rate is £500 per month, but the stairs make this less attractive, so he lets it for £450 per month. If he is interested, he will need to pay £900 as a one-month deposit is required. He will, in due time, also require a reference from a previous landlord. (He obviously cannot provide a reference but feels sure he can fake something.) John says he will take it and give the landlord £900 cash now. (He does not want the landlord to see his pile of cash, so he goes into the bathroom and removes £900) The landlord comments that he is not used to cash but seems happy. Let me show you the garden. It is shared by the six bedsits, and at the moment, there will be 9 of you living here. The garden seems very pleasant with two benches and a table. The landlord says, 'By the way, I am John too. I think I should take you to the nearest local, which is very good, and allow us to get to know each other a little better. Which is what they do. The landlord seems a decent chap, but he would not want to spend too much time in the pub with him. From his conversation, he learns nothing of interest. As they are leaving, the landlord says, 'Almost forgot. This key is the front door, and this is the key to your room.'

John returns to the bedsit and climbs the stairs, and lets himself into his room. He is quite pleased with himself. His writing story seems to have ticked the right boxes, and he can stay here as long as he wants. The rent at £15 per night is cheaper than Maude's and the place is also cheaper than Truro's and has a cooker and a decent TV. He checks his funds - after paying the rent, he has £4,060 left in the kitty. If he can keep his living expenses down to say £10 per day, with the rent, he would be able to last about 162 days. Not that long. He must find employment. He should have asked John. He still has his copy of the West Briton and looks at the jobs, but nothing suitable. He unpacks his bag, which doesn't take long and thinks about the girl in the coffeehouse. Does he fancy her? Yes, anything in a skirt. He better go and see her and express his thanks.

He arrives back at the coffeehouse, and there she is. He gives her a big smile and says, 'We're neighbours.' She asks him if he wants lunch and tells him the crab toastie is great. He orders it along with a coffee. She is right, the toastie is great. Not very busy, so when he has finished, she joins him at his table. She has got nice blond hair, medium length, and under her apron, what looks like a pretty good figure. Yes, he can be friends with her. She opens the conversation.

'I have never met a writer, it is so exciting. Is your book a novel, and what is the storyline?' (A very direct question. To be honest, he had not thought this through.)

'I do not know yet. I had written about a quarter of a book in London, but it was rubbish and I dumped it in the bin. I have come here for new inspiration. Over the next few days, I will work out my plot and then start eagerly writing. Unfortunately, I will not be able to devote all my waking hours to writing as I need a job to pay the rent and to eat. I would prefer cash as I have a personal hate of tax and NHI. Any ideas?'

She has no idea, alas. They talk a little more and decide to meet later and go to the pub - the shepherd's pie and sausage, and mash are very good.

He leaves her. Time to stock up. There is a local Co-op. He buys things for breakfast, beer and wine, but does not bother about lunch or dinner. It still comes to £13, which is above his daily budget.

She has told him that she lives in number 1, and as he knocks on her door, he realises they have not exchanged names. She opens, 'Hi,

I'm John, and I think we have a date.' She replies, 'Hi, I'm Sue, and I was not aware I had a date tonight,' and laughs. A good start, it is nice to meet a girl with a sense of humour. They make their way to the same pub where he was with John earlier. The first person they see is John, who makes some comment about their being together, which he doesn't get. Hopefully not rude - he is too old to fancy her, surely.

They both order a pint of Doombar and each pays. They take some menus to the table. She apparently loves sausages, so they both order sausage and mash.

He says to her, 'You know a little about me, but I know nothing about you. Tell me all about yourself.'

'Not a lot to tell, to be honest. I was born and brought up here. I did quite well at school and got my A levels with good grades. My parents persuaded me to go to University. I went to Cardiff for three years and studied French. My second year I spent in Paris, which was fun. I graduated last May and came home. The only job I could get was in the coffeehouse, which does not say much for a University education. I do some translating work, but it is intermittent and does not pay that well. For a couple of months, I lived with my parents, but after the freedom of my years away, I could not stand it, so I found the bedsit which is owned by a friend of my father, and here I am.'

He looks at her a little more. She is quite attractive, but dressed tonight for winter, which is not showing anything of her figure. But she is University educated - good, so not some dull girl. He thinks he could get on with her. What can he say now without giving himself away? Why not talk about the writing? Their food arrives, so they concentrate on eating. Not too bad. They finish and decide on another pint.

If John is going to be a writer, he would have liked a computer or an iPad to do the work. In his present financial position, he doesn't think he can afford either unless he can find something cheap second-hand. He probably needs a typewriter, so he says to Sue:

'When I was in London, I used to do my writing on a typewriter. That typewriter annoyed me so much because nothing ever any good came out of it. When I left, I just abandoned it, but now I need to find another one. Funds are a bit limited, any ideas where I could find another?' He thinks that sounds rather good. She has no idea but says there is a Car Boot Sale on Sundays on the edge of town and offers to take him there - you never know. He makes a joke about a second date, and she laughs with him.

They finish their drinks and head back to the bedsit. As they are going in, he says to her (because he rather fancies her and the night is yet young, 'Would you like to climb the stairs and come into my place and share a bottle of wine with me?' She readily agrees. They enter his bedsit, and she comments on how tidy it is. Only just moved in. She also comments on the double bed, which surprises him, but qualifies it by saying all bedsits have doubles to accommodate couples. He wonders if there is anything in her mentioning the bed.

He finds a bottle of red wine, which is all he has and has trouble finding glasses, but eventually locates two wine glasses, which are good quality. They sit on the sofa together and chink glasses.

She says, 'And I don't know that much about you either. You seem a lot older than me and must have many experiences to tell. How did you earn money in London to pay the rent? Where did you live? Have you ever been married? Did you have a girlfriend in London whom you left behind? Do you like it here so far, and is it going to be a good place for your writing? And lastly, you are not very smart in appearance, your beard is straggly, and I would say your hair is too long.' A lot of questions he is going to have to be careful with.

'To start, I am thirty years old (a slight exaggeration as he is nearly 35)and have not had the pleasure of all life's experiences yet. Money has always been a problem for me, as working interferes with my writing. I do not like to pay tax, so most of my earnings were from casual cash-paying jobs. Don't ask me what I have done, as it is not an impressive CV. I lived in a bedsit in Clapham near the common, which cost me a lot more than I am paying here. I have to admit that I have never been married. I have never proposed to a girl because the right girl for me has never come along. I had no girlfriend in London whom I left behind. I have only been here for less than one day, and so far it seems fine. You are probably right about my appearance. For a long time, I have had nobody to look good for, and I guess I have let it go a bit, but I have saved a fortune at the barbers. Does that answer all your questions? Before you reply, let me ask you a couple. Do you regret University? Do you have a boyfriend?'

'Thanks. Your answers are clear and concise, which I like. I have met too many men who are incapable of answering a simple question, and it seems all they can do is tell fibs and lie. (Well, everything considered, that is a good reply and she doesn't think I am a liar, which, as we all know, I most certainly am). I do not regret University. I thoroughly enjoyed every minute of it, especially my time in Paris. My only regret is that it did not prepare me for gainful employment. I have applied for a couple of full-time translator jobs but have not yet been successful. Will keep trying, and hopefully at some point in the future will be able to get out of the coffeehouse. I had a lot of boyfriends in Cardiff, and in the last year, I was close to an Engineer. I thought it might go somewhere, but he hot-footed it to Dubai for the money, and I have not heard a word from him, and to be honest, I couldn't care less. I have no boyfriend at present. All the guys around here are too small-town for me. That's what makes it so good to have met you.'

Well, that all sounds very nice.

He pours her another glass of wine, which she willingly accepts.

She then says it is nice and warm in here and takes her jumper off. She is wearing a white shirt underneath, and for the first time, he gets a view of her breasts, which look inviting. The top three buttons are undone, and he can see her cleavage and a white bra. He supposes he had better follow suit and takes off his jumper.

She grins at him and says. 'Fancy undressing on our first date. There is only one thing you can do, and that is to kiss me.' What an invitation. Does she want me to completely undress her? He is not sure. Anyway, he starts to kiss her, and it is all tongues. He has an immediate erection, and she is sighing happily. He is not sure where to take it from here, but decides to do nothing but kiss. This goes on for a long time. A lot of sighing, but he is not going to take it any further. She looks at her watch and says I better get going, as doing breakfasts tomorrow. She declines another glass of wine but then says unexpectedly, 'I think we should have a second date tomorrow night. I get off work at 3 and would love to cook you dinner. I am in number 1, come knock on my door at 7.30 armed with a bottle of your excellent red wine.' He readily agrees, and they have a last kiss goodnight.

He goes to bed feeling quite happy with life.

The next morning, he gets up with a spring in his step and makes himself breakfast. I have nothing to do until dinner time. How can I fill my day? He hears noises in the garden and sees that there is a gardener. Maybe this might be my chance to get some work done. He wanders down to the garden. The bloke looks just like Rod. He introduces himself as John, the new tenant. The bloke doesn't seem to want to talk much, so he thinks he might as well be direct. 'I am a poor writer who still needs to earn to pay the rent and eat. Any chance of a job with you?'

The bloke looks at him questionably. 'I don't know if writers are going to be any good at gardening, but now that you mention it, I may be looking for some help. I have a problem with servicing my clients, which is why I am here on a Saturday. A month or so ago, an old friend of mine called me up. He had lost his second in command and needed assistance. I agreed to help him and I now go three days a week to this writer's house. It is worth it as the pay is very good, so spend the other four days doing five days' work. I tell you what, come out with me tomorrow and Thursday through Saturday. I will pay you £80 per day at the end of the week. If you shape up, I will take you on full time Thursday through Saturday, which will enable me to have Sundays off with my family, who have hardly seen me for the last month.'

This is a very interesting offer. Should he ask for £100 per day, as £80 is hardly minimum wage? Better not. He will get £320 this week and then £240 per week thereafter. So he has replaced me as Rod's helper. Hopefully, I will not be asked to go to Le Carre as his disappearance would be hard to explain.

He accepts the offer. The bloke whom he now knows as Tim will pick him up here at 8 tomorrow morning.

He wanders back to the Co-op and buys an expensive bottle of wine and a sandwich for lunch. Nero d'Avola, which should go down well. He avoids the coffeehouse and returns to his bedsit. All going well, he thinks. Got a girl and a job, what more could I want? He spends the afternoon reading. At 6, he treats himself to a beer. Then he has his first shower in his new bathroom. He attempts to comb his hair and make his beard look more presentable, and puts on chinos and a blue shirt.

He knocks on number 1 at just after 7.30. She answers the door and greets him with one of her lovely grins. She comments that he is looking very smart. He is not sure what to say about her. She is wearing a white vest and showing her shoulders and arms, and he thinks he detects a bra underneath and a very short black skirt and black tights with no shoes. Basically, she looks jolly sexy. She says, 'Welcome to our second date.' He guesses this must mean something. She accepts his bottle of Nero D'Avola and says, 'Great, as I am treating you to Italian tonight.' She goes into her kitchen area and opens a bottle with a pop. Surely not champagne. No it is not, as she brings him an Aperol Spritz with Prosecco, he assumes. They clink glasses. He tells her about his job offer and trial with Tim. He is worried that he will not be any good at gardening, a slight untruth as he had his experience with Rod, but this is probably a good untruth and should not catch him out. He then tells her that he will have to miss the third date as he will be working tomorrow. She says no matter she will still go to the Car Boot sale and see if she can find him a typewriter. They agree on a maximum spend of £30.

They finish their drinks, and it is now time for food. She opens the wine and brings two plates to her small table. It is a mixture of cured meats, cheese, olives and artichokes, which she jokes is her Sicilian Board to go with the wine. It is a delicious starter. She hurries away and comes back with two plates of homemade lasagna. It is again delicious and a hell of a lot better than the microwave he used to eat. They chat away happily like long-lost friends. He is feeling very relaxed with his new friend, or is it a girlfriend? They finish their food and retire with their glasses to the settee.

The kissing starts almost straight away, and she is sighing again. Where is this going to go? He is not sure. After a while, he feels her breasts, which feel very, very good, and he is met with more deep sighing. He decides he will leave it up to her to make the next move. She does not make the next move, so basically nothing else happens. Time rushes on, and it is now midnight. He has to leave as he is working in the morning. As he is leaving, she tells him that on Sunday evening, she is going to her parents' for the Sunday Roast. If he likes, she will get him an invite and come and knock on her about 6.30. A long, last kiss goodnight.

John is lying happily alone in his bed. There could be something here. He can even imagine making love to her, and he feels pretty certain she is not going to set him up and accuse him of rape like that bitch Penny. He really does hate her. If he had known that she had been sacked, he would have been so glad for some reason that leads him to think about Karen. In some ways, he is glad he is rid of her, and Sue seems a much better bet.

Up early, and he puts on his working clothes and boots and wanders outside. Tim is on time. He wants to ask about the writer, but decides to ignore it and wait for Tim to mention it. They go to three houses for two hours each and have a pub lunch. Tim does not talk much. He thinks he has done all right with the jobs he has been given. They get back around 4. Tim says you did all right today, which is praise indeed, and he will pick him up on Thursday at 8 again.

Too late to go to the shops for wine, so he will just have to take one of his lesser bottles. He has a shower and puts on his best chinos, a white shirt and a jumper. Nearly 6.30, so he knocks on Sue's door. She presents him with a typewriter which looks nearly new. They wanted £40, but she managed to knock them down to £20. Well done, girl. Tomorrow he will start writing. He will leave it at her place and pick it up on his way home.

It is a short stroll to her parents' place. They live in an imposing Victorian villa. Why should we want to leave there and move into a bedsit - after the freedom of University, she must have needed her own place. Her parents are very welcoming, and they start with a gin and tonic. He is a bit worried that his long hair and beard will put them off, but it seems the opposite. He is apparently the first man Sue has ever introduced to her parents, and they are very pleased to make his acquaintance. It all seems very nice.

The roast chicken with all the trimmings, with rhubarb crumble to follow, is to die for. They all share his bottle of wine. After they have finished eating, the father suggests they have a game of Scrabble, which is his favourite game. Father wins and seems pleased. Although it is still quite early, they take their leave. John is given an open invitation to come anytime. As they are wandering back, John comments on his welcome despite his long hair and beard, and he cannot believe he is the first man she has taken back. She tells him that it was her father's joke. Over the years, she has taken quite a few of her beaus back. She thinks that despite his flaws, he made a good impression.

They get back to her room, and she takes off her jumper and tells him to remove his. She is wearing the same white blouse with buttons undone. 'This is our third date now. Still early, so a lot might happen.

I am ready if you are.' That sounds like a very open invitation and he is feeling a little nervous.

We are not going to go into details, but after a lot of playing, they end up in her bed making love. She has condoms, which, given his past experience, is a relief to him. Their love making is very sexual. Lying in bed, she tells him that it was great and it has been a long time for her. He tells her likewise. At around midnight, she says he should stay the night, and they make love again. She is up at 7.30 and brings him a glass of OJ and a coffee. She gets her breakfast in the coffeehouse. She will be off to work now, and he leaves her carrying his typewriter. She will give him a knock after 4 when she returns from work.

Back in his own place, he makes another cup of coffee and makes himself some toast. Sitting down, he thinks that was great, and it doesn't feel as if it is going to come back and bite me. He gazes at the typewriter. Well, I will need some paper. He had spotted a WH Smith in the High Street. He might as well go there and get some, which is what he does.

On returning, he puts the typewriter on his table and inserts a sheet of paper. He has said he is a writer, but he is not. He also said he would spend some time planning his book. That is what he will do over the next three days. What is he going to write about? Does he want to write about the real world, or is he a fiction writer? He thinks he will go for fiction, but then he needs a storyline. He does not think he wants a murder mystery or a story involving the police. Maybe a children's story. He spends the whole morning thinking about this and realises that he has writer's block.

He goes into town and gets himself a sandwich in M&S for lunch. Should he get something for dinner to share with Sue - not sure he can be bothered. He returns with just his sandwich.

He must get over this writer's block. Recently, he has been reading Le Carre because he worked for him. He has written a lot of books.

How does he start a book? He doesn't know, and he never got the chance to ask him. All his books are very different. He must start somewhere. Where am I to start? His brain has gone blank, but he must write something or his story about being a writer will not hold up.

Chapter 18

While John has been settling into his new life in Wadebridge, the Truro Inspector has continued to be busy. One day, he is thinking through the murder case. We have a suspect, but is he really a suspect? He decides that he needs to compare the Colin Bucket DNA with the DNA which the found at the murder scene. This takes a couple of days. The result is that there is no match. That means that Mr Bucket's only crime is running away. We still need to find him and bring him to justice but my priority needs to be the murder. He goes over all the files, and the reality is that all they have is the sighting of the white van. They have been successful in getting DNA from all the local white van drivers but no matches. The only conclusion is that the white van is a red herring, and they need another line of enquiry. He goes back through all the witness statements, and there is nothing that seems to need to be followed up on. They are getting nowhere. What can he do?

Penny arrives in Antigua and gets driven to a beautiful hotel. She has a nice room with a balcony overlooking the sea, which is a glorious blue. Nearly time for dinner. First, she will go to one of the bars and see if there are any interesting young men whom she can attach herself to. The bar has about 8 couples happily drinking and chatting away. She has a rum punch and is a bit glum. Might as well have dinner then. She goes to what looks like the main restaurant. Has she booked? No. You have to book dinner here, but not too busy tonight, so we can fit you in. The restaurant is full of couples happily eating together, but with no sign of any unattached men. She realises that with the time difference, it is now very late, so she retires to her room. She wakes up very early, and breakfast has not been served yet.

She puts on her bikini and a beach dress and slips on her sandals, and goes down to the beach. Nobody about. What can she do? No idea. She just sits on a bed chair. After about an hour, there is activity in the restaurant where she had dinner last night, and she spots, yes, another couple sitting down. At least she can now have breakfast. The breakfast is not too bad. What is she going to do with her day? I know I will go and ask at reception. The receptionist is very smiley. Lots to do here. We have a spa where you can get many treatments, there are tennis courts, there are paddle boards and sailing and water skiing, for which you have to pay. What takes your fancy? None of the above. Her first morning, she just lays in the sun and has a swim in the sea. In fact, her whole month there is an utter bore. She hardly talks to anybody the whole time except the staff who are always pleasant but this is not for her, and she is relieved when it is time to go home. She will be able to concentrate on a new career.

Karen is not having a great time either. Nothing from Paul and she is not communicating with anybody except Colin's parents. She is sure hoping that something is going to happen in her life. From time to time, she still thinks about Colin. As the days go by, he goes down further in her esteem. How could I have ended up with such a bastard. She is pretty sure the right thing to do would be to get a divorce, but for the time being, she cannot be bothered. Jonathan will be going to school full-time in the Autumn and that will be her opportunity to get back to work. It will be doubly good as she will be meeting new people and having something like a proper life.

Maude can still not really believe that John was a runaway. He seemed like such a nice chap and she thought all he said was true, but it patently was not. They had dinners out together, and she cooked him Sunday roasts and made him breakfast every day and even washed and ironed his clothes. But it was all just one big con and she fell for it. Her life had, however, got a whole lot better. The house is sold with a completion set for 31 March. She will be quite rich. She has started looking for a flat to buy in Newquay but hasn't found the right place yet. The best bit will be being able to spend time with her family.

Nicola soon forgets all about John. She had been taken in by him and she thought she would have liked their relationship to flourish, but at the end of the day, he was just one big con. She is grateful to Jasmine and Elena for their detective work and hopes they are enjoying Rome. She will touch base with them again on their return and compare notes.

John spends the rest of the afternoon trying to overcome writer's block but gets nowhere. All too soon, here is Sue, who seems full of the joys of spring. Have you written anything on your new typewriter? No, just going through the planning stage, not quite an untruth but fairly close. And then she says, 'Not made love in your bed yet, so let's have a go.' Which is what they do. He is unable to offer her dinner and she is unable to offer him dinner, so they go back to the pub and drink Doombar and eat shepherd's pie. They go back to his room and make love again. She stays the night in his pad. In the morning, he gets up first and gives her OJ and coffee. He will make her dinner tonight. She goes off to her job.

He thinks he would like to make her a nice dinner and so he goes to M&S. For starters, he buys two Coquilles St Jacques, which can be heated in the oven. For the main course, he buys two pork chops, potatoes and cabbage as well as apple sauce and some more wine as he has nearly run out. He spends the rest of the day trying to plan his book, but gets nowhere. He wonders if he should write a book about an alleged rape and the culprit's escape from bail. He could write his story, but that would be dangerous, as the police might follow up with his publisher, and he could get caught. That will not do. He is devoid of any other ideas, but is going to have to write.

She turns up as promised and asks about his book planning, to which he can only give a vague reply. She does not seem impressed. She doesn't seem in the mood for bed either. They end up watching Pointless, which she likes, but he doesn't get. Time to have a beer and start dinner.

She seems a bit impressed with his efforts in the kitchen. After dinner, she is back to her loving ways, and they go to bed, and she stays the night. OJ and coffee in the morning again for her. She goes off to work, and they do not discuss what to do that evening, which he finds a little strange - has she gone off him?

He sits down for a book planning session. He suddenly has an idea. Why not write a children's story for grown-ups? He can portray an idyllic childhood, but then something goes wrong. His heroine, who is a girl, loses her parents in an air crash. There is nobody to look after her, and she has to go to an orphanage and then into foster parents. She is not a happy girl. At long last, she is adopted by a lovely couple, but she can never love them because she adores and misses her parents. He is not sure where it is going to go from there, but it is a start and to him sounds good. He gives his book a working title, 'Eight Miles High', to bring in the element of the air crash. He gets out the typewriter and paper and starts writing. He finds he is really into it, and by late afternoon, he reckons he has 5,000 words, and he is yet to get to the air crash. Will he go into the gory details? He will decide when the time comes. He is so engrossed in his writing that all he has to eat the whole day is a piece of toast. Sue knocks on his door just after 4.

We forgot to make any arrangements for tonight, so she is still on board then. He suddenly remembers he has work at 8 in the morning. They decide to go to the pub again for dinner and to sleep alone in their own beds.

They get to the pub and find a table. Back to sausages tonight. She asks about his book and he tells her he has now started and already has 5,000 words. No, she cannot see it; she will have to wait until it is finished. He reckons he will be writing 3 days a week, Monday through Wednesday, and he would like 100,000 words, which will be about six weeks. They have a big kiss at her door and he gets back alone to his flat. She is going to cook for him again on Thursday night, and he can stay even if he has to get up early to go to work.

Tim is with him promptly at 8. They go to four places today and have another pub lunch. Tim says nothing about his three days at the writer's place, so he doesn't ask. In fact, Tim does not say much at all. He learns only that he was born and bred here and has been a gardener since he left school. He has a wife and two teenage kids who are an endless bother. He doesn't ask John any questions about his writing, which is a relief.

We are not going to go into lengthy details about Sue and his love life and eating arrangements, but jump forward a month.

After the first week, Tim told him that he liked having him around and was happy to make their arrangement permanent. He resists the temptation to ask for more money. His book is progressing well. It has moved forward considerably with nearly 90,000 words. His heroine went to drama school because she wanted to be an actress and then moved to Los Angeles to further her career. She inherited a lot of money from her deceased parents when she was 21. She married a man so that she could stay in the USA, but she is not happy with him. He wanted it to have a happy ending to reflect his own happiness with Sue, but at the moment, it is not going that way. He is not sure where to take it.

Then something big happens. It is a Friday night, and Sue is cooking again. He mentions that tomorrow he will be paying another month's rent. She says, 'To my mind, it is stupid for us to both be paying rent as we spend so many nights in each other's places. I think we should commit to each other and move in together. The rent will be half, and we could afford a better lifestyle. I think I prefer my place as there are no stairs, although it is a bit more expensive. What say you to moving in with me and paying me half the rent or £250 per month? This is like a bolt out of the blue and totally unexpected. He is very fond of her, and it seems like she is fond of him. The savings in rent would be good, and he could get his deposit back. Would he have to give notice? He doesn't know. At the same time, as far as he is aware, he is still a married man, and would it be right for him to set up home with another girl? He needs to give her a response. 'I would be delighted to live together. Ever since we met, I have continually looked forward to seeing you, and having a permanent relationship will suit me fine.' He hopes he has sounded convincing. She just gives him a huge smile and says, 'Let's get on with it then.' She says she has a written rental agreement, which he never got. She rummages around in a drawer and produces it. There is no requirement to give notice, so they decided to contact the landlord in the morning, and he can move in with her straight away.

This is making him very happy, and to think he was nervous of sleeping with her in case she too accused him of rape. A rent of £250 per month will be great. He can earn that in three days working with Tim and may even be able to save a little after all his expenses. She then says, 'If we are going to live together, then I am going to cut your hair and trim your beard to make you look more presentable.' They spend the next hour and a half with her, bringing his appearance up to scratch. He looks in the mirror and is pleasantly surprised; she has done a good job. She then tells him she would prefer it if they kept it a secret from her parents, to which he readily agrees. Now we are going to get into dangerous territory. She says,

'Now that we are going to live together, I need to know more about you. We have never discussed your upbringing or past, and I seem to know very little about you except that you are a writer with a gardening job and did not have a girlfriend when you left London. I would like to know the following -

Where were you brought up?

Where did you go to school?

Did you go to University?

Have you ever had a proper job, and what was it?

Are your parents still alive, and if so, do you communicate with them, and do they know you are living in Cornwall?

Do you have brothers and sisters, and are you in contact with them?

Do you have aunts and uncles?

How did you become a writer? Have you had any books published? Why did you live in London, which must have been expensive?

Who has been the love of your life?

This is quite an extensive list of questions. He is going to have to be very careful in his answers.

'Firstly, I have to tell you that you are the love of my life today, and I think I can honestly say that I have never met a girl who matched you at all. (not bad for an opener) I have not talked about my past with you because, in many ways, it seems irrelevant. Since you are now asking, I can tell you that I was brought up in Essex and went to Brentwood School and did A levels. My grades were not good enough for University, so I became an articled clerk and did exams and became a Chartered Accountant. Accountancy was not for me. About the time I qualified, I had a terrible experience as my parents were both killed in a motorway accident. I inherited some money. I decided that, as I did for the time being not need to work I would become a writer. I have finished four novels, but never found a publisher for any. I have no brothers or sisters or aunts or uncles because both my parents were single children. I think that answers all your questions, but feel free to ask anything else.' That did not sound too bad and basically seems pretty reasonable. She is frowning a little what can be bothering her.

'That is all very interesting. I would never have taken you to be a Chartered Accountant. Your appearance is completely different from what you would expect. Because you have those skills, why are you taking a low-paid job as a gardener? On a completely different subject, have you ever been abroad, and where did you go? My only trip abroad was when I spent my year in Paris, which I think made me a bigger person. I would guess you have been all over the place.'

The Accountant bit is quite easy, overseas could be more difficult particulars as he is currently without his passport.

'As I told you, Accountancy was not for me. If for my job I wanted to be an Accountant, I would have to cut my hair, shave my beard and wear a suit and tie and worst of all, pay tax. I am very happy being a gardener outside, and although the remuneration is low, I find it highly satisfying. I would not say I have been all over the place. When I was a teenager, I used to go on foreign holidays with my parents, mostly to Spain. We drove through France a couple of times, but I have never been to Paris. When I was an articled clerk, I went to Greece on a couple of cheap holidays to Corfu and Rhodes, which I quite liked. I have never been out of Europe. I would like to go to the USA one day, and New York, Los Angeles and the Grand Canyon are on my bucket list. My passport expired three years ago, and I have not renewed it. 'That sounded all right, I think. Her questions seem to have ended. John says he might as well clear out his room. He packs everything into his one bag and empties the fridge, and returns to Sue. She seems surprised by his meagre belongings and wants to ask him why he has so little, but she does not. They go to bed.

The next day, he goes off early to work as usual. She phones the landlord, who will be around when she has finished work. The landlord comes round and she explains that John is moving in with her. He has left his keys with her, and they go upstairs to inspect. Everything seems to be in order. The landlord makes out a cheque to her for the deposit, as he is not sure of John's surname, and neither is she. How can she be living with someone and not know their surname? The landlord, who, as we know, is friendly with her father, asks if she has told her parents of the new arrangements. She replies in the negative, and he says he will keep mum.

After the landlord has left, John returns from his day's work. She tells him all that has gone on. She will bank the cheque, and he will pay her no rent this month and then £50 next month to make them even. There is then the matter of the key. There is only one. They decide that she will get a duplicate made so that they can each have a key.

John and Sue settle happily into their new arrangement. Nearly every Sunday, they go to her parents for the roast, which is a nice affair. They show no sign of knowing that they are living together, and they do not feel inclined to tell them.

Another three months pass. Not much has changed for them, but every day they seem to grow closer. They have never had a disagreement, and life seems rosy. John has finished his book. It did not have a happy ending, but I will not spoil it if you get to read it. That could be difficult because, despite John's efforts, he is not able to find a publisher. He has copied it about 10 times and sent it off with great hopes. The responses have all been negative. Sue read it and thought it was a great story and should be available for the whole world to read. He would have liked to have been able to consult John Le Carre on how to get published. Then he has an idea. One day, he tells Tim that he has written a book but is having much difficulty getting published. He knows that three days a week, Tim works for a writer. Here is a copy of my book. Could he possibly give it to him and see if he has any ideas? Tim says he has hardly ever seen the writer, and most of their dealings are with the wife for him, but he will give it a go. Let's see if anything happens. In the meantime, John decides he must write another book, but finds he is back to writer's block. John and Sue have a routine for eating. He cooks on Monday and Tuesday. She cooks on Wednesday and Thursday. These are dry nights, and they do not drink alcohol. They then go out on Friday and Saturday to the pub or a restaurant and have a drink, and to her parents on Sunday. For both of them, it is very pleasing. Sue has had a major change in her working arrangements. She has managed to find an agency that gives her a lot of translating work and pays better. This is more what her education was meant to provide her, and she has ditched her full-time job in the coffeehouse and now only works there on Saturday, which means they spend three days a week together in the bedsit in a kind of domestic bliss.

Finally, John has an idea for a second book. He rather likes sad stories, so let's make this one sad. He starts off with a couple in an ideal relationship, just like him and Sue, and they have two small children. Well, not like him and Sue, as they have no kids yet, and it is something she never talks about - and she is now on the pill, which makes it all the more unlikely. The husband is a geologist, and he travels overseas a lot. He has him in Nigeria, and he is kidnapped, and a ransom is demanded. When the ransom is about to be paid, there is a gunfight, and he is accidentally shot dead. This is the end of the world for his wife, and she spends a desperate time. She starts smoking cannabis to make her life a little better. So far, so good and a good bit of sadness. Then she meets a man whom she likes a lot, and he says he is a widow. What he does not tell her is that he killed his wife with laburnum poisoning. Their relationship progresses, and he asks her to marry him. She is not sure because she loved her first husband so much, but she eventually agrees. A few weeks before they are to be married, they have a drunken evening and smoke a little cannabis. He then tells her that his wife was a dreadful woman and that he murdered her. She is gobsmacked. She does not know what to do, but eventually goes to the police and reports that this man had told her he murdered his wife. This is as far as he has got, but he gives it a working title of 'The Telltale.' He should be able to finish it in a few days. He thinks it may be better than his first book and allows Sue to have a read. She, as ever, is enthusiastic and cannot wait for the ending. He is not sure where to go with it, but he will work it out.

A few days later, Tim says to him, 'The writer (he still does not know who the writer is) has read his book and thinks it is excellent. He believes that with his influence, he can get you a publisher which your book deserves. But first of all, he would like to meet you to discuss the options. He has suggested I bring you along to his house one day, and we can get the ball rolling.' This is not what John wants to hear. If he goes along with this, no doubt Rod will be there, and the whole thing will raise a lot of ugly questions, like why did he do a runner. He is going to have to find a way out of this, but he is not sure of what approach he should take.

'Thanks, it is great news that the writer thinks it is excellent. I do not think it would be right to take up his time as he must be very busy writing, and I am not sure what I would be able to say to him. Could you just ask him if he could kindly submit my book to his publishing contacts?'

Considering the circumstances, he reckons that it is a good response to a potentially difficult situation. Tim says Okay, he will do that, but he may be missing an opportunity. John cannot afford to let his desire to have his book published put him in danger of arrest.

He gets on with finishing The Telltale. The wife killer is arrested and brought to trial. He is found not guilty of the murder of his wife, but here is the rub. His heroine is accused of perjury and has to stand trial herself and is found guilty, and is sentenced to a period in prison. Her whole world has fallen apart again. She had thought she was doing the right thing by reporting him, but that does not seem to be the case. Book finished. He takes a number of copies and sends them off to prospective publishers. You will not be surprised to hear that all his appeals are rejected. John Le Carre is put out that John could not be bothers to come and see him. He would have liked to meet and have a discussion with another writer. He does nothing more with 'Eight Miles High', which seems destined for obscurity.

Sue likes the end of his book. His lie in coming to Wadebridge was to say he was a writer, and he thinks he has managed rather well to live up to that expectation. What he still finds a little strange is that she has never mentioned his meagre belongings. He would have thought she would want to know why, as a 30-year-old man, he had so little. Surely he would have books, CDs and movies and a lot more clothes, but she has never asked. The reason she has never asked as to be honest, she failed to notice. She was just so happy when they moved in together that nothing else mattered. Their 3 months of living together have been great, and she adores him a little more every day. She does not think she has ever been in love, but she thinks he may be the first man she has loved. What does she like most about him? Going to bed is very fine, but above all, it is his honesty. All the other men in her life from when she first started dating at 15 have always seemed as if they had something to hide, and quite a few of the blokes she has been with told untruths - it could have been about other girls, money or anything, but all of them lied at some point and she found them out. John, on the other hand, is not like that, and she feels sure he has never told her a lie (how wrong could she be, because in reality, everything about John is a lie. You cannot be a runaway from the legal system and be deemed honest. We probably feel sorry for Colin and what Penny did to him, but at the end of the day, we know he is dishonest, and all is a fallacy.

We haven't written about Penny recently. She had thought that getting another job would be easy. In the three months that she has been back from Antigua, she has been active in trying to find employment. She has signed up with three employment agencies and looked at jobs advertised in the Financial Times and elsewhere. There are two problems. The pay is not that good, like she was used to, and the jobs themselves are mostly pretty dull. She liked her old job a lot, and there was always a thrill in IPOs. She cannot find anything to match that. Although she did get redundancy, that seems to be being used up very fast, and she really needs to get back to work. She has been for about 8 interviews. She did not want any of the jobs, but at the same time, she was not offered any positions. Not good. She needs to get onto this fast. Our readers are probably pleased with this news, as we have never liked Penny. I think we all agree that what she did to Colin was the pits and serves her right.

Karen is not doing much better. We are now in June, and she has enrolled Jonathan in a nearby school, and he will be starting in September. She has also signed up with two employment agencies. She is looking to be a solicitor from 10 to 3 to allow her to get Jonathan to school and then pick him up at the end of the day. Such jobs are few and far between. She will just have to keep trying. Paul is at the back of her mind, but she has had no contact with him, and she thinks going to him and asking him for a job is not on. She wonders if she could go back to her old employers, who thought highly of her. She contacts them and gets a good response and is invited for an interview. She is interviewed by one of the partners with whom she had worked before. It seems to be going well. She explains her requirements for working hours, and that does not appear to be a problem.

Going well then. It is the end of the interview, and she is looking forward to the job offer, which can only be a formality. She is shocked when the partner says, 'I am sorry, but I do not think you will be able to fit in. Firstly, the working hours that you have requested will not meet our working practices, and secondly, I think you have been away from the business for too long and will be at best rusty. Sorry to disappoint you. Thank you so much for coming to see us again. It is always a pleasure.' What a blow, and was he flirting with her at the end? She leaves a little down in the dumps. Something will come up, she thinks.

She has also been considering taking Jonathan away before he starts school, to the Mediterranean sun and not Southwold, where Colin took them due to his lack of a passport. Because it is nearing the school holidays, the prices are through the roof, and she decides against it.

So we have two girls, both unsuccessfully looking for jobs. We certainly do not feel sorry for Penny, but we should sympathise with Karen. It is not her fault, and all we can do is wish her well.

Karen has not met any men in this time. We are not sure how she is going to meet another man. Her best hope will be in a new job.

The police have made no progress in their murder enquiry, and as we know, Colin or John is still a free man. There is not much going on in the search for him, for which he should be grateful.

Chapter 19

It is now Summer and the weather is sunny and warm. One Sunday, Sue suggests they go to the ocean. She tells him that in the old days she and her friends used to take the bus to Padstow and then walk along the coastal path to Trevone, which has good swimming. Let's do it. He is not too worried about going to Padstow because he was only there a couple of nights and will not be remembered, but he does have a problem. He has no swimming shorts, and he tells her so. You mean you came all the way to Cornwall and left your swimmers behind. Silly boy. There is a local shop which sells swimsuits, and he buys a pair which he does not like much. She has put her bikini on before they left and is carrying a hold-all with two towels. They have to wait 30 minutes for a bus, but are then on their way. When they arrive in Padstow, she leads him to the coastal path, and it is about a 30-minute walk to Trevone. There is a nice beach cafe and they have a pasty and a beer sitting in the sunshine. Time to get on the beach. He puts the towel round him and changes into his swimmers. She glances at his body, and he feels a bit embarrassed. She takes off her clothes. She sure looks good in a bikini. Into the water. Blow me, it is cold. She swims off like an expert. He paddles around, not enjoying it much. He wants to go back to the beach, but better wait for her. It seems ages for her to return. She says it was great - how was your swim? He wants to say not that great but just mumbles. On their towels, and he is shivering. She gets him a hot chocolate but doesn't have one herself. She is lying in the sun looking like a goddess. He recovers and stops shivering. After about an hour, she says, another swim then. He did not realise that he would have to do it again. Into the cold water, and she invites him to swim with her. He tries but cannot keep up and returns to the shallows. He will not wait for her this time, so he returns to the towels. A bit shivery but not as bad as last time. At long last, she returns and makes an idle comment about his swimming. They spend another hour sunbathing. We'd better be getting back, as we don't want to miss the roast. They take the coastal path back to Padstow and have to wait ages for a bus, and arrive back in Wadebridge just after 7. Hot foot it home, a quick change and over to her parents. Her Mum does not seem to mind them being late. The chat is all about the trip to the beach. Her father says he envies them. If the weather is nice next Sunday, why don't they all go to Trevone? He will drive them, which will save the bus fare. It is so agreed. Then the father goes on, 'John, it is so nice to see you and our Sue getting on so well (he does not know that they are living together and shows no signs of any suspicion in that direction), and I have to say that you are by far the best man she has ever brought home. What I like about you is that you seem straightforward and honest, and I could hardly hope for better for her.' (That is indeed a compliment. He thinks I am straightforward and honest. I wonder what he would think if he knew my circumstances, and whether he would take kindly to us living together.) They make their way home. Sue seems very happy and full of life, and they make love.

A normal week. Sue is busy with her translating. John is thinking about his next book. He would like to make his story into a book, but as we have already discussed too dangerous. Maybe not as dangerous as dating, he has failed to find a publisher. He spends his days tapping his pencil and getting nowhere. Sue has been used to him tapping away on his keyboard and asks if anything is the matter. No, just thinking about what to write in my next book. He does his three days' work with Tim. He enjoys being with Sue on the first three days and finds he misses her company when he is gardening. But the weather is very good and it is so nice working outside. He can hardly believe that in his old life, he was office-bound. This life seems so much better. Does he prefer Sue to Karen? He guesses he does. In his old life, it was all monotonous. He thinks back to his last days with Karen in Southwold. No sex as she slept with the boy each night. Sue would never let that happen - she is always fun, unlike Karen, and I think I am in love with Sue and I think she is in love with me. I wonder where this is going to take us. As the story moves forward we are going to find out.

The next Sunday, the weather is still good, and it seems like they should take advantage of her father's invitation. They go round to her parents and take the drive to Trevone. Much better than the bus and walk. Sue and her father are straight in the sea and swimming out. Her mother says she likes swimming, but does not like to go out so far. He goes for a gentle swim with her. The water is a little less cold, warming up with all the sunshine. He is not shivering today. Her mother is chatty, but he is not taking much notice. Sue and her father return. Her mother has brought a picnic, which is not too bad. John comments that she will be feeding them twice today - no matter. John stands a round of beers, which seems appreciated. After they have let their lunches go down, Sue and her father are back in the water. John and her mother decide to stay on the beach and are ridiculed when the others return. John thinks this is so nice to be a family on the beach and making fun of each other. When he ran away at first, he had lost all of that and, to be honest, was lonely and scared of what might happen. He no longer feels lonely, and he has a new family to have a good time with, and he is no longer scared. It is over six months since he disappeared and he is still a free man and long may it be so. They return in good time. They turn up for the roast a bit early and the atmosphere is cheery. This is how life should be.

On Monday morning, John works out the framework for his next book. He needs to get writing again to maintain the pretence that he is a writer. He decides to do a follow-up to The Telltale. He will visit the lady in jail and explain to her the anguish that she has done nothing wrong. She will write a book detailing her experience and maintaining her innocence. Somebody, maybe a retired policeman, will get hold of her book and follow up on her story. This policeman will find evidence that she was telling the truth and that the likelihood is that the bad man did indeed murder his wife, which is what he had admitted to her and why she went with her story to the police. The man will get arrested again and brought to trial. It will be a full-blown trial with a jury. He will be able to select twelve very different people with different backgrounds and prejudices of their own. The man will need a defence. He did not murder her, she committed suicide. That can be easily proved with the suicide note, which she allegedly left, but he is unable to produce such a note. This will be a real courtroom drama. He is not sure how it will end, but for the time being, he will give it a working title, 'My Back Pages.' He gets writing, which seems to impress Sue.

The next Saturday, they are in their usual pub chatting away. Sue says, 'I am enjoying my first Summer with you, and our two visits to the beach have been terrific and it looks like we will all be going again tomorrow as the weather is still so nice. To make it a perfect Summer, I think we should try to get away to the Mediterranean, where the weather is always perfect and the sea is warm. I have been fiddling around online and discovered that Ryanair have twice weekly flights from Newquay to Alicante and Malaga. I am sure that Tim would not mind you taking a week off, and we could jet off together to warmer climes. I am sure it would be easy to find a cheap hotel somewhere near a nice beach. What do you say? 'What can I say. The obvious thing is that not possible as I do not have a passport. How do I explain that? Well my old passport expired, and I did not bother to renew it as I was not intending to go abroad. Which is what he says. She frowns at him and almost glares. 'Well that's easy then. When did your passport run out? I am sure that you can submit it and get it renewed, no problem.' He has to reply.

'It is not as easy as you say. I was a bit of a jerk and threw the old one away. I do not remember the expiry date, and I certainly do not have the number, so I would have nothing to go on.'

She is not easily satisfied. 'Well, to make it easy, just apply for a new one.' He can see that she is not going to let this go. The only thing that he can do is waffle about the procedures, the need for a birth certificate, etc, which he does not have. He mumbles about the procedures and his lack of a birth certificate. It looks like they may be about to have their first row. They leave the pub and walk home. The silence between them is overpowering. She goes off to bed in a huff. He thinks I have a real problem here. Not having a passport was always going to be my downfall. The last thing I want to do is lose her, but with this problem, it could be so. I have got to think on my feet.

But the next morning, it is all very different. She wakes him up with a glass of freshly squeezed OJ, which is their Sunday treat and says, 'I am so so sorry. I cannot believe that we had our fast confrontation (not sure he would call it that) over something so stupid. I can well understand that you do not have a passport (actually, she doesn't understand at all, as he has had to lie again) and who needs to go to the Med when the weather is so good here. Please forgive me, and let's go and have a great day at the beach. He tells her that she is forgiven, but feels a bit two-faced, as at the end of the day, it is all his fault.

They have a good day at the beach. The water is a little warmer, and he swims out with her some distance, which seems to please her. They have the normal roast with her parents and go home and make love. As he falls asleep, he thinks all is well then. But we know that cannot be. At the end of the day, he is living a lie, and we feel sure this is going to come back to haunt him. It simply is not possible to live a double life. It may be something simple like her wanting to go abroad, and as we know, it will be impossible for him to get a passport, as he is living his life as a made-up person.

The next month is pretty much the same routine. They miss one Sunday as it is cold and rainy, but they do go three times. Sue seems very happy with life, and she never mentions their confrontation, and being sensible, he just ignores it. He feels that every day he is loving her a little more, and her feelings seem to be the same. They smile and laugh a lot together. It all seems so much better than the relationship he used to have with Karen. He wonders sometimes if he had not had to run away, whether he would have stuck with her. He reckons he probably would have because he had no idea what he was missing. But now he has run away and found a new life, which he finds completely satisfying. However, at the back of his mind, there is always this nagging feeling. I am living a lie, and one day it is almost inevitable that I will be found out. He tries not to imagine what would happen if she found out. For the time being, he will just play the writer and the loving live-in housemate.

He finishes My Back Pages and again goes through the boring process of submitting it to publishers. He is still waiting for replies, but after the first two books, he is not too hopeful. In order to maintain the pretence of being a writer, he will have to start another one. Sue has liked all his books and is very encouraging. He asks her if she has any ideas on how to get a publisher. She spends a lot of time researching the internet and gives him the names of some smaller publishing houses that she has identified. He will take more copies and send them off, and see what happens.

It would be nice to get published and maybe make a bit of money. From a money point of view, it all seems to be going along okay. He is making £240 per week from gardening with Tim. This is about £960 or so per month. He has to give Sue £250 for the rent, which leaves him with about £700 per month. Their dinners out normally cost about £30 each. As they are doing it twice a week, that costs about £250 for the month. They share all the bills, and water and electricity are about £80 per month. They have a kitty for food and supplies, and he normally puts in £200 per month. By his calculation, he is spending about £200 per month less than his earnings, so he has not had to take any money out of his cash reserves - all to the good and it is now well over £4,000. It has certainly helped having the gardening job and moving in with Sue. She does not like to talk about money. He has no idea whatsoever how much she is making from her translation work, and he doesn't like to ask. He reckons she is probably making more than he. The reason we are talking about money is that our story is about to take a sudden turn or a twist.

They get through August and are now into September. Their last visit to Trevone was on the August bank holiday and with the weather, it now looks like it will be over for this year. He makes a strange discovery. She likes watching football. On Saturday nights, they always watch Match of the Day, and on Sundays after the roast with her parents, they watch Match of the Day 2. Karen had no interest in football and he thinks it is very nice to share the football with Sue. Another plus point for her. On Sundays, they have got into the routine of buying the Sunday Times and spending the morning lounging around reading. After a quick lunch, if the weather is okay, they walk along the Camel trail towards Padstow or the other way towards Bodmin. One week they hire bikes. He finds it exhilarating, but Sue is not a natural rider and does not get on with it, so they revert to walking.

On their return one Sunday, he makes her coffee. Neither of them are partial to tea. She says,

'I have been thinking about our life. We have been living together for over three months now, and for me, every day has been a joy. It looks like we have become an item, which makes me very happy. There is one thing that is bothering me, and that is that our place is a little small. When I go to my parents I feel envious of the space. I do not think we need all that space, but a proper flat with a bedroom and a living area, and a proper place to eat would be a lot better than our cramped surroundings here. As you know, I love the internet and I have been searching for local flats available for rent. The best one I found is just round the corner. One bedroom, a living room and a terrace with a view of the Camel. Costs £1,200 per month. Perfect, but with our current jobs, I do not think we would be able to afford it. I could certainly do more translating work, but that would not bring in that much more money. Which brings me to you. You are a qualified accountant, and I feel sure that you could get a job earning £30,000 per year or more. You would probably need to get your hair cut and shave off your beard and buy a couple of suits and some smart shirts, and get at least one tie. I have yet to see you in a tie, but I am sure you would look very sexy. I feel sorry that it would probably mean that you would have to give up your writing, which I know you adore, but it is not bringing in any income, and I have to tell you that I think your books are brilliant. What do you think?'

This is the twist that he had not been expecting. He loves being in the bedsit and it has become a real love nest, and it is nice always being so close together. He is not sure that a bigger place would provide the same atmosphere, and they could lose that loving feeling. Then there is the problem of getting a job. He can deal with the suits, shirts and tie, but he most certainly does not want to go back to looking like Colin. With his disguise, he has survived a long time in his present look and going back to the Colin look would be a risk. Then there is the job. He has no identity, no NHI number and no references. He cannot prove he is a Chartered Accountant, and it seems highly unlikely that anybody would employ him. The worst thing about all this is that he can see it developing into their second row and, more importantly, an opportunity for her to delve into his lies. He really is on a sticky wicket here, but he is going to have to give her a reply.

'My darling, I had not expected that. I am more than happy here in our love nest, which in all respects seems to me to be ideal. I never imagined that you did not like it here and were hankering for something bigger. I am afraid that I fear that a new place would mean we would lose everything that we have built up here as an Accountant. I have already told you that it was not for me. With what I am doing now, I have the best of both worlds. I spend three days per week outside, which I love, and the other three days writing, which I also love. It would be a real wrench to give up the two things which I love, to be an accountant in an office, which I certainly would not love, just to get a bedroom and a living room and somewhere to eat.'

Well, that really did sound pretty good, and the reference to a love nest was in itself brilliant. I wonder how she is going to react.

'I hear everything you say. I do love our love nest, and I have never been happier in my life. You are everything to me, and I do not think that I will ever be able to love another man. (This is rather good, she has declared her love for me, I'd better tell her I love her too in my next reply) But I think we need to think about the future. I truly feel that our relationship is going somewhere, but it is hard to imagine growing old together in this bedsit. I do not think it would suit us in our seventies, eighties or nineties, and I think we need to plan for the future together. I take your point about not wanting to be an accountant and your love for the open air and writing. For the time being, I will be happy to carry on as we are, but we have to move forward. When we have dinner tonight, I am going to ask my father's advice on how we can move forward.'

Well, that was not too bad. It could have been a lot worse, but what is she going to say to her father? As they are getting ready to go to her parents, she asks John for copies of his books, which she can give to her father. He has no spare copies to hand, but says he will get a copy done tomorrow.

Off to her parents. As always, they start with a G&T. Sue says to her father.

'Daddy, we need some advice. (He looks a little concerned, and John is concerned that she is now going to tell him that they are living together.) You may not be aware that I am desperately in love with John and he is at least very fond of me. For the last few months, we have been living together in my bedsit. (He was obviously not aware and looked a little shocked) We (I thought this was her, not we) are trying to plan our future together, and the first stage would be to move out of the bedsit and into an apartment. I have found a great place but it is £1,200 per month compared to the £500 we are currently paying. I am doing well with my translating, but John is spending three days a week writing which is his mission in life, but not remunerative at the present time and not earning a great deal for his three days of work. John will give you copies tomorrow of the last three books he has written whilst he has been here. The bottom line is that we cannot afford to move. What we need from you is your advice as to how we can increase our income and move on.'

Her father is frowning a little. Is he going to make a comment about them living together?

'I feel privileged that in your hour of need, you come to me for advice. I will have to think very carefully about ways that you can increase your income. I am sure your mother, as well, is so glad that you are so taken with John. He is an excellent character, and we, too, are very fond of him. I look forward to reading his books.'

That didn't say much.

Over the roast dinner, the chat is normal, and no further mention is made of Sue's plea for advice.

They leave in time to catch Match of the Day 2.

The next day, John gets copies of his book and delivers them to her parents' house. Her father is at work, so he has to give them to her mother, who invites him in for a cup of coffee. He doesn't really want to, but agrees. In the end, it is all quite pleasant and her mother makes no mention of them living together. He can tell she wants to ask all about it, but she shows restraint.

Nothing much happens in the next week. John and Sue are still the best of friends and she shows no sign of any grudge from his refusal to be an accountant.

Time for the Sunday roast again.

As usual, they start with G&T. Her father says

'I have had an interesting week. I managed to read all three of John's books and finished My Back Pages yesterday afternoon. I must say that I was really impressed and your books are a lot better than some of the airport fiction that is thrown at us these days. I have also been thinking about your income problem. I have found it very hard, if not impossible, to find a way for John to substantially increase his income from his three work days. But there is always a solution. You, Sue, are our very dear and only child. We have been quite lucky in life and own our own house without a mortgage and have a good deal of savings. One day, this will all be yours when your mother and I have left this world. Well, it won't be all yours as there will be Inheritance Tax to pay. What your mother and I would like to do is to give you a little of your inheritance early and propose to give you £600 per month for half the rent on the apartment. That will mean that your monthly outlay will only go up by £100, which I hope you can afford. There is one caveat. On alternate Sundays, you have to ask us round for the roast and we will need a G&T before we sit down.'

Sue and John both look at him in astonishment. Sue says,

'I cannot believe what I am hearing. You are being so generous, and you are going to be our saviour. I do not know how to thank you. All I can do is thank you very, very much. It will be a pleasure to cook for you on Sundays every other week. Thanks again.'

The rest of the evening is spent in good humour on all sides. As they are walking home, Sue says

'I cannot believe our luck. First thing tomorrow, we will call the agent and see if we can get a viewing. 'For John, this is all moving a bit fast. He genuinely likes living with her in the bedsit, and his excuses were real. He is not sure whether he wants to be beholden to her father, as it will give him a degree of control over their affairs. At the moment, they have been able to be their own people, but this gives another dimension to life. Nevertheless, he will have to go along with it. Maybe she will not like the flat and finds she prefers their love nest - not likely, he thinks. As is customary, they watch Match of the Day 2 and have great sex. Sue seems very happy.

The next day, they had hardly finished breakfast, and she was on the phone with the agent. They get a viewing at midday. They arrive and have to walk up three flights of stairs; perhaps this will put her off. He has to admit the flat is very nice and he particularly likes the terrace. It comes furnished and all is good quality. They will not have to buy anything. Sue is all wow and super. She says to the agent Can he give them a couple of moments alone. He goes back out onto the terrace. Sue says this is brilliant - we have to have it, do you agree? What can he say? They rejoin the agent on the terrace and tell him that they would like to take it and move in as soon as possible. He says, 'Come back to the office then.'

It is a short stroll to his office. His first question is about joint tenancy. Yes. He asks about their current living arrangements. He then says they will be given a lease for one year at the fixed rent. After one year, the lease will be renewable for a further period at a rent reflecting the then market. Do they agree? Yes. Next, he will need to verify their identities. Passports or driving licences should be sufficient. He will also need details of their bank accounts from which the rent will be paid. This will be in the form of a monthly direct debit. In addition to the rent, they will need to provide a security deposit of one month's rent to cover any damage to the property. The landlord will pay the building insurance, but they will need to arrange cover for their personal possessions. Lastly, he will need a reference from their existing landlord to cover timely rent payment and maintenance of the property. All being well, they should be able to do this in a couple of days, and they can be in by the weekend. Any questions. John obviously has a lot of questions. He cannot prove his identity, and he has no bank account. Should he raise this now? He thinks better not. It looks like Sue will have to be the sole tenant.

This does cause problems. When they go back to the agent and explain John's lack of a passport or driving licence and their wish for Sue to be the sole tenant, he is not a happy man. They do manage to get a decent reference from their existing landlord. It drags on, and they are still in the bedsit the next weekend. John had been expecting

Sue to make a fuss about his lack of a driving licence. She does not, and he wonders why - does she have some doubts about his identity? Everybody else did. She is an intelligent girl and must be holding her comments back for some reason. To make the agent happy, Sue's father signs a document as guarantor, and Sue becomes the sole tenant. A move-in date is agreed for Wednesday. They give notice on the bedsit and the landlord refunds Sues deposit without any hassle. On Wednesday, Sue goes to the agent and gets the key.

John's belongings are easy to move, but Sue has a lot more stuff. They go to see her mother and borrow two suitcases. It is not so far to the new place, and they struggle to get it all there, and the stairs are a drag, but at last they open the door to their new flat. Sue makes John carry her over the threshold. She is over the moon and cannot stop gleefully laughing. 'We have done it, and here we are. This will be our new love nest.' They have dinner at home and share a bottle of champagne to celebrate. John looks at his new surroundings. It all looks pretty smart. It is almost on a par with his old place in the Barbican. It has been a difficult journey getting here, but he feels that at long last he is now on the right road. Life can only get better from now on. He was so right to run away, even though there was a lot of angst and worry. It would have been totally wrong for an innocent man to go to prison.

The next morning, he has to go back to his old place to catch up with Tim. He tells him about the move, but he is not at all interested. He does show a little more interest when he drops him off at his new place at the end of the day, 'going up in the world.' Well, yes, he is, but he is a long way from where he used to be, but he cannot say that.

Chapter 20

It is three months or so leading up to Christmas. John and Sue get into a nice routine in their new flat. It is not quite the same as the love nest but they are still making love at every opportunity. Sue, in particular, seems very happy in their new place. John is happy that she is happy. As requested, they provide the Sunday roast on alternate weekends, but Sue is different; she always cooks Italian which her parents seem to enjoy. They have received an invitation for Christmas lunch at her parents. John would have liked to spend it alone with her, but finds he has to agree. She then starts worrying about presents that seem endless. They go to a small bookstore and find an expensive first edition of Dr No by Ian Fleming for her father, and in an antique shop, an art deco brooch for her mother. At long last, she is pleased. He wonders what she will buy for him and then he has to buy for her. She will need more than one present. He goes back to the antique shop and purchases an Art Deco necklace, which he thinks she will like. He should buy her clothes, and he does not want to buy underwear or nightclothes; something to go on top will be fine. He spends the afternoon wandering the local streets and finds an upmarket ladies' boutique where he buys her a cashmere sweater. That will do.

Christmas comes all too quickly. They get up on Christmas morning and squeeze oranges and have croissants and proper coffee. Sue says it reminds her of Paris. She would so like to revisit one day. It is now the present time and she hands him one neatly wrapped parcel. He hands her two parcels and she says, 'What a lucky girl!' He opens his first, and it is an iPad. He has always wanted one of these and gives her a big kiss. She says the days of the typewriter are now over as you can write your books on the iPad. She is right, it will be brilliant. She opens her presents and seems very pleased, and gives a big return kiss. They dress smartly and go to her parents.

Her father has opened a bottle of champagne to celebrate the day. They then exchange presents. Her father is very taken with his book and cannot believe it is a first edition. Her mother seems to love her brooch - how clever. She is given her presents, which she unwraps. He cannot remember what they were, but at the back of his mind, boring best describes them. He is given a very smart Ralph Lauren shirt and a Ralph Lauren sweater. Looks like they are trying to smarten him up - good luck. The Turkey lunch and Xmas pudding are all brilliant. They wash it down with two aged bottles of Margaux. Probably the best one ever, and he tells her mother, and she gives him a gorgeous smile. He seems well in with this family. They really like him almost as a son. He wonders what their reaction would be if they knew his true story. After lunch, Sue helps her mother clear away and John has a glass of port with her father.

They have a game of Scrabble, which her father wins. Nobody wants to watch The King's Speech. Does anybody want anything else to eat - no, thanks. They then watch Love Actually, which he has never seen. It appears that this family watch it every Christmas Day. He rather enjoys it, particularly when Colin Firth's manuscript blows into the lake. He comments that this has never happened to him, and they all laugh. Her mother goes off to make turkey sandwiches, and they happily eat them with mince pies. It is getting late, so they head home. John thinks that was certainly a lot better than last Christmas. I have come a long way in a year. Not sure if I am blessed, but life seems pretty good.

Life is not so good for the other characters in our story.

Penny could just not find a job, but her money is running out, so she has to do something. The last thing she wants to do is go backwards but this is precisely what she does. She sees an advertisement for an auditor at the firm where she did her articles and applies. She is interviewed by a partner who is well known to her. He looks at her CV and fails to understand why she is applying for her old job when she has made so much progress. She gives an incoherent reply about the problems of commerce and her longing to return to her roots. He does not seem to understand her one iota, but nevertheless, she is offered a junior position at less than half her previous salary and accepts. She will not be able to afford many dinners out and not many trips to the shops, but at least she will be able to pay the mortgage and eat. Also, she is in a good position to make it with a young, upcoming accountant. She has now been in this job for three months. To say the work is dull would be overstating it. She has to spend her whole time watching the pennies. She has been to two social drinks with others in the firm. No budding young accountants for her, and she has to admit she finds conversation difficult. Everybody is bustling with energy and enthusiasm, but she has none. She wonders how she can improve her life. Her plan to get rid of Colin worked like a dream, and she should have got his job and been on the way to a directorship, but that bitch, Deborah, got in the way and got rid of her. Did she suspect the truth of her scheme - who knows? But she has to think about the future now. Her mortgage is crippling. She is on a low fixed rate but only for another six months. She is not sure if in the current market she will be able to match it. She does have a spare bedroom, which she could let out for an enormous sum, but there again, she is not sure if she wants to share. She could sell her pad and find a cheaper and smaller one, or even rent. Since she bought prices have gone up and she should show a tidy profit, but she likes her pad - why should she be forced to downsize? The answer is simple, because what you did was dreadful, and you deserve everything you get.

On Christmas Eve, she finds herself on the train headed to Godalming. She is spending Christmas with her parents and her brother and his wife, whom she cannot stand, and their three children. Her father picks her up at the station and gives her a peck on the cheek - there has never been much love between father and daughter, and to be honest, it is the same with her mother. Her brother is the golden boy and has given them three grandkids. They arrive home, and all she gets is a peck on the cheek from her mother. All she can hear is the noise of the kids. Is it going to be like this for three nights?

They sit down for supper with the kids. She detests having to eat with kids. Her brother's wife is a solicitor and has just been made a partner in her firm. She rabbits on forever about her business life, and Penny is hardly listening. She asks her what she's doing now that she lost her job - well, that was cutting. Penny says she has returned to the profession - must be a come-down after your high-flying job. Not at all. How long is she going to have to put up with this? After Christmas, her brother and his family are all going to Antigua to enjoy some winter sun, and there is a lot of talk about that. Is Penny going away? No. The kids are taken to bed. Some peace at last. Penny does not want to spend time with them and retires early.

On Christmas morning, very early, all she can hear is children's shrieks. She stays in bed as long as she dares. Goes to the bathroom, which is empty and has a long bath. Twice, there is a knocking at the door but she ignores it. She returns to her room and gets dressed and goes down. A lot of snide comments about the late hour. Breakfast is over, but she manages to get herself a glass of OJ. She is given about five presents, which she opens absent-mindedly, but she cannot for the life of her remember what she got. She has forgotten to bring her presents down and it is very embarrassing as she has bought nothing for her brother, his wife or the kids, as she had not been told beforehand that they were to be part of the party. She goes to get her parents' presents. They do not open them, and one of the kids demands to know where is hers. She explains the circumstances not too clearly. The whole morning, the kids are so noisy, and it is driving her head in. She thinks I could have been a mother and had to put up with this. Abortion was certainly the right thing. She then has to sit down with them all and eat turkey with all the trimmings and Christmas pudding. The kids just go on and on with their noise. She hates it all. It is a nice day, and her father proposes a walk. It will be good to get out, and she goes to fetch her coat. The walk is the best thing so far about this awful Christmas. They return and watch Love Actually. She has always loved this movie, but it is again spoiled by the kids who will just not keep quiet. It is still early and her mother prepares supper of cold turkey, baked potatoes and mince pies. The kids are put to bed at what to her seems far too late. Her father then proposes a game of bridge. She does not play, so she is left out. They are playing in the dining room, so she retires to the TV and watches something boring. All she wants to do is go to bed, but thinks it would be rude; however, they are being rude by excluding her. She goes to say her goodnights and gets more snide comments. Boxing Day is even worse as the weather is bad and there is no walk, and the kids continue to make life hell. She will catch an early train back tomorrow and get out of this terrible place. So, not a great Christmas for Penny, but we think she probably deserved it.

It is not much better for Karen. Her mother is off on a Christmas Cruise, so she reluctantly agrees to spend it again with Colin's parents. It all seemed the same as the previous year. Jonathan is now at school, but she has not been able to find a job. She must get one in the New Year as the savings are dwindling. And another thing, she needs a man in her life. Life without Colin has not been fun. They get through most of Christmas without a mention of Colin. That is, until Boxing Day evening, when his father says, 'Another year had passed and here we are again without Colin. We managed to find out that he had gone to Cornwall and informed the police. They seem to have been totally ineffective in finding him. This could be because they have made little effort to find him. He is not accused of murder (although, as we know, he was the prime suspect at one time and they made considerable efforts to find him), and it is probably not a priority. He has presumably hidden himself well. None of us has heard a word from him for over a year. I wonder sometimes if something has happened to him. He was a caring chap and we might have expected something to say he is all right but we have nothing.' Karen had not really wanted to talk about Colin and his father; raising it in this way to her mind is not good manners. She does not want to get into a lengthy discussion about Colin, and she just says, 'Thank you for remembering Colin.

His absence at Christmas is a great loss to us all. I miss him every day and it is not fair for Jonathan not to have a father.' She thinks that will wrap it up, but it does not. They have a long conversation about guilty or not guilty and a lot more besides. She really does not need this.

To be honest, she is glad she is going home tomorrow. What will the conversation be next Christmas?

It is now rapidly approaching the New Year. John and Sue decide to have an evening at home with home-cooked food and champagne. Sue goes to a fishmonger's and sources langoustine and a lobster. They start with the champagne. You could not imagine a happier couple; love is in the air on both sides. The langoustine starter is very good, and then Sue produces Lobster Thermidor, which they eat with French Fries. After dinner, they put on some music (her collection of CDs because as we know, John has none) and opened a bottle of wine. It is all very pleasant and just before midnight they put on the TV and watch Jools Holland see in the New Year. Sue is looking reflective, and she says, 'I bless the day we found each other. You are the first man I have truly loved and I think the love is mutual. We are a few minutes into the New Year, and I think it is time to reflect on how we are to move forward. The thing that I most desire is for you to ask me to marry you. I have developed a longing to be your wife. When we are married, we can have kids. I would like three, as I think I was deprived of being an only child. What do you say?'

John had not been expecting this. She wants me to propose to her. I could propose to her, but if we did get married, I would probably be a bigamist unless Karen had divorced me. I am already on the run, so another crime like bigamy would hardly matter. And she wants to have kids with me. I already have a son, and to be honest, he was a pain. I like being alone with Sue, and I am not sure I want to spoil it by having kids. Kids would also mean the need for a bigger place, which we can ill afford. So much to think about, but I am going to have to say something.

'I cannot believe that you want to marry me. I am not sure I have anything to offer you apart from my love. My main aim in life is my writing. I have completed three novels but have failed to be published. My earnings from gardening are very little. In order to live in this flat, we are having to rely on the generosity of your father. I would love to have kids with you but we would need a bigger place, and we would never be able to afford it.' He thinks that was a good reply, but how will she respond?

'You are not going to ask me to marry you then. Do not be afraid that I will say no because I have already said that is what I want you to do. My parents are both very fond of you, and I am sure that they would be delighted if we got married. They will be even more delighted to be grandparents, and I feel sure that my generous father would help us with somewhere to live.' She seems to have got it all worked out. But she needs a response. There are two things I could do. Propose to her, it's not like we are going to be married tomorrow. Best not beat about the bush.

He gets down from the settee and kneels in front of her, 'Sue, my dearest, will you give me the honour of marrying me?' All she can do is shriek, but he thinks she has said yes. She calms down and puts on her practical hat. She wants to get married as soon as possible; no point waiting. Church would have been nice, but they are not religious, so the Registry Office will be fine. Honeymoon should be in Paris as presently off season in the holiday resorts, and lastly, she will come off the pill so they can start family planning. Well, she surely has thought it all through. In a strange way, he feels as if he has been trapped. They go to bed and make love, and she says, 'Next time, you'll be able to give me a baby.' While he is not an expert, but guesses it may take a little longer.

They get up late on 1 January. After breakfast, she starts playing with her iPad. In order to get married, they will need a marriage licence. For that, you need a passport - problem. John agrees that he will apply for a passport, although, as we all know, that is not going to happen. There is some discussion about the timing of his passport application, and they agree should not take too long at this time of year. John reckons he has now got a month at best to pretend he is going through the process. What will happen then? Well, to put it bluntly, it will all be over, and he is going to lose her. This makes him very sad. He does not want to lose her. Why was he so stupid as to propose marriage? What's done is done, and he is going to have to move carefully forward. He may be able to explain his lack of a passport, but probably not. His best chance is to say early on that he has no birth certificate but in the back of his mind, he knows there is a process for claiming that document. He cannot do that because, technically, he does not exist.

Chapter 21

Over the next three days, he is working with Tim. Sue has got him the form for the passport application. He tells her that he does not have a birth certificate. The next day, she presents him with the process for obtaining a birth certificate. She is not giving up. He tells her he will have to do it on Monday. She is not very impressed by his delaying tactics.

On Sunday morning, he gets up and opens the curtains. There are three police cars and a white police van outside. What is going on? Have they found him and come to arrest him? There is quite a lot of coming and going but there is no knock on the door. He relaxes a little. Must be something else. He goes out to buy the Sunday Times and nods to a man. Back with the papers and they share reading. Football results do not matter as they watched Match of the Day last night. Liverpool is top of the league. Shortly before lunch, there is a knock on the door, which he answers. Two men are standing there. They introduce themselves as an Inspector and a Sergeant and show their warrant cards, which he doesn't really take in. May they come in? Naturally. Can I offer you tea or coffee? No thanks. Is he about to be arrested? It is not looking good.

The Inspector says, 'The reason we are here is that sometime after 6, last night, a woman in one of the ground floor flats lost her life, and we have reason to believe foul play. We are interviewing all the tenants of the block to see if they can give us any information. May I start by asking your names and dates of birth?' John and Sue both give their names and dates of birth. John has to make up his. 'Secondly, how long have you been tenants here?' They give this information and their previous address. 'Thirdly, what time did you get home last night and have you seen anybody unusual in or around the premises?' Sue reports that she got home from work at about 5.45 and John reports that he got home from work just after 6. They both have to explain their jobs. They went to the pub for dinner and drinks and returned in time for Match of the Day. Neither saw anybody in or around the premises. The Inspector tells them the victim was an elderly lady who had full-time care. Her carer left at 6 when she was very much alive and returned this morning just before 10 to find her dead. Neither had ever met the lady in question, probably because she didn't go out much. The policemen have been noting down all they have said. It seems to be the end of their enquiries, and they take their leave. Sue is very upset that somebody has apparently been murdered on their block. Could they be next? Don't be stupid.

They watch the early evening local news. The main story is the murder. They go to her parents for the Sunday roast. There is a lot of chat about the murder on their block. They recount the meeting with the inspector and his sergeant. They do not think they are suspects. For some reason, in all the excitement, they forget to mention that they are engaged.

They are not suspects, but the police are mystified. The forensic team has been there all day. The pathologist has declared that she died from a stab wound to the heart, and a frail old lady would have stood no chance. No sign of any defensive injuries. The pathologist puts the time of death between 6 and 8 the previous night. And there is no sign of any forced entry, which suggests the lady admitted her attacker. Was the attacker known to her? They will have to check her acquaintances to see if they can determine any. The inspector and the sergeant are mulling over the probabilities when the sergeant suddenly says, 'You know we interviewed that Match of the Day couple on the top floor, well the man reminded me of someone, but I cannot think of the context. Perhaps we should do a check on him to see if he has a criminal record. They check with his name and date of birth, but no record of any offence. This is bothering the sergeant because he feels sure he recognised him. And then it comes to him. The missing rapist who came to Cornwall. He has to dig through the files for ages, but eventually comes up with the identikit picture of Colin with long hair and a beard. The inspector agrees with the sergeant that there is a strong likeness. Should they go and arrest him? They think it over. His DNA is on file. They could revisit him and his girlfriend and take DNA samples and say they have found DNA in the lady's flat and are taking DNA from all the residents for comparison purposes. It is too late to do it tonight. An early morning call would look odd, and he probably goes to work, so they decide to return at 6.30 the next evening.

At 6.30, they are knocking on the door and John answers. The police show their ID again. They tell him about the DNA and the need to take DNA from all the residents to be able to eliminate them from their enquiries. John and Sue both provide samples and the police leave.

John is vexed by having to give a DNA sample, but there was no opportunity to avoid it. Had to be done. He supposes that they will just compare their DNA with the matter recovered from the crime scene, but maybe they will go further and do a more thorough check and identify him as the alleged rapist. He thinks over his options. His relationship with Sue is shortly going to come to an inevitable conclusion. The police having his DNA is a real downside. Is it time for TURN 4 and where would he go? He decides to stay put for a few days, as he will not be losing anything.

The two policemen return to the station. During the day, they had obtained Colin's DNA from Truro. The Inspector in Truro is very excited about their possible sighting and will come over to their station later. On their return to the station, they sent Colin's DNA and John's DNA on a motorbike to the Royal Cornwall Hospital in Truro, which is the nearest place for a DNA match in with a note expressing urgency.

When it is received at the hospital, it goes through the normal channels and after about three hours or 10pm, it arrives in the appropriate laboratory. There is one person on duty. He picks up the package and notes the urgent. Why is it always urgent with these people? Not much to do, so he might as well get on with it. He finds a match for the two samples. Police are obviously doing their job and phones Wadebridge police station with confirmation of the match. The inspector is still there as this has got to be big. It is now nearly midnight. A bit late to make a call here, thinks. The Inspector from Truro does not agree. We should do it now. Which is what they do. At 12.3O they are knocking on John's door. John eventually opens the door, dressed in a dressing gown and apparently nothing underneath. He looks at the inspector and he says, I know not why 'What the hell.' The inspector says, 'Calm down, young man. You may remember that you gave us a DNA sample earlier this evening. I am here to tell you that your sample has been matched with one Colin Bucket, who is an alleged rapist who skipped bail over a year ago. I have to inform you that you are now under arrest. (he then gives the speech, anything you may say may be given in evidence, etc). You are to be taken to the police station forthwith.' John cannot believe this is happening. It is less than 6 hours since he gave his DNA and here we are. He should have done TURN 4; it was stupid of him not to have gone on the run after he had given his DNA. He decides to say nothing.

Sue has heard all of this and she too cannot believe it. John is on the run from bail because of an alleged rape. That is not her, John. But wait a minute. He has never had many possessions, which fits in with a man on the run. He has no passport, which is not normal. She starts to believe he truly is a runaway. How did she fall for such a thing, and she thought they were going to be married and have kids and live happily ever after?

John is allowed to dress, but only under the watchful eye of the sergeant. He is not handcuffed but is led to a waiting unmarked police car, which takes the short drive to the police station. They have to sign him in with the desk sergeant. He is identified as Colin Bucket, taken to a drab interview room with just a table and four chairs and a recording device. They all sit down. A man who has not seen before identifies himself as an Inspector from Truro and adds that he has been trailing him for over a year and now we have you. You are entitled to legal advice. No thanks.

First question 'Is your real name Colin Bucket?' No Comment. The questions go on for over two hours, and his only response is No Comment. The police seem unconcerned with his attitude. It is now nearly three in the morning. He wonders if he could claim mistaken identity but that seems futile. At the end of all this, the Wadebridge Inspector says you will now be transferred to a holding cell. In the morning, you will appear before magistrates here. The Crown will set out the case against you and ask for you to be held in custody pending your trial. I think it is fair to say that is what will occur. Following that hearing, you will be transferred to London and imprisoned on remand until your trial. John is not at all pleased to hear all this. No point in asking for legal assistance - he is just going to have to accept a period in prison and then a trial. He cannot be found guilty as he is totally innocent.

He does go to the Magistrates' Court, where indeed he is remanded in custody. He spends one more night in the holding cell. He is allowed a bag with some fresh clothes, a toothbrush and toothpaste, which he assumes Sue packed. The next day, he is driven with the sergeant to Bodmin station. In the back of the car, he is handcuffed to the sergeant and they catch the train to London, which takes about four hours. When he wants to have a pee, the sergeant joins him handcuffed in the cubicle. He wonders what would have happened if his need was greater. They arrive in London and are met by two police officers. The sergeant uncuffs him but transfers the cuffs to another. They get in an unmarked white van and drive for a while. He sees the outline of what certainly looks like a prison, and here they are.

He has no idea of how long he is going to be imprisoned here, and will probably be until the trial, whenever that may be. He feels unsure as to how he is going to survive. All we can say here is that he hates every moment of his time in prison. His hate for Penny increases daily.

On Tuesday, Sue goes to see her mother and tells her the whole story of what has happened. Her mother cannot believe it. John was such a good-standing young man. There must be some mistake. Sue admits to her mother that she has thought it all through and it seems to her there is no mistake. She was taken in by a man on the run. She does not tell her mother that they were engaged; better in the circumstances to keep that a secret. She goes through his possessions very carefully. There is nothing there to provide any identity. No bank cards, cheque books or driving licence. She had not been expecting a passport, and there was none. And she finds over £4,000 in cash - where did that come from?

Karen is informed of Colin's arrest. Well, at least he is alive, but she finds that she now feels nothing for him. She is informed of the procedure for visiting. Why should she visit him? She has nothing to say. In fact, Karen never visits Colin whilst he is on remand. His father visits him once. Colin protests his innocence and says he was set up. His father agrees wholeheartedly with him, but at the back of his mind, he reckons guilty as charged. Innocent people do not run away.

Penny is also informed of his arrest. A new Court date will be set and she will need to be ready. To her, this is not pleasing. She set him up to get his job. She didn't get his job and then lost hers and now she is in lowly employ. A part of her wishes she had never done it because, if anything, it was a backwards step. And now she is going to have to go to Court and tell outright lies, which she really does not want to do. If he is found guilty, he is going to prison for a long time, particularly as he ran away for over a year. She could change her story, but that is impossible. She will be charged with perjury and no doubt end up in prison herself. She is just going to have to do it. Will she just give her evidence, and that will be that, or will she be subject to cross-examination? She is not looking forward to that, as any weaknesses in her story could be exposed. She assumes there will be a jury. She will need to play to their sympathies.

Colin is not surprised that Karen has not visited him. Did she divorce me? He thinks not as his father would have mentioned it. I could have been a bigamist. He did not enjoy his father's visit. Pleading his innocence did not seem to go down that well, and he is going to have to convince a jury of his innocence. He manages to get in touch with Chuck and will have a meeting in a couple of days.

Chuck arrives as buoyant as ever. He starts off by telling Colin that it was a bad move to run away and an even worse move to get caught. If he is found guilty, his sentence will be increased. Colin tells him a bit about his run away and how he was caught by DNA because of the murder. Chuck says the Crown have applied for a new trial, but no date has been set. It could be six months or more. Colin says, 'Does that mean he will stay imprisoned for all that time. Yes. Chuck goes on to say that we will need a first-class barrister and has a couple of minds whom he has worked before. There are two things which will be key in the trial. The jury - his barristers will train him to play to the jury to get the best possible outcome. Penny - she will give her evidence and expect everybody to believe her. If what you say is true, it is all a complete fabrication. The barrister will need to attack her in every way possible and reduce her credibility to zero. I may have just the man for that. Lastly, we get to costs. 'This is not going to be cheap. I have had discussions with my firm and we propose a fee of £10,000 plus VAT or £12,000, which is payable immediately. The barrister's fee will be around £30,000 plus VAT or £36,000. We are responsible for this fee and would need you to pay upfront when you instruct us. I am asking you for a total payment of £48,000 now.'

Colin cannot believe what he is hearing. The cost of his defence seems enormous, and it is required to be paid now. He had around £4,000 in Wadebridge, which he assumes Sue now has, and he is pretty sure she is not going to send it to him as she will feel hard done by. That leaves his wife and his father. Karen has not even been here to see him. She was left a reasonable amount of money when he ran away but will she give him £48,000? In reality, it is his money, so she jolly well should, but women are strange creatures and you can never tell. His father probably has the money but his suspicion is guilt. He could go to Court with no legal representation, but that could be fatal. He could try to find a cheaper alternative but he would still need the money from Karen or his father. He is stuck between a rock and a hard place. He tells Chuck that at the present time, he has no money as he left all his wealth with his wife. He will try to see if he can get her to pay up. He explains the absence of Karen's visits and he cannot tell how she will react to a demand for legal fees. Does Chuck's firm do pro bono to which he gets a resounding - No.

We seem to be getting into a very difficult situation here. Colin has no way of communicating with Karen. He could send a letter to their old address and hope it gets forwarded somehow, or perhaps better to phone his father and get Karen's contact details.

He phones his father (this is before his visit and he is a little more helpful) and finds Karen has moved to another flat in the Barbican, and gets the address and a phone number.

Should he write or call? He decides to write:

'Dear Karen, I am writing this to you from prison, where I am being held on remand until the trial. We are still awaiting a date for the hearing.

You and Jonathan have always been the love of my life and I think you deserve some explanations.

It is true that I had sex with Penny. This is the one and only time that I have been unfaithful to you, and I truly regret it. The sex was consensual after a business dinner when we were celebrating a successful IPO. I left her flat in the early hours. She then decided to set me up by damaging her wrists and saying I had tied her to the bed and raped her. She was ambitious and wanted my job. You could say I was a fool to have fallen for such a trick and you would be right. As you know, I was arrested and bailed to appear in Court. My legal advice was that I was on very thin ice. I assure you that I was totally innocent and I was further advised that I would be looking at a very long prison sentence for aggravated rape.

I am sorry that you had to put up with Southwold, but I had no passport to go overseas.

I thought through all my options. I did not want to go to jail as an innocent man, so I decided to run away. For over a year, I kept my profile low, and I do not think there was ever any risk of my arrest. I expect the police had photographs of me. A while ago, I was using the name John and sharing a flat in Wadebridge, Cornwall, which is a pretty town on the Camel river and a murder was committed in one of the flats. The police had DNA from the crime scene and came to take DNA from all the residents, in six hours, which to this day I do not know why so fast the police came to my flat and arrested me as Colin Bucket. I was taken to the Magistrates where I was remanded in custody. I was taken handcuffed on the train to London and I have been in prison ever since. I am innocent, and it feels so wrong to be in prison.

Anyway, the point of this letter. In the hopefully near future, although the date is yet to be set, I will be back in the Old Bailey. As you can imagine, I am going to require legal assistance. I have had a conference with a solicitor and he is demanding £48,000, including VAT, to arrange my representation, which includes the barrister's fee. I have no money in the world, and I am going to need your assistance to pay this fee. When I departed, I left you with cash and investments of a considerably greater value, and I am now asking you to help me out in my hour of need.

I look forward to hearing from you.

Love as always to you and Jonathan

Colin'

He thinks the letter reads rather well and he will await her reply.

Karen received the letter and cannot believe the tone. He has run away and left me, and now he wants me to give him £48,000. The first thing she does is get in touch with Colin's father and tell him about the letter. He says he will need a copy, and she posts it to him. When he has had the chance to read the letter, he calls her. 'This is a very difficult situation. Colin is my son and your husband, and he is in a difficult situation without money. I have no idea how much money you have and really, I do not want to know but it seems certain to me that he will need legal advice and somebody is going to have to pay. I have been doing some research. He would probably be eligible for legal aid as he is without funds, although the Court may deem your funds as his when he would not be eligible. The disadvantage of legal aid is that you have no choice in who you get, and the probability is they will not fight very hard for you. Colin, in his situation, will need a hard fighter with guts. I have contacted a solicitor friend of mine who has quoted £12,000 plus VAT to cover his fees and a barrister, which is a lot less than Colin's demand. This would cover everything, including the trial. I do not think that you should be put in a position to pay his legal fees, and I therefore propose to pay these costs myself as he is my son and I would like to help. If you are in an agreement, I will write to him accordingly.' Karen cannot believe he is being so generous and it lets her off the hook, and she agrees. His father writes Colin a letter with his proposal.

Colin receives the letter. He had been expecting a reply from Karen, but it appears she has no wish to correspond with him. Looks like it is all over for her, too. He doesn't care that much. At least she did not just ignore his letter and pass it on to her father. Colin is not that sure about Chuck. In the early days, he was all get up and go with private detectives and all that, but at the end of the day he seemed to doubt the real story. Typical of his father, he has found a cheaper alternative but he has been gracious enough to offer to pay. A new solicitor would not have Chuck's baggage and would be able to approach it with fresh eyes. His father is probably right about legal aid. Not the best defence and Karen may have to pay in any case. He calls his father and thanks him for his generosity, and his father says he will get the ball rolling.

About two weeks later, Colin is told that a solicitor will be coming to see him tomorrow. He will have to meet the solicitor in his prison uniform, which will not make a great impression. He goes to the barbers and gets a haircut and his beard shaved so he is more presentable and no point now in trying to look different. He is taken into a room. A very pretty dark-haired girl in a black suit and white blouse is waiting for him. She introduces herself as Penelope Catchpole and she will be his solicitor. He is hoping against all hope that she does not ask him to call her Penny, as he couldn't stand it. Firstly, she asks him to explain why he ran away. He pleads his innocence, which is a good start, and says he had been advised that her case was very strong, even though it was all lies and he saw it as the only way out. He tells her the circumstances of his capture. She is looking reflective 'I too am going to advise you that her case appears very strong. We are going to have to prove to a jury in Court that her injuries were self-inflicted and she was aiming to set you up because she wanted your job. I have never in my experience come across such a case but the important person to prove your case will be the barrister. I have spoken with my partners and we have identified the ideal barrister for you, who has had a similar case and won. We intend to instruct him and at our next meeting, which will be next week, I will bring him along. We have checked with the Court and no date has yet been set for the trial. I am sure you find that frustrating, but the good thing is that it will give us time to get your defence in order. Just as an aside. About your capture. You say that the police visited you on the day of the murder. My suspicion is that you were recognised and they returned with the spurious DNA for all residents. You were probably their only DNA but they needed it to formally identify you. Not good practice but there is nothing we can do.' She takes her leave and he is sorry to see her go. In prison, it is only men and you have no idea who you might be dealing with. Her comments about his arrest are interesting but as she says nothing we can do.

About a week later, she returns with the barrister whose name is Mr Lingard. He is casually dressed without a tie, which strikes him as a little odd. But then he starts talking and it is a different ball park. 'I have defended a number of rape cases and I am sure Miss Stackpole will have told you that I have a good success ratio. The key is that in the majority of cases, the supposed victim is lying. Your case is a bit more difficult as the supposed victim has presented the police with injuries and your sperm. Your defence is consensual sex, and you most certainly did not tie her up and the injuries were self-inflicted. She was ambitious and after your job. Our job is to prove that she set you up. As part of your defence, we will need to find credible witnesses who can confirm the desire to set you up. I will go to your old company and try to find such a witness. The next thing we will do is attack her sex life, which I have done many times and will do again. Any questions?' Colin does not really have any questions. He is mightily impressed with Mr Lingard. He seems like a real fighter, which is exactly what he needs. Mr Lingard says he will get on with it, and they leave.

In the next five weeks, he hears nothing.

He is informed that he has another legal meeting tomorrow.

Miss Stackpole and Mr Lingard again. It is nice to see them again.

Penelope starts by telling him that the Court date has been set for the first week of September. That six months away means he will have been in this place for close on nine months. He wants to complain but doesn't. Mr Lingard then says, 'Some good news, I hope. I visited your old company and interviewed your assistant and secretary but they were not much help. I had sort of hoped that I would find Penny in your old position, but I did not. You were replaced by an outsider and then Penny was sacked for incompetence. I did manage to interview your replacement, who is called Deborah. What she told me was very interesting. Your Penny did not take kindly to her appointment and acted as if she was the boss, always trying to take over and run meetings. This made Deborah very suspicious of her and she feels sure you were set up and Penny held a major grudge against your successor. She has no proof but has agreed to appear on our side as a witness and put forward her suspicions.' Colin says that sounds like good news and Mr Lingard confirms so. Penny got the sack - serves her right, and hope she is suffering like me. Colin then brings to the attention of Mr Lingard the detective work of Chuck. He tells them that Penny was observed having an abortion. He tells them that Penny had told him she was on the pill and it must have been part of her plan for him to deposit his semen to provide DNA evidence of sexual intercourse. Mr Lingard nods and says, 'Very interesting.'

The next six months drag on and on. Colin has two meetings with his lawyers, but not much to report. At the end of August, they return. First of all, Mr Lingard tells Colin what he must wear for the Court. A smart suit, nice shirt and a different tie for every day and do not forget to have clean shoes. No prison uniform. After some discussion, Penelope says she will get it sorted. They try to determine the length of the trial. They agree probably between four and five days. Mr Lingard then spends a lot of time asking him questions and correcting his answers where necessary. This takes over two hours. At the end, he says, 'Good to go then.'

Colin now has a week before the Court. He spends a long time practising his replies. On the Friday before Court, Penelope comes along with his wardrobe. He has a smart blue suit which fits, five white shirts and five ties and a pair of black shoes.

Penny, meanwhile, has spent a lot of time with the prosecutor rehearsing her lines and responses to cross-examination. She tells the prosecutor that she cannot understand cross-examination, as what she has to say is completely clear and should be taken verbatim. He has to correct her thinking, but goes on to say that he is sure she will be fine, as she has nothing to worry about, as she is telling the truth. At the back of her mind, she knows this is not correct and feels nervous about cross-examination.

Karen and his parents have decided to attend the trial. Her mother has made some excuse and will not be coming. Karen thinks as ever, she will not be there to support me when I need it most.

Chapter 22

It is now the day of the trial. Colin is permitted to go to the barber early and get a haircut and shave. He puts on his new blue suit, shirt and selects one of his ties. He looks at himself in the mirror and is pleased with what he sees. He will be believable in front of the jury.

He is taken to an unmarked white van without handcuffs, and they take about a 20-minute drive to the Old Bailey.

He is shown into a room where Mr Lingard, who is wearing a wig, looks suitably ferocious to him, and Penelope is seated. Mr Lingard compliments him on his appearance. Good. He goes on to say that the first thing they will do is select a jury. He wants as few women as possible on the jury as they are more likely to sympathise with a woman, and by the same token, the prosecutor will desire all women. Let's see what happens. As an aside, Colin asks why they are in the Old Bailey, which he thought was only for major criminals. It is explained that it is because of his residency in the Barbican.

They proceed into the Courtroom, which to him seems quite small. They sit at their bench, just the three of them. On the opposite bench are seated six gentlemen. It looks like the prosecution is putting a lot into this, and he comments to Mr Lingard, who tells him - No worries, most of them are superfluous and we have everything we need.

The judge enters, and they all have to rise. He is an imposing figure and Colin feels a little daunted. The judge opens proceedings by saying We will now select a jury. There is a real farce. Mr Lingard opposes all the female potential jurors, and the prosecutor does the same with the males. This has been going on for over two hours and it is nearly lunchtime. The judge hammers his gavel and says, 'Enough of this nonsense. It is clear to me that the prosecutor wants a female jury and the defence want a male jury. I will not stand for this and I have it in mind to report both of you to the Bar Council for your antics. I hereby declare that counsel on both sides will no longer have the right of objection to potential jurors. After lunch, we will bring in the next twelve plus two reserves and swear them in.'

They adjourn for lunch. Colin would have liked to go to the pub and have a drink for once, but his police minder tells him he has to stay in the Court. They go to the cafeteria with the minder in tow. He sits at a table away so at least they can converse. Mr Lingard says that was a bit of a drag, and we will have to put up with what we get.

They return to the Courtroom. The judge does not seem in a very good mood and the twelve plus two are sworn in. We are now going to tell you about the jurors, but without names, as that is forbidden by law.

The jury consists of six ladies and six gentlemen, which neither the prosecution nor the defence wanted.

1. A 62-year-old woman who has been happily married for 38 years to an Indian doctor who is now a senior consultant. They met when she was a young nurse and he was a newly qualified doctor. They fell in love and married. She now lives with him in a flat in the Barbican, and they have a holiday home in Cornwall which they visit as often as possible. They have two daughters in their early thirties. The eldest is single and works in Silicon Valley in California. The youngest is a recently married lawyer also living in London. She retired from nursing to look after the family. In the last 15 years, she has been involved in local politics and sits on the City of London council as an independent. They are reasonably wealthy. She has a loving relationship with her husband. In London, they go to the theatre at least once a week and eat out maybe three times a week. Apart from visits to Cornwall, their only recent travel has been two trips to California to see their daughter.

Sex is not high on her agenda. She was a virgin when she got married. In the early days of marriage, it was something you did to have babies. After the babies, in other words, for the last thirty years, there has not been a lot. She has never been unfaithful with another man, and we cannot imagine she ever would. She does not drink a lot of alcohol and never more than a couple of glasses of wine. She never drinks at home and has never taken recreational drugs.

2. A 50-year-old English lady married for 29 years to a successful lawyer who is a partner in a small City law firm. They have lived in a Georgian house in Islington for the last fifteen years and have a small mortgage. They have a son and daughter in their twenties who live away and are both single. The daughter is gay, but both parents have accepted and they remain a happy family. She has a loving relationship with her husband, and they too enjoy eating out but prefer the movies. She is the headmistress of a local primary school. In the Summer, they rent a house in Suffolk for six weeks and entertain friends and family. In Winter, they go skiing for the February half-term, and last year they went to Vail. She had numerous lovers in her teens, but since getting married, she has remained faithful. Sex is still high on her agenda as it always has been and she is still having sex at least twice a week, even at her age. She drinks a lot over the weekend with her husband. She has smoked weed about fifteen times, but nothing else.

3. A 45-year-old English lady has been married for nearly 20 years to a successful engineer. For the first fifteen years of marriage, they lived in Australia, where he worked in the oil industry. They now live in a Victorian house in Islington. They have two daughters aged 13 and 15. Finances are fine. Another loving relationship, and she plays competitive badminton with her husband. A lot of holiday time is going to badminton tournaments. Still enjoys sex, but these days it only seems to

be about once a week, although they always have a good fuck
if they win a title. She has been a faithful wife. She is a stay-
at-home mum. She likes a good drink and, on occasion, has
been known to get legless, but then regrets it and goes on the
wagon for a while. She has smoked pot twice, but it did
nothing for her. She would rather get pissed.

4. A 59-year-old English woman divorcee. She got divorced 10
    years ago because of her husband's adultery. She got a good
    settlement and bought a pleasant two-bedroom apartment in
    Highbury with plenty left to live on, but she did return to
    teaching chemistry in a private school. She has little social life
    except below and rarely goes away. She was also having an
    affair when her husband was found out. She loves sex, and
    presently she is sleeping with two married men who buy her
    nice dinners and then go back to her place for bed. They never
    stay the night. Not too bad, and about once a month, she has a
    one-night stand. A moderate drinker who has never smoked
    dope.

5. A 19-year-old English girl who works as a secretary in a firm
    of City accountants and lives at home with her parents in a flat
    in Highbury. She is always broke and has to borrow from her
    parents. She has had a lot of sex, from holidays in Spain, where
    she would pull a different bloke every night, to pulling blokes
    in the pub or at parties back home. She reckons she has slept
    with upwards of 50 blokes, but Mr Right is nowhere in sight.
    Her ambition is to trap one of the rich accountants she works
    for. She drinks a lot and is often legless. She started smoking
    dope in the playground at school and still does it often. She
    has taken cocaine twice, but did not like the feeling.

6. A 40-year-old never been married Jamaican woman. She has
    two teenage kids and is living on benefits in a dingy council
    house in Highbury. She makes some undeclared money but is
    always broke. She has sex rarely and only drinks if somebody

else is paying. In her younger days, she smoked a lot of dope and took cocaine, but not much now.

7. Our first man. A 40 year old English pilot working for British Airways. Married for 10 years to a stay-at-home mum of two kids who have just reached school age. Finances are tight with their mortgage on their pad in Islington and he cannot persuade his wife to go back to work as an estate agent. He loves flying, but his social life not that great as always tired on his return and needs to relax before his next trip. Holidays will be a subsidised trip on a BA plane. Sex with his wife these days seems to be a shag before he leaves and a shag when he gets back. He tried to be faithful, but three years ago, he had his first night with an air hostess. Since then with some success, he has tried to get laid on every trip, which is the prerogative of a captain. He doesn't think his wife suspects. He likes a drink but has to watch it when he is flying. He has never taken drugs.

8. A 40-year-old single English man. A partner in a medium-sized practice of chartered accountants in the city of London. He too lives in the Barbican. He was engaged to a lovely lawyer who was the girl of his dreams in his twenties. She dumped him for a lawyer. He has never got over her and hasn't fallen in love since and he reckons he has not had sex for more than 10 years. Has loads of money. For holidays, he likes to be on the golf course. His favourite is Pebble Beach in Monterey, California. He drinks a lot. Partners have lunches and wine, and cognac at home in the evening. Never taken drugs.

9. A 56-year-old gay man who lives with his male partner in a Victorian terrace in Islington. His partner is independently wealthy, and he is involved in charity work, mostly fundraising for the Air Ambulance. He and his partner enjoy eating out and going to the movies. Their prime recreation is walking in Regents Park to trips in the UK or abroad. He has

always been faithful to his partner and has no interest in other men. He is a moderate drinker with a couple of glasses of wine most nights. Never taken drugs.

10. A 45-year-old plumber married for over 20 years with three teenage children. He lives in Highbury in an old Edwardian four-bedroom house, which he bought as a wreck and turned into a nice place to live. His wife works in a supermarket, and money is tight. He is a loving and faithful husband. He drinks a few pints at the weekend and has never taken drugs.

11. A 60-year-old married man who has recently been made redundant from his job at the local council. His wife of 35 years is a maths teacher. They have two grown-up married children. They live in a 3-bedroom house on a housing estate in Stoke Newington. Finances seemed okay until he was made redundant, but he is now relying on his pension. His wife is retiring soon, so money will be tight. They do not go out much and watch a lot of TV. About five years ago, he had a fling with a Secretary. The sex was great, but he was careless, and his wife found condoms in his wallet and he had to own up. An uneasy reconciliation and she rarely lets him touch her. He now suspects her of an affair. Holidays are normally in Majorca, and he gets pissed every night on Sangria and Bacardi. He, too, has never taken drugs.

12. And lastly, a single 38-year-old man who is a failed entrepreneur. He lives in a modest rented flat in Stoke Newington. To keep up appearances, he drives a newish BMW and is always smartly, if a little flashily, dressed. Finances are tight, and he has been bankrupt. He has no girlfriend but uses his charms to get into girls' knickers for one-night stands. He is a moderate drinker and has smoked dope and taken cocaine.

13. This all takes a load of time and it is now approaching 4. The judge says there is no point in starting and he adjourns the Court until the next day. Colin manages a couple of words with

Mr Lingard, who assures him that the jury can be handled. He is taken back to prison.

The next day, he again dresses smartly but with a different tie and makes his way back to the Old Bailey.

The judge comes in. The first thing he does is to direct Colin to the place for defendants. He makes his way slowly, if a little gingerly, and he can feel the eyes of the jurors scrutinising him. That was all wrong. He should have moved with confidence.

The prosecutor is requested to make an opening address. It is very bland. That man you see tied up and raped a woman etc, etc. Mr Lingard is then requested to make his opening address. He seems much more alert. 'Ladies and gentlemen of the jury, we are here today to hear a case of rape. There was no rape, which we will prove to you and you are sure to find the defendant not guilty.' Short and sweet, Colin likes his robust approach.

The prosecutor may now call his first witness, and naturally, it is Penny. She makes her way to the witness stand, looking apprehensive, which pleases Colin. She is sworn in. The prosecutor asks her to describe the circumstances of the relevant evening. She nervously begins, and the judge tells her to speak up.

On the night in question, I had dinner with the defendants and two others in a nice restaurant to celebrate a successful IPO.' At this point, she is interrupted by the judge, who says she will have to speak English as he suspects the jury has no idea what an IPO is. Colin thinks this is quite good as the judge has twice reprimanded her. She explains IPO apparently to the judge's satisfaction and continues. Penny continues 'The two others left the restaurant early. I had a bottle of calvados in my flat, so I invited the defendant back to my place. I poured him a calvados and the next thing I knew, I was being tied to my bed. He removed all my clothes and raped me. He then left and somehow I managed to untie myself and went straight to my local police station, where I reported the matter.' Colin is a little astonished at her statement, which seems very short. The prosecutor is then asked by the judge if he has any questions for the witness. He replies that the witness has been very clear. Mr Lingard is now asked if he has any questions. He rises 'Thank you for your clear testimony but I am afraid I will have to ask you a couple of simple questions. Firstly, you offered to take him back to your flat to drink calvados. When you arrived back at the flat, you stated that you gave him calvados. Did you by any chance put on any music to enhance the mood?' She replies that she cannot remember, as the events of the night were so traumatic. He continues 'Thank you. I am sure the jury will understand your lack of remembrance. Secondly, as you have described it, you were alone with him drinking calvados in your living room but now we are in your bedroom and he is tying you to your bed. How did we get to the bedroom? Did he drag you there or did you invite him into your bedroom?' Her reply is that she cannot answer that question due to trauma. Mr Lingard sighs, 'We are in the living room but then in your bedroom, but the witness is unable to tell us how she got there. I am sure the jury will be wondering how you got there. My third question is whether you now say you were able to untie yourself. I have never had both my hands tied to a bed, and I have to admit in the event that it happened to me I would have no idea about how to untie myself. Did you use your feet or something else?' She replies that she continually wriggled her hands until at last one became free and she was able to release herself. Mr Lingard nods, 'Your fact that you have said you were tied up is fundamental to this case. We are unsure how you got to the bedroom and I have to say I feel unsure as to how you managed to untie yourself. If what you say is true, then it would have to have been a very loose knot for you to wriggle free. From your evidence, you have not told us how long this took. From the timing of the events to your arrival at the police station, it must have been short. Again, it will be up to the jury to determine your evidence. Onto my next question. How many men have you slept with?' At this point, the prosecutor jumps up and objects. He is overruled and Penny is told she has to answer. She replies about 10. 'And this was all consensual sex with kissing beforehand and after, with making plans for future dates.' Her response is 'Yes'. Mr Lingard had not been expecting this response as she had basically admitted to consensual sex. ' I am not sure that I understand you. You have told us that all the men you have slept with have been consensual, but you have accused the defendant of rape, which does not add up.' Penny is now looking very flustered and says she did not include the defendant in the reply because he had raped her. He continues 'The defendant was your boss. It has been put to me that this is all a set-up and your ambition was to get rid of him and get his job.' She replies that before the episode, she had great respect for her boss and thoroughly enjoyed working for him. Why then did she apply for his job after he was dismissed following the incident? She replies,

'I never wanted his job, but when the opportunity arose, I applied.' Mr Lingard says to the Court

'The witness says she never wanted his job. But we think she did which is why she applied. She was only able to apply because she had set him up. Later that will be for the jury to decide.'

One last question. 'Have you ever been on the contraceptive pill.' Answer 'No.' 'And have you ever had an abortion?' Answer 'No.'

That is the end of his questioning and Penny's evidence.

It is now lunch and the judge adjourns until after lunch.

Colin has lunch with Mr Lingard and Penelope. No sign of Penny or the prosecutor and they wonder where they can be. Mr Lingard thinks his questioning and ability to put doubt in the minds of the jury went very well.

Back to Court. The next prosecution witness is a doctor who explains he took a semen sample from Penny. It was later found to match Colin. The doctor is asked by Mr Lingard if there were any signs of forced entry, to which the answer is No.

The next prosecution witness is a policewoman who details the injuries to Penny's wrists and she provides photographic evidence, which is shown to the Court and the jury. She tells the Court that Penny told her she received the injuries when she was tied to her bed by the defendant. It is time for Mr Lingard to cross-examine. 'Has the policewoman ever seen similar injuries?' To which the answer is No. 'In the opinion of the policewoman was the supposed victim was tied tightly.' The prosecutor interrupts and Mr Lingard is admonished by the judge for using supposed. The policewoman is asked by the judge to answer the question. She replies, 'From the extent of the injuries she would think that the victim was tied very tightly.' Mr Lingard 'If, as you say, she was tied very tightly, what would the victim have had to do to untie herself?' The policewoman responds, 'I am afraid I am unable to answer that question.' Mr Lingard is not going to let this go. 'You have told us that in your opinion the victim was tightly tied. The victim said in questioning that she wiggled her hands and was able to release one tie. It did not take her that long to report the matter to the police and be photographed, which you have kindly brought with you. If the victim was tightly tied in your opinion, would wriggling enable her to untie herself.' The policewoman gives the same reply. Mr Lingard says 'Ladies and gentlemen of the jury we have heard here today that the victim was tightly tied. The police witness is unable to enlighten us as to how the victim would have escaped from the ties. I will leave you to draw your own conclusions.'

The next prosecution witness is the Inspector from Truro. Before the prosecutor is able to begin, Mr Lingard makes an objection. The defendant is not charged here with anything to do with his bail, but only rape and he does not understand why the prosecution is bringing this up. There is some discussion and the judge rules that the witness can go ahead.

The Inspector details the police actions in trying to find Colin. He is then questioned about the arrest of Colin. Did the police have DNA evidence from the crime scene and did they take DNA from all the other residents? The answer to both these questions is No. The Inspector has to finally admit that Colin was identified by one of the officers on the murder case when they made their preliminary enquiries and they need to get his DNA to prove it was him. The Inspector is then asked some questions about Sue.

It is getting late in the day and the judge adjourns.

Colin is able to have a short meeting with Penelope and Mr Lingard, who tells him that he thinks it is all going very well. He does not imagine that the prosecutor will have any more witnesses and Colin should prepare himself to take the stand tomorrow.

Karen and his parents have sat through all of this. Karen is pleased that his barrister is raising doubts.

The next morning, Colin pays particular attention to his appearance and is back at the Old Bailey.

The prosecutor says he has no more witnesses. It is time for the defence.

Colin is moved from the defendant's box to the witness stand and has to take the oath. Mr Lingard asks him to recount to the Court, to the best of his ability, the events surrounding the night in question.

'I can remember the night very clearly. I treated my team to a good dinner in recognition of their good work. Two of the team left early and Penny invited me to her flat to drink calvados. When we arrived at her flat, she poured me a calvados and put on a CD by Norah Jones to set the mood. We started kissing and one thing led to another, and we made love. She told me she was on the pill so we had unprotected sex. It was the first time I had been unfaithful to my wife but I felt no guilt. I remember clearly that as I was leaving, she said to me she hoped this would not be a one-night stand, which I took to mean that she had really enjoyed making love with me. It came as a complete shock to me when I was arrested the next day and accused of rape.' Mr Lingard 'Thank you for your clear testimony. You have only told us that you made love but did not tell us the location.' To this, Colin replies that it was in her bed. 'Did she lead you into the bedroom.' ' Yes.' 'In your lovemaking, did you ever tie her up?' 'No.' Mr

Lingard knows he is now going to shortly hand him over for cross-examination, but he needs to set the scene for the set-up and deal with the bail.

'Your defence is that you have been set up because Penny was a very ambitious woman who wanted your job. Did you know that after you were removed from your job, she applied to take your position?' Colin replies, ' You are right, this was all a set-up as she wanted my job. I did not know that she had applied for my job.' Mr Lingard, 'We now get to your bail. Why did you run away?' Colin now thinks he has a chance to shine. 'I did run away because I was advised that even though I had been set up, the evidence against me was very strong and there was a high risk that I would be sent to prison. I knew my innocence of the alleged crime, and I could not face going to jail as an innocent man. That is why I ran away. It was unfortunate that there was a murder in my block of flats, and I was identified by one of the investigating officers.'

Mr Lingard now addresses the jury 'As you have heard, the defendant admits to making love to the victim, but he did not tie her up and he did not rape her. She invited him back to her flat and set the mood with calvados and music. When it was time for him to go home, she hoped they would do it again. There can only be one explanation for her actions, and that was ambition. He is innocent of all charges.'

He hands over Colin to the prosecutor.

'What we have here is a clear case of aggravated rape. Your only defence seems to be that you have been set up because of her ambition to get your job. In my book, with the evidence we have before us you can only be telling untruths.' Colin had expected something like this and he has been well trained and all he can say is 'What is your question?' ' The prosecutor says he has no questions because the facts are clear.

Colin has been in the witness box for a little over 45 minutes. He had been expecting something a lot longer. They feel their points have been well made.

Mr Lingard calls his first witness, Deborah whom he introduces. Mr Lingard asks her to describe her relationship with Penny. 'It was clear to me from day 1 that she resented me getting the job. At meetings, she was always looking to take the lead. There was something there that I did not like and after a while, it seemed obvious to me that she had cleverly engineered the demise of her old boss and after all her efforts, could not stand the fact that she did not have his job. I knew that she had applied and been unsuccessful. We were doing an IPO and she made a fundamental mistake with a profit forecast and we had to let her go.' Mr Lingard says to her, 'I want to be clear here. My client's defence is that he has been set up. Are you saying in your estimation, he was set up?'

To which the reply is 'Yes.'

It is now the turn of the prosecutor. 'I cannot believe that you can come in here and say that the victim set up the defendant. We have all the evidence here to show what really happened and you have the cheek to come in here and say something different. I move that the evidence be struck from the record and the jury be told to disregard the evidence.'

The judge is almost glaring at the prosecutor and told that he is denied.

The next witness is the private detective who followed Penny to the abortion clinic. He tells how he followed her there, where she spent over two hours. The prosecutor asks no questions.

That is all the witnesses for the defence.

It is now lunchtime.

Colin has lunch with his team, and Mr Lingard thinks it is all going well.

They return to the Court, and the prosecutor is asked to make his closing statement.

'Ladies and gentlemen of the jury, we have spent one and a half days examining the evidence of aggravated rape by tying up the victim. We know from the semen that the defendant had sex with the victim, and we know he achieved this by tying her up. We have seen photographic evidence of her injuries. It is as clear as can be what happened and there can only be one outcome of your deliberations - guilty. As an aside I can also inform you that the victim did not have an abortion; she was visiting the clinic on behalf of a friend.'

Mr Lingard cannot believe that yet again the prosecutor has been so short. He is going to take a lot more of the court's time.

It his time to take the stand.

'Ladies and gentlemen of the jury. I am afraid that I have a lot more to say than my learned friend the prosecutor, and I would be grateful if you would bear with me. The whole prosecution case is based on two things. Firstly, the presence of the defendant's semen and secondly the injuries to the wrists of the victim, which are attributed to her being tied up by the defendant. I have to tell you that the defendant has pleaded not guilty because he did nothing but have consensual sex with the defendant. Let us deal firstly with the semen. The defendant's semen was present because he had consensual sex. She invited him back to her place and then set the mood with calvados and music. You will remember that when asked, she could not remember music, but the defendant is clear on this point. After some kissing, she led him to her bedroom, where they had consensual sex. In the evidence of the victim, she was unable to explain the circumstances of their being in the bedroom due to trauma. She could not have told the truth, which is that she led him there. Now to the sex itself. In her planning, she was clever and needed his semen as proof that he had sex with her, so she told him she was on the pill and they had unprotected sex. Joy, she would have her sample of his semen. That backfired a little as she became pregnant and had to have an abortion. The explanation of visiting a friend is not believable as she spent more than two hours, which is far longer than would be necessary to make an enquiry on behalf of a friend. Next, we get to tying her up. The defendant most certainly did not tie her up. The police evidence was that the knot was very tight, and here she has made another mistake. She made marks on her wrists to signify having been tied up but these marks were too severe. The question arises, how did she manage to undo the ties? The police were unable to offer an explanation. The reality is, it was easy as she was never tied up and just made the marks herself. Why did she go to all this trouble? Simply, she wanted his job, and after he was released by the firm, she made her play, but with little success. We have heard evidence from the defendant's successor that, in her opinion, the victim was obsessed with his job and most probably set the whole thing up. I do not know why the prosecutor thought it necessary to bring up the bail question, as the defendant is not charged in this respect, but I will deal with it. If he was innocent, why did he run away from bail? He had been badly advised that he faced a prison term and saw it as the only way out. He now has my advice, and his innocence is as clear as can be. The victim wanted his job and saw a perfect opportunity to set him up, which she did. She allowed him to make love to her with unprotected sex to get his semen and then made marks on her wrists, but as has been demonstrated too much, and reported to the police that she had been tied up and raped. The defendant is totally innocent, and I feel sure that your deliberations will come to the same conclusion. '

The judge thanks both counsel for their closing statements and then goes through some administrative matters with the jury. As it is late, he tells them that he will now adjourn the Court and they will return tomorrow to give their verdict.

Colin is able to have a short conference with Mr Lingard and Penelope. They both seem pleased and upbeat.

Meanwhile,, Karen and his parents retire to the cafeteria. Karen says it certainly looks like he was set up. If I were on the, jury, I would find him not guilty, and I am sure the jury will agree. His father concurs, and his mother does not say much. Karen takes the short walk home, collects Jonathan from school, and sits down to think. He is not guilty and will be released. Where does that leave our relationship? He will be shattered by the experience. Do I want to get back together with him? To be honest, she doesn't know. After what he has done, being unfaithful, disappearing and all that, she feels unsure whether she could ever love him again. If he is found guilty and sent to prison, she will definitely divorce him.

Chapter 23

It is now the next day, and the Court convenes. The judge sent the jury to their room.

There is an air of anticipation in the room.

The 62-year-old English lady who is married to an Indian doctor is elected Chairperson. She says the first thing they will do is go around the room to get the various opinions, with ladies first.

The first to talk is the 50-year-old English lady married to a lawyer. ' There is no doubt that sex occurred between the victim and the defendant. They both tell completely different stories. The victim says that she was tied up and raped. The defendant says they had consensual sex. The defence put forward a number of arguments as to why the defendant had been set up. In my view, there are two things which point to this. The lack of clarity as to how they got to the bedroom, and the apparent tightness of the ties, which may have been difficult to undo. On the other hand, I was impressed by the evidence of the victim. If she did go through all that, it must have been very difficult to go to Court, and I find it hard to believe she set him up. For the time being, I am sitting on the fence. ' She is thanked.

Next up is the 45-year-old English lady married to an engineer. She says she agrees with everything the First Lady said, and she, too, is sitting on the fence.

The 59-year-old divorcee is next to speak. ' As has been said here, we are looking at two different stories. I was divorced about ten years ago, but I have always liked sex and am still getting my fair share. I have a pleasant apartment and, from time to time, take men back for sex. When I take a man back for sex, I like to set the mood with a nice drink and music, which helps a man relax. The defendant's description of the evening fits in with what I would do to entice a man with whom I wanted to have sex. I think she lured him into having sex with her and then set him up. The thing that she did wrong was to make her injuries too severe, and it is beyond me how she would have been able to untie herself. My verdict is innocent.'

We now have the 19-year-old English girl. ' I am not sure why I am here, as I thought I would be too young for jury service. As the previous ladies have said, we have two different stories, and we have to decide who we believe. I live at home with my parents and have never taken a bloke, or I mean a man, home to have sex with, so I am unable to comment on moods. I have, however, had sex with quite a few blokes, and all I can say is that it is always different. Some blokes are just sweet and cuddly, whereas other blokes can be more forceful. I do not think, however, that I have ever been raped. Now to the matter in hand. Did they have consensual sex, or did they have sex and something went wrong, which made the victim plead rape? I am afraid I do not know either way and will also sit on the fence.'

The 40-year-old single Jamaican girl is next. ' I too am finding this hard. The prosecutor has just said Here are the facts - guilty. The defence has looked closely at the facts and raised doubts in our minds. Did I like the victim? No. There was something about her which seemed calculating, and she was playing her own game. Did I like the defendant? Yes. I have met a lot of blokes in my life, and I think I am pretty good at spotting the bad ones. This defendant seemed to me to be one of the good ones, and in hiding difficulties, he was believable. I think he is innocent, and he had consensual sex, and it came back to bite him. '

The chairperson comments that we have now heard from all the ladies, and we have two innocent and three on the fence. Let's hear what the men have to say.

First to speak is the 40-year-old English pilot. ' This seems to me a clear case of who is telling the truth. The victim told her story very well and was believable. The defendant was likewise. One of them is not telling the truth, and it is for us to determine. I am a pilot flying sophisticated pieces of machinery. What we rely on is a trustworthy ground crew to make sure that our planes are fit for the air. Every time I fly, I have to expect that the ground crew have performed properly. It has been known for aircraft to fail pre-flight checks, and this results in internal enquiries. The remiss ground crew will always be found. Our task is more difficult as we have to determine who to believe. I incline to believe the defendant. Why do I not believe the victim? I think she may have been clever and planned it all. She was clever to get his semen, but not so clever as to get pregnant, and she was not so clever as to not be able to explain how they ended up in the bedroom and again not so clever with the extent of her so-called injuries. My vote is for innocent.

The second is another 40-year-old English accountant. ' I have never been accused of rape. I have never raped anybody. If I were accused of rape, I would make sure I got a jolly good lawyer. What we have here is a prosecutor who says Here is the evidence, find him guilty. And we have a defendant with a jolly good lawyer who has done his best to make a conviction doubtful. I wonder where he got his lawyer from; we can be sure he is not legal aid. As has been said, we have two stories, and we have to believe one. On balance, I tend to believe the rape, and I think the defendant's clever lawyer is just a bit too clever for me, and I would say guilty. ' The first guilty, then.

The third is the 56-year-old gay man. ' I have always had great faith in the police. We have been presented with evidence of rape. I consider that the police would have looked at all aspects of the case before they brought charges. For these reasons, I vote for guilty.'

This jury is not going as expected. The five ladies have not found him guilty, and now two men are finding him guilty.

Time for the 45-year-old plumber. 'This is my first time on a jury. It seems to me we are being asked a difficult question. Who is telling the truth? What is not in doubt is that sex occurred. What is in doubt is whether he ties her up to have sex. We have seen photographs of the injuries to her wrists. The police have told us that it would have been very tight. The defence is that he did not tie her up, and they have given sound reasons as to why this must have been self-inflicted. I did not like either the victim or the defendant, who both seemed as if they were holding something back. On balance, my view is that the victim set him up, and I would go for innocent.'

Next to last is the 60-year-old man who worked for the Council.

'It has been fascinating listening to you all. The question here is the truth. It seems that the majority are saying innocent, but a couple of my male colleagues have gone for guilty. I can see the evidence of his guilt, but I have also carefully noted the points raised by the defence. I do agree that the defendant has a jolly good lawyer, but at the end of the day, I just don't know, and I will sit on the fence.'

The last is the 38-year-old failed entrepreneur. ' I have good looks and used them to go with a lot of girls. I like that one of my fellows has never been accused of rape. What would I do if I were accused? I would look at the evidence, and if it didn't look good, I would probably run away. That seems to be what we have here. The defendant looked at the evidence. He was advised that he was going to prison and ran away. He got caught and found himself a good lawyer. A good lawyer will always make us think, but my gut tells me that he ran away because he was guilty.'

The chairperson then sums up by saying. 'The men have said three guilty, two innocent and one fence. In total, we have four innocent, three guilty and four on the fence. It is time you heard my view. As many of you have said, our job here is to determine the truth, and we have two different stories and are being asked to make a judgment as to what the truth is. Looking at both sides, I can see the clear evidence of rape, and I can see the clear evidence that the defendant has been set up. I have to tell you that I, too, am going to sit on the fence, which puts me in the majority. That will not please the judge, as the Court needs and requires a verdict. I think the only thing we can do is go back to the judge and ask for direction.

They go back to the judge and tell him they have been discussing all day and have a deadlock. The judge says he is sorry to hear that. If at all possible, he would like the matter to be settled, as he would not want to have to order a retrial and make the witness have to testify again, which he believes would be distressing for her. In these circumstances, the Court would accept a majority 10-2 verdict rather than a unanimous one. As it is late, the judge adjourns until the next day. Colin has a brief moment with his counsel, who tells him that this is good news as he has not been found guilty.

The jury returned the next day to their room. The chairperson says 'I think the judge has clearly told us that we have to do our best to reach a verdict. I sat on the fence for my first vote. I have listened carefully to you all. On balance, I do not think that the jurors who found him guilty have thought it through properly, and I can now vote not guilty. I will ask the others who sat on the fence to now update us.'

The first to speak is the 50-year-old woman married to a lawyer. 'I would have liked to discuss this with my husband, who is a lawyer, but I have played it straight. I think he would have said case not proven, particularly because of the apparent tightness of the knots, and would have advised me to say not guilty, which is now my verdict.'

Next to speak is the 45-year-old woman married to an engineer. 'I, too, have spoken to nobody but would have liked the opportunity. I said the first time that I agreed with the lady who spoke before me, and I am going to agree with her again and give you my vote as not guilty.'

We now have the 19-year-old girl who says she tends to agree that the case is not proven, and she, too, will vote not guilty.

The chairperson comments 'Thank you, ladies. We four who were sitting on the fence have now all said not guilty, which means that all six ladies have now voted not guilty. Before we started, I would have expected the ladies to convict and the gentlemen to protect their own, but this does not seem to be the case. It seems to me that the crucial evidence is the tightness of the binding. It seems that the probability is that she would not have been able to easily release herself, which means she did it herself for her own ambitious ends. I will now ask the men for their thoughts.

The 40-year-old accountant is the first to speak. 'I voted guilty because I thought the defendant's lawyer was a bit too smart. But I have listened to what you are saying. The smart lawyer did not tell us about the tightness of the binding. It was the police who told us. We were able to look at the photographic evidence, and there appeared to be deep scars from the tightness, and it seems to me that it would have been very difficult to get out of it. I now think it was planned, but the so-called victim made a grave error when inflicting her injuries, and I will change my vote to not guilty.' The chairperson says that by her reckoning, we now have 9 not guilty, 2 guilty and 1 on the fence and asks the 60-year-old Council worker who was sitting on the fence to update them. He says he has listened to all the arguments and is now going to say not guilty.

The chairperson comments that we now have ten innocent people and asks the gay man and the entrepreneur if they would like to comment on their guilty verdicts, but they both decline.

The chairperson presses a bell, and a member of the Court appears, and she says the jury has a verdict. They are ushered back into the Court.

They have to wait for a time for the judge, but he finally appears. He asks the chairperson if they have a unanimous verdict, to which she replies 10-2, which satisfies him. She declares the verdict as not guilty. The judge nods almost as if he himself would have voted not guilty and speaks. 'Mr Colin Butcher, you have been found not guilty and are now able to leave the Court a free man. The jury has found that you did not tie up and rape the woman as you were accused. That means that the jury has found that the alleged victim made up the story and lied to the police, which is a serious offence. I will be writing to the Director of Public Prosecutions with a recommendation that this matter should be looked into. The Court is now adjourned.'

Colin goes down into the Courtroom and shakes the hand of Mr Lingard and Penelope and thanks them very much. To him, it is all a huge relief because, after all, he was totally innocent and was set up. He hopes Penny is really going to be in trouble and asks a question about it. All Mr Lingard can say is that he will not be defending her. They then ask him how he is going to celebrate. He has no idea, but first stop at the pub would not be a bad idea. Karen and his father then join them (but not his mother), and they all agree to go to the pub which is just next door.

In the pub, his father orders a bottle of champagne and five glasses. They all chink glasses and make a lot of toasts. Time is dragging on, and the lawyers leave. Karen says the three of them should grab a sandwich in the pub, which they do. Colin has a pint of beer. It sure feels good to be free.

Karen suggests they now go back to her place. Colin wonders where her place is and soon finds out, another flat in the Barbican. They enter, and there is his mother looking very grey. She asks about the verdict and shows little response when told not guilty. Must have been obvious, or Colin would not have been here. His parents leave shortly, and he is left alone with Karen. She is looking very serious, and he wonders what she is going to say or if he should say something. To be honest, he is not sure what to say.

She starts 'I sat through the whole trial. You said that you had consensual sex with her, and she says you tied her up and raped her. I have known you a long time, and I never believed you were that type of person. I never really liked Penny, and setting you up was a terrible thing to do. I think the jury was probably persuaded by the ridiculous injuries she inflicted on herself. She would never have been able to get out of that. I truly hope the full force of the law comes down on her. We now need to get to what we are going to do about you. By sleeping with Penny and then running away, you have killed anything that ever was between us. After you ran away, I thought about divorcing you, but I took no action. During your trial, I have been reflecting on this issue, and I have concluded that I am now going to sue for divorce. Your affair and absenting yourself are good grounds. There are a number of matters to be considered, amongst which are Jonathan and money. I am prepared to make you an offer. Jonathan will come into my care, and you will have access on alternate weekends from Friday to Sunday evening. Money - I will make over to you half the cash and investments, which will amount to just over £100,000. You will not be permitted to stay in this flat.'

Colin can hardly believe she is being so direct. Does he want to divorce her? He supposes so because, after all, he did want to marry Sue and maybe be a bigamist. He has no love for Jonathan, and alternate weekends sound like the biggest drag out. He could make excuses and do it as little as possible. She wants half my money. I worked my balls off to make all that money, and she contributed little, and now she only wants to give me half. But he will have to reply.

' You are saying a lot of things. Your desire for a divorce is the most damaging to me. My affair, as you call it, was the only time I have been unfaithful to you in our entire marriage. It was not the right thing to do to sleep with my assistant, and into the bargain, she set me up because she wanted my job. I had to leave because my legal advice was not strong, and as an innocent man, I faced the prospect of going to prison for a lengthy time, which I could not face. When I came back with my father's help, I was so lucky to find Mr Lingard. He was not like my previous lawyers and managed to prove the setup. So, as I am saying, it was not really an affair but a one, and I had good reasons to run away. Do you still think you truly want to divorce me? (he is not quite sure why he has asked this because, as far as he is concerned, he wants it too.)

At this point, she is looking a little nervous, and he dreads her saying she still wants to be married to him, but this is what she says.

'I am certain that I want to divorce you. Before the trial, I was not so sure. I sat through the whole trial, and I have to tell you that if I had been on the jury, I would have found you guilty. You are right that you were lucky to find Mr Lingard, a clever lawyer who got you off. I now feel nothing for you, and the only way forward is divorce.' Good, he thinks. I'd better carry on.

'In the event of divorce, you mentioned Jonathan and money. I am happy to agree to both your proposals, which I think will make the process a lot easier. I assume you have not yet started the process, but I would be more than happy to be involved from the start. I do not know how long these things take, but hopefully, being uncontested, it will not take too long. Onto matters of practicality. It will be my intention to see if I can get my old job back, and in the event that I am not successful, I will look for similar employment. You made no mention of my future earnings. I assume when we divide the money, you will not be looking for any further money from me from my prospects. She replies that she had not considered it, but it seems to her that he should be made to take responsibility for the costs of raising his son, and she will take advice on the matter.

He continues ' You have to understand that at the moment I do not have a penny in the world. When I left, I left behind my bank cards and driving licence. If you found these, I would be grateful for their return. She replies that they were destroyed.

He wonders why they were destroyed, but carries on.

'Without a penny in the world, I am in a bit of a pickle. Apart from the clothes I am standing in, I have nothing, not even a toothbrush or razor. I can understand that you do not want me to stay here with you, but I do not think I know anybody who would give me a bed for the night, and I do not fancy sleeping on the streets or in a homeless shelter. That means I need some money now to get going. It is still early. Do you think we could go to the bank and withdraw some funds as part of my payoff (not sure why he used the word pay off)? Perhaps £2,000.'

She is still looking nervous, but after a lot of humming and harring, she eventually agrees. They go off to the bank almost immediately and withdraw the £2,000.

Outside the bank, they discuss the way forward. Tomorrow she will start the divorce proceedings, and he agrees to come over in the evening to plan tactics and, as she points out, see his long-lost son.

She walks off briskly.

He considers what to do. He needs some more clothes - shirts, underwear and socks as well as the toothbrush and razor. He makes a quick trip to Boots and M&S, and all his worldly goods are now in one carrier bag. Now he needs to find a bed.

After a lot of agonising and asking around, he finds the Easy Hotel in Shoreditch, where he manages to get a room for £63 per night and books 5 nights.

It is Thursday night, and he lies on his bed and thinks about his options.

The first thing to do is get a job. Tomorrow, the first thing he will do is return to his old place of work and see if he can get his job back. If nothing is going on, he will ask them for a reference. If he is not successful, the next stop will have to be an employment agency. He knows of only the agency that got him his last job, and he will go back to them. He then starts to wonder if that is what he really wants. He has to admit that after he ran away, he did enjoy outdoor life, and he did enjoy writing books. Could he go back to Wadebridge and see if Sue will have him back? He would have a lot of explaining to do, but she was a great girl, and he did so much enjoy the life he had with her. He decides he will just see how it goes. He goes out and finds an M&S and buys a sandwich and a bottle of wine with a screw top and takes them back to the Easy Hotel and has dinner alone and finishes the bottle of wine. Brushes his teeth and goes to bed. Sleeps well and does not wake up until 9.30.

He showers and shaves and brushes his teeth and puts on a new shirt, underwear and socks and gets himself into what he calls his Court suit. He has a quick breakfast at Starbucks and heads in the direction of his old job.

The receptionist remembers him. He explains he needs to see the MD on an important matter. She does not seem that impressed with his request. What is an important matter? He explains it is to do with his dismissal. After a long time, he is shown into the Boardroom. He sits alone for another age, but eventually the MD arrives. He does not look like he is in a good mood and seems to be glaring at him. Colin opens

'Thank you for seeing me. It has been a while, and I have missed being here. You are probably not aware, but yesterday I was acquitted of the charge of raping Penny. The jury agreed that I had been set up and found me not guilty. For me, it has been a very trying experience, and I now need to get my life back together. Which is why I am here. I loved my job and working with you, and I think it is only fair that I should be reinstated as I did nothing wrong. My reinstatement would make life much easier for all of us, and there would be no question of a legal case for unfair dismissal.'

The countenance of the MD has not changed.

We have been following the trial because of the potential damage to the reputation of this firm. We are well aware that you were acquitted. Your acquittal, however, does not change the tenure of what happened. You took advantage of your position to have sex with a subordinate. It is my view and that of the Board that what you did was entirely wrong. We think that what you did was despicable, and there is no place for such a person in our organisation. Your position has been taken by a person in whom we have the utmost faith. You will not be reinstated or offered any other position in this firm. Oh, and by the way, good luck with unfair dismissal. We have taken legal advice on this matter, and you do not stand a chance. I bid you good day. 'And he walks out of the room. Colin realises he didn't even ask for a reference, but he has to accept he is not coming back here. Time to visit the employment agent.

They cannot see him until Monday, so he makes an appointment.

Friday afternoon and the weekend are difficult. All this waiting. He sees a couple of movies to waste some time, but cannot remember them. He eats cheaply to save money, but has a stock of wine in his room and drinks a bottle each night all to himself. He wonders what Monday will bring, and his thoughts keep returning to Sue. On Sunday night, through his alcoholic haze, he suddenly remembers he was supposed to see Karen on Friday night to talk about the divorce, but he totally forgot about it with everything else. He will go and see her tomorrow evening.

Monday comes, and he makes his way to the employment agency. His interview is with a girl he has never met, and he does not find her very attractive. She has his file, which is a good start. First things first. Mobile telephone number and contact details. Not a good start. He'd better get a pay-as-you-go and let her know the number. He gives his father's address and phone number as contact. Next recent employment. Gardener is not going to sound so good, so he tells her that he has taken a break since leaving his old job and has been writing novels. Why did he leave his old job? He might as well tell her the truth, which he does. She seems a little shocked. Does he have references? No. What was his salary and bonus structure, to which he can reply. Now the bad news. There are currently no openings available at his salary level. He would be prepared to work for less. She gets out another file and says she cannot see anything suitable at present. If anything comes up which may be suitable, they will certainly contact him. He leaves disconsolate.

He does, however, buy a mobile and phones her with the number.

Hangs around for the rest of the day and goes to see Karen at about 6. All apologies for missing Friday. She doesn't seem to mind. Jonathan is there, and he shakes his hand. Jonathan asks him where he has been, and he tells him it is a long story. Will I be seeing more of you now than before? Yes. Jonathan is asked to go to his room.

Karen has been busy with the divorce, and she hands him some papers for him to sign. He doesn't really read them but signs them anyway. She tells him that the papers will be filed tomorrow, and they will then have to wait 20 weeks for a conditional order. He reflects that 20 weeks is not too long to wait. He will be well out of it. He starts to think about the money. The bank account was joint, and the investments were all in his name. He says to her.

'I think we agreed to split the money. As you know, we had a joint bank account, and the investments were in my name. I suggest that we sell all the investments and deposit the proceeds in the joint account. I will open a new account in my sole name, and I suggest you also open an account in your name. We can then split the joint account and put one-half into each of our new accounts.' She says she had not intended to split the money until the divorce was finalised. This surprises him, and he tells her that he could sell the investments and put the money in his new account, and then they would have to make some adjustment one way or the other when the divorce is finalised, and it seems much easier to do it now in the way he has outlined. She does not seem happy with this, but eventually agrees. He is a little worried that he will sell his investments and then she will not let him have his half, but he is a signatory on the joint account, so he can just transfer the money to himself. And that is in fact what happens. In the middle of the following week, he has a new account with £105,000 and a new credit card and debit card. He has also managed to get his passport back from the police. He feels set up for life.

Chapter 24

He may be set up for life, but he is still staying in the Easy Hotel. In the last 10 days, he has been to two more employment agents and phoned the original, but a job does not seem in sight. He thought he was set up for life, but the £105,000 will not last forever, and he really needs to start earning again, and he needs a proper place to live. Without an income, he will not be able to get a mortgage, and buying a place is out; he will have to find a place to rent. He dismisses the idea of the Barbican as he does not want to be close to Karen. He hopes his only contact with her is when he collects Jonathan on alternate weekends. He has not yet made arrangements for his first weekend with Jonathan, as he cannot take him to the hotel. He now has an iPad and starts searching for possible flats. He sees about four flats in Blackfriars and Smithfield. They are all over £2,000 per month, and three are only one bed. His preferred option is a 2-bedroom Georgian conversion in Middle Street, West Smithfield, for £2,448 per month. Walking distance to the City and a bedroom for Jonathan - sorted then, and he signs up for 6 months and gets a small discount for paying all up front, but it is still over £14,000, and it is only part furnished, and he will need to get some bits and pieces, which will only add to the cost.

He moves in on a Friday with just him and his limited wardrobe. It does not take long to unpack. The flat has a washing machine and a tumble dryer. He strips down and washes everything which he has not been able to do in the hotel. It will be nice to have clean clothes, and he does need some casual clothes - jeans and sweaters would be nice. When it is all clean and dry, he dresses again, but he only has his suit. He goes out and buys a pair of jeans and two sweaters. Gets home, puts on his new jeans and a sweater and feels like a new man. He decides to go and visit Karen and offer to take Jonathan off her hands, as he is now set up.

She doesn't seem very pleased to see him. He explains his new living arrangements and offers to take Jonathan. She obviously does not want to give him up, and there are a lot of excuses about the divorce still in process, and not knowing if the new place is suitable for a young boy. They take a short walk to Middle Street with Jonathan in tow. It surprises him that she says it will be okay, and they make a date for him to pick him up next Friday evening to return Sunday evening.

During the next week, Colin spends a lot of time job searching without any success.

It is Friday evening, and he is not in the greatest of moods, but goes to pick up Jonathan. To him, the two days and nights are a total drag. On Friday evening, he takes Jonathan to an upmarket burger place. There is little conversation, and all Jonathan seems interested in is where he went when he was away. On Saturday, they take a walk to the Tower of London, where Jonathan has never been, but he doesn't seem too impressed. Dinner at home. What can he do on Sunday? They take a boat to Greenwich. He drops Jonathan back a little early at 4 pm. Karen asks him if he had a good time. All he can say is yes, and he offers no more.

Colin can hardly believe that he is going to have to do this every two week, but he makes arrangements for the weekend after next before he leaves. Jonathan does not really say goodbye to him, and there are no thanks for his efforts.

Colin is pleased to be home and gets drunk. In his drunkenness, he thinks about his life. It is good to be nearly divorced. His two days with Jonathan were no fun at all, and it was close to a nightmare, and he is going to have to do it every two weeks. His job prospects are not looking that good, and he is not sure how to move it forward. He rather likes his new flat, but it is expensive and he will not be able to afford it long term. Where is he going to go from here? He enjoyed writing, but he failed to get published, and there seems little point in writing another book. Gardening jobs in the City are likely to be nonexistent, and that will not be the way forward, although he does like the outdoors. In his musings, he gets back to thinking about Sue. He must have loved her, or he would not have asked her to marry him. Shortly, he will be divorced and will be free to marry her. What does she think of him now? He has to admit he has no idea. Should he try to make contact with her again? Is she still in the same flat they shared, or has she moved or gone back to living with her parents? He could write her a letter and send it to her parents, but that would be very impersonal. The best thing to do would be to turn up in Wadebridge, knock on her parents' door and find out her whereabouts. But that seems stupid, there is probably no way she would want to see him after what happened, or maybe it is worth giving it a go. He gets no further in his musings as he falls asleep on the sofa.

He wakes up on Monday morning feeling very uncomfortable after his night on the sofa, and he has a big hangover. He makes himself some coffee. Did I decide to return to Wadebridge and try to make it up with Sue? He thinks he did. Was that the drink talking? Time to think about it clearly. He does. Summing up the situation on all accounts, it would be the best thing to do. My life is going nowhere, and I need to try to rekindle a lost love. He decides he will do it tomorrow and get a train to Cornwall. He checks the train times on his iPad. He goes out and buys an overnight bag for his travels.

And here we are the next day on the train going to Cornwall. He arrives in Bodmin about 3 pm and takes a bus to Wadebridge. It is now around 4 pm, and he goes to Sue's coffeehouse. She is not there as she was only working Saturday. He spends a long time over his coffee and is tempted to ask after her, but resists the temptation. Nearly 5 pm, and time to bite the bullet, and he makes his way to her parents' house and knocks on the door.

Sue opens the door and is shocked to see him, and is speechless. Colin is not speechless.

'Hi Sue. It is so good to see you looking so well. I have certainly missed you. If you will permit me, I have a very long and complicated story to tell. I could well understand if you do not want to hear my story, but I think we owe it to each other.' She is still speechless, but eventually says

'I never expected to see you ever again, but here you are. I missed you at first, but to be honest, over the last few months, I have completely forgotten you. I am not sure that this is the right place for storytelling with my mother around. I will get my coat and we will go somewhere else.' He can hear her having a conversation with her mother, but cannot hear the words. Has she told her that Colin has returned? He will never know. She is back at the door with her coat. They make their way to their favourite pub, which he takes as a good sign.

They order two pints of Doombar and settle at a table.

'Well, what's the story then?'

Colin has not rehearsed his story, which was an oversight, but he will just have to make it good.

'Everything I have told you about me is a lie. (he now has to quickly decide whether to tell her the whole truth, including Karen and Jonathan, but for some reason thinks better of it.) In my old life, I was a successful businessman working all hours in an office. I earned a healthy salary and lived in a nice apartment in the Barbican near where I worked. I then made a bad mistake. I had consensual sex with my assistant after a business dinner. What I did not know was that she was ambitious and wanted my job. She made ligature marks on her wrists and reported to the police that I had tied her up and raped her. I was arrested and charged. My legal advice was that, although my defence was that I had been set up, the evidence against me was very strong and I would be sent to prison for a long time for aggravated rape. I knew I was innocent and could not face prison for something I had not done, and I decided to abscond from bail. My first stop was Truro. I grew my hair and a beard as a sort of disguise and got a good job gardening, which I enjoyed after the long years in the office. There was then a murder, and the police wanted DNA from men associated with white vans. I knew the police had my DNA, so I had to decamp to Newquay, where I stayed for a while. I was acquainted with people who became suspicious of me, and it was time to move on again. I first went to Padstow for a couple of days, but didn't like it. I then came to Wadebridge, where I was lucky enough to meet you. All seemed to be going well until there was another murder at our flats and we were interviewed by the police. The police obviously had mug shots of me in my old life, and they must have made enquiries in Newquay and updated my image with hair and beard. One of the officers who interviewed us about the murder must have recognised me, and as you know, I was arrested. I was kept a couple of days in the Wadebrige police station and then transferred to London and remanded in custody. I spent nearly six months in prison before my trial. I had a very good lawyer who proved to the satisfaction of the jury that the so-called victim had self-inflicted the injuries and set me up. I was found innocent and released a free man. I have since been trying to get my life back together, but with little success, and have been unable to get my old job back or any other job for that matter. I started thinking about you and the wonderful times we had together, and decided that I just had to see you to find out if we had any hope of a future. So here I am, and it feels so good to be back talking to you.'

Sue has quietly listened to all he has to say, but now she has to respond.

'You are right, it is a long and complicated story. I am not sure you have told me all. In your old life, you mentioned you had an apartment. Did you live alone or with a girlfriend, fiancé or even a wife and kids?

A short but telling question. Is it time to tell the whole truth, or should he brazen it out? He thinks he does still love her, but some things are best kept secret.

'I lived alone.'

This does not seem to satisfy her.

'Did you have a girlfriend or fiancé in London, and have you ever been married. Did you connect with any of these after your acquittal?

She is being very direct, and he is going to have to say something.

'At the time of my arrest, I had no girlfriend, which is probably why I had sex with a girl at work, which was wrong of me. I have never been engaged or married, and there was nobody to connect with.' He reckons that is a reasonable answer, but a long way from the truth. The problem now is that he can never tell her the truth. He would so like to be able to tell her the truth, but she would not want to hear it.

She is mulling this over.

'I am not happy. When we were together, I was in heaven. You were the man of my dreams, and you asked me to marry you. The lack of a passport, which I guess the police had prevented you from getting a marriage licence, so we could never have got married in any case. Did you ask me, knowing it could never happen? That I will never know. More unsettling is that our whole relationship was based on one big lie. Everything you told me was an untruth, but I still fell for you. If you had been upfront and told me the truth, would I still have loved you and wanted to be your wife? That again I will never know. To me, this is all so confusing, and I need some time to think it all through. Are you going to be here long?'

He replies, 'I can be here as long as it takes.'

She says 'In that case, give me a couple of days. Come round again on Thursday evening and you can take me out to dinner. In the meantime, I will have a long chat with my parents about it all. On more mundane matters. After you were arrested, I gave up our flat and went back to living with my parents. It seems better now than when I first returned from university, and we get along fine. My translating work is going well, and I am making a good living and saving lots of money. I have nearly enough for a deposit on a place of my own, which I can get with a mortgage. And the murder at our flat. It was the carer. Her trial was recent, and she was sentenced to twenty years. Thinking about what you said, her actions led to your arrest. I wonder what would have happened to us if you had not been recognised.'

They finish their drinks, and he escorts her home.

He checks into a local cheap hotel for three nights.

He is lying on his bed thinking about his conversation with Sue. Her questions were very direct. It is a shame that he has had to tell her more lies, but it seemed the only way. She does not appear to be rushing back into his arms and wants to spend time discussing it all with her parents. In the past, they did seem to like him, and her father was generous with the rent support. Will they still like him when they hear the true or almost true story? He is going to have to wait 48 hours to find out.

It is a drab and dreary 48 hours for him. He calls for her on Thursday evening. He takes her to what was their favourite pub. She wants a beer, and they find a place to sit and order some food. It is just chit chat and nothing serious. He decides he will wait for her to bring it up. They finish their food, and he returns to the bar and gets two more beers. Is she going to get serious now? He sits down, and she says

'Thank you for the beers and a nice dinner as always. (Good start, he thinks) When you told me your story the other night, I told you that I needed time to think and talk with my parents. As I said to you the other night, our whole relationship was based on one big lie. You have now told me what you say is the truth. I believe you as far as it goes, but in my mind, it does not all add up. Your marriage proposal was a sham. You had no proper identity and could never have got a marriage licence. So why did you ask me? I cannot fathom it one bit. At the end of the day, you had no reason to propose marriage as we were happily living together, and I never, to my mind, hinted that I wanted you to propose. So why did you do it? No reasonable explanation. We then get to the question of girlfriends, fiancés or wives. You have said that none of these applied. I find the lack of a girlfriend unlikely. You are an attractive man, and it is difficult to believe you have had no girlfriend. Then I started thinking perhaps he didn't have a girlfriend because he had a wife. She became aware of the rape allegation and kicked him out. Even worse, you may have had kids. You would not have been able to tell me that, would you? Which brings me to the crux of the matter. You started our relationship with one big lie. On balance, I think you are still not telling me the whole truth, and I think you must have a wife and one or two or maybe three kids. What I am trying to say is that I do not trust you, and I would like you to go away and leave me alone and never try to make any contact whatsoever in the future. When you were arrested, we were over, and we are still over and will remain over.'

Colin cannot really believe what he has just heard. She has hit the nail on the head. He must compose himself and give her a reply.

'I am very sorry to have heard what you have just said. I can understand that trust must be difficult after my first lie. My first lie was necessary because of my difficult situation. Everything I told you about my circumstances was the truth and nothing but the truth. You are basically accusing me of being a liar and even suggesting I am a married man with kids. Nothing could be further from the truth. What I really want to do is get back into your heart, and I would like you to tell me what I have to do because I would do anything for you.'

Sue had not been expecting a response of this nature, and she is almost taken in. She thought she had made it abundantly clear that she wanted nothing to do with him, and here he is pleading like a lost dog.

She has had long discussions with her parents, and they, too, were clear that she should not be fooled again. But she will have to respond.

'What you say is very heartening. I thought I was very clear that there is no way back to my heart for you. As they say, don't get fooled again. I could give you a long list of requirements which you may or may not be able to accomplish, but I have no intention of pursuing that line. You have to understand it is over, and I never want to see you again. I do not like walking alone at night, so you can walk me back to my door, and we can say our final adieu.'

She is being very direct. Should he plead like a lost dog? No, he thinks better of it. He just walks her home, and they say adieu without as much as a kiss.

He gets back to his lodging and lies on his bed. She doesn't trust me. Who can blame her? My second story was not the truth, and it has come back to haunt me. My only hope is to tell her the whole truth, which I could do in a letter. The trouble is that to her, the whole truth could just be another lie. It is all useless, and I think I will have to just consign her to history.

The next day, he returns to London. Over the next few days, he still considers writing a letter, but never does.

Time to get his life back in order. Two things are essential. A job and a girlfriend.

One month on, and he has been unsuccessful on both counts.

Chapter 25

We have not heard much about Karen for a while. She seems to be in the same situation as Colin. No job and no boyfriend. She thought it would be easy to get back to work with her qualifications but none of the City firms want to employ a single mum. She is with two agencies and has had seven or eight job interviews but no offers. She thinks she will need to set her sights lower and look for a small practice somewhere, but has little idea how to go about that.

On the romantic front, nothing. How is a single mum going to find a man? She has no idea. She is basically a stay-at-home mum with zilch social life. She had liked Paul a lot but the feelings were not reciprocated.

What is the future going to hold for her? It is difficult to see her situation changing. What she needs is a job to fill her days better and give her the chance of finding someone new. Our story is not going to go that far so we will never know her future. Do we feel sorry for her? Yes. She was a loving wife and mother who did nothing wrong and her whole life was thrown into chaos, and she lost her husband. If she had thought it through better, she should have forgiven him for what he said was his one and one indiscretion and tried to repair the marriage. She thought otherwise, and now here she is as a depressed and lonely single mum without much hope for the future.

Penny seems to be no better. She hates her job and the pay is terrible. There is no man in her life. It seems to be a struggle to pay the mortgage every month but she likes her flat and does not want to downsize. She is not prosecuted for perjury, which is something. She is often reflective and a part of her tells her that she is glad Colin was found not guilty - he did not deserve a prison sentence. She realises that her mistake was the ligatures, which were too tight and she would never have been able to get free. It was a good idea but it seems to have come back to haunt her. And how could she have got it so wrong on the Profit Forecast which has been her undoing? If she had not been so concerned about Deborah, she would have done a proper job. But she didn't, and look where she is now. In our hearts, we are cheering her downfall.

Life for Sue is a lot better. She feels that she did the right thing in dismissing Colin from her life. Their relationship started with a lie, which can never be a good thing. She still feels that in his new story, he was missing key details and she feels convinced he had a wife and probably kids. Well rid of him then. She starts to look for properties to buy. A flat comes up in their old block but she cannot face going back there with all the memories. She has a long talk with her father. He likes having her back at home but he realises she has to move on and make her own way. He agrees to give her a substantial contribution to her deposit. She can now go a bit more upmarket. She is not sure if Wadebridge is the right place for her. It is a bit insular with a lack of attractive men. She decides she will look further afield and views properties in Truro and Padstow. She doesn't like Padstow that much, although it is good for the beach and decides on Truro. It would be good to have two bedrooms, as she could let out a room to help pay the mortgage and, more importantly, to have a companion. She is not ready to live alone. Her budget is £200,000. Surfing the internet, she finds she can afford a house in either Daniel Street or Carclew Street. A house appeals. She phones agents and gets appointments to view. She spends nearly a whole day in Truro viewing properties. Her favourite is a lovely two-bedroom cottage in Daniel Street. She tells the agent she will have to come back with her father and makes an appointment for Saturday morning.

They arrive back on Saturday morning and her father agrees it is very attractive. They retire to the Thomas Daniel just down the road for a coffee. Her father tells her that the house is fine, but he is not so keen on her moving so far away. He has really enjoyed her company over the last year or so, when she moved home, and Truro seems a long way and he cannot see them seeing much of each other. Sue listens carefully but she has made up her mind for Truro.

She starts the purchase process and within 6 weeks, she has the keys. Her mother and father drive her over with all her things and she is ready to settle in. It takes her about two weeks to find a tenant for the second bedroom. The girl is a nurse working at the local hospital. The nurse has day shifts and night shifts. They get on fine and from time to time go out for a drink together, normally at the Thomas Daniel. Apart from that, she does not really have a social life, which can be a little boring. She is not really sure if she wants to meet men, as after her experiences with John/Colin she is unsure if she will ever be able to trust a man again. Not a great position for a young girl to find herself. Her translating is going well and with the rent for the second bedroom, the mortgage is easily paid and at the end of each month, she is able to transfer a little to her savings. She may be financially okay, but we cannot help feeling sorry for her. She has no social life and no man in her life, and it is difficult to see how she will ever be able to let herself trust another man.

We are going to have to end with Colin. At the present time, he has no job and no girlfriend. It would have been interesting to take the story further and see how his life progressed but we are not going to do that. We are going to pass judgement on him.

He was a successful businessman who used his position to have sex with his assistant. The words of his former MD, who said that his actions were despicable. We are minded to agree with this assessment. We may have had some fun and adventures with him when he ran away from the trial but at the end of the day, what do we think of him? Not a lot.